Praise for other books by Graham Seal

Great Australian Stories

'The pleasure of this book is in its ability to give a fair dinkum insight into the richness of Australian story telling.'—*Weekly Times*

'... a treasure trove of material from our nation's historical past ... you don't have to be Australian to enjoy it, but it helps.'—*Courier Mail*

'This book is a little island of Aussie culture—one to enjoy.'—*Sunshine Coast Sunday*

'Numbskulls, drongos, bunyips, whingers and cockies all feature in this book of legends, yarns and tall tales from our rich tradition of Australian storytelling ... Great fun.' —*Scoop*

Great Anzac Stories

'... allows you to feel as if you are there in the trenches with them.'—*Weekly Times*

'They are pithy short pieces, absolutely ideal for reading when you are pushed for time, but they are stories you will remember for much longer than you would expect. Fromelles, the Fuzzy Wuzzy Angels, the grim humour in horrific circumstances, or the heroism of a person will haunt the reader. There is so much here: victories and defeats, help and hindrance, memories and wilful forgetfulness, and much that has never before been published.'—*Ballarat Courier*

'... rewarding reading ... a valuable document.' —*Sydney Morning Herald*

'A compilation of yarns about Aussies at war, *Great Anzac Stories* provides an in-depth look into the bravery of all those involved.' —*4 x 4 Australia*

'... a book that will clarify many of the Anzac myths and settle a few arguments.'—*The Senior*

'This book represents just a small selection of stories of courage, calamity and some humour in a comprehensible form.'—*PS News*

Other books by Graham Seal

Great Australian Stories
Great Anzac Stories
The Soldiers' Press: Trench journals in the First World War
Outlaw Heroes in Myth and History
*Dog's Eye and Dead Horse: The complete guide to Australian
rhyming slang*
Echoes of Anzac: The voice of Australians at war
Inventing ANZAC: The Digger and National Mythology
Tell 'em I Died Game: The legend of Ned Kelly

GRAHAM SEAL

LARRIKINS, BUSH TALES & OTHER GREAT AUSTRALIAN STORIES

ALLEN&UNWIN
SYDNEY·MELBOURNE·AUCKLAND·LONDON

Allen & Unwin
83 Alexander Street
Crows Nest NSW 2065
Australia
Phone:(61 2) 8425 0100
Email: info@allenandunwin.com
Web: www.allenandunwin.com

Cataloguing-in-Publication details are available
from the National Library of Australia
www.trove.nla.gov.au

ISBN 978 1 74331 996 3

Set in 12.5/16 pt Adobe Caslon Pro and 10/16 pt Shannon Std by Bookhouse, Sydney
Printed and bound in Australia by Griffin Press

10 9 8 7 6 5 4 3 2 1

Contents

Introduction:
The Great Australian storyscape

THERE IS A great Australian story, made up of many, many stories. These are tales large and small, personal and public, funny and sad, wild and woolly and sometimes just weird. Taken together, they sum up what Australians are, how we came to be and how we like to think of ourselves as a people. They also suggest something about how we might be in the future.

I think of this as the great Australian storyscape, a never-ending flow of yarns, legends, myths, jokes and anecdotes that we tell each other over time. Stories by Australians, for Australians, about the Australian experience. Some of these tales are borrowed from elsewhere and adapted to our needs in accordance with the tradition of making do and improvisation. But most are home-grown. They tell about the past, both as it was and how we wish it might have been. But because they are still being told, re-told, rediscovered and otherwise recycled by word of mouth, in print and, increasingly, on the internet, they also speak to us in the present. These tales are worth the telling and the hearing or reading because they give an insight into that larger national story of which they are all a part.

Readers of the earlier *Great Australian Stories* will be familiar with the approach and format of this sequel. In a few cases there are updates or new angles on some of the stories included in the earlier book. The evolving history of the piratical 'Black Jack' Anderson is one of these. The yowie and friends continue to fascinate many of us, and so I've taken the opportunity to get up to speed with the latest on hairy figures and similar creatures.

Some readers wondered why there was nothing on Ned Kelly in the first book. I thought that readers might be tired of the Kelly saga but judging by the swag of recent books and television shows on the subject, it seems not. So there is a whole Kelly chapter here, beginning with an overview of the events of 1878–80 but focusing mainly on the rarely mentioned aftermath of the outbreak.

You will find here tales both true and less so from Australia's rich history and folklore, beginning with a selection of Indigenous legends and settler stories of the wide, brown land. This is followed by selections on the early unwilling emigrants, as well as free settlers attracted to the 'plains of promise' in search of a better life for themselves and their children. Many of the early settlers did not come of their own free will; a few tales of the convict days reflect their troubles as well as some of their unusual reactions.

The love of 'a fair go' is an important element of national identity, as is travelling across the vastness of the country and carrying a swag. The hardships of pioneering and economic depression and of the battler feature in the section on 'Doing it tough', while the sometimes forgotten experience of colonial children deserves attention as well. We also have our fair share of unsolved crimes and other mysteries that nag at the nation's memory, and these are also touched on.

Finally, most of us have to work for a living. Working life is a primary source of the kind of dry humour that gets us through the working day, and beyond, and there were just as many experiences of work to laugh at in the past as there are in the present.

A few themes weave their way through this collection. Together, these themes sum up the distinctive experience of the Australian people and how they have talked about it, written about, sung about and laughed about it.

The land itself features in many stories, either directly or by implication: understanding it, travelling across it or trying to make a living from it and the challenging environment that famously produces fire, flood and drought, often at the same time. From the earliest times, we hear about hardship, struggle, tragedy and conflict. But these troubles are balanced by hope, optimism, celebration and the need for equality and fairness. Making do and getting by are wired into the Australian way of life and state of mind. No matter what the situation, someone comes up with a way to make things easier, faster, safer or just better, and in the most difficult situations, laughter often comes to the rescue. The people in the stories, and sometimes those who tell them, range from the ordinary to the extraordinary. Occasionally, they are just plain odd. They are reproduced faithfully and like many historical texts, some contain language and express attitudes that may be considered offensive today—you stand warned.

Tall tales and true. A few sad ones, a few strange ones and a lot of yarns. A couple of curiosities for good measure. All seasoned with the characteristic spice of the 'great Australian slanguage'.

Graham Seal

Acknowledgements

MY THANKS TO: Rob Willis, Olya Willis, Maureen Seal, Mark Gregory, Peter Austin, Robyn Floyd, Mary Newham and the descendants of Olga Ernst (Waller), Elizabeth Weiss and staff at Allen & Unwin as well as all the unknown—but not unheard— spinners of yarns and tellers of tales who help us to laugh, cry and perhaps think about things anew.

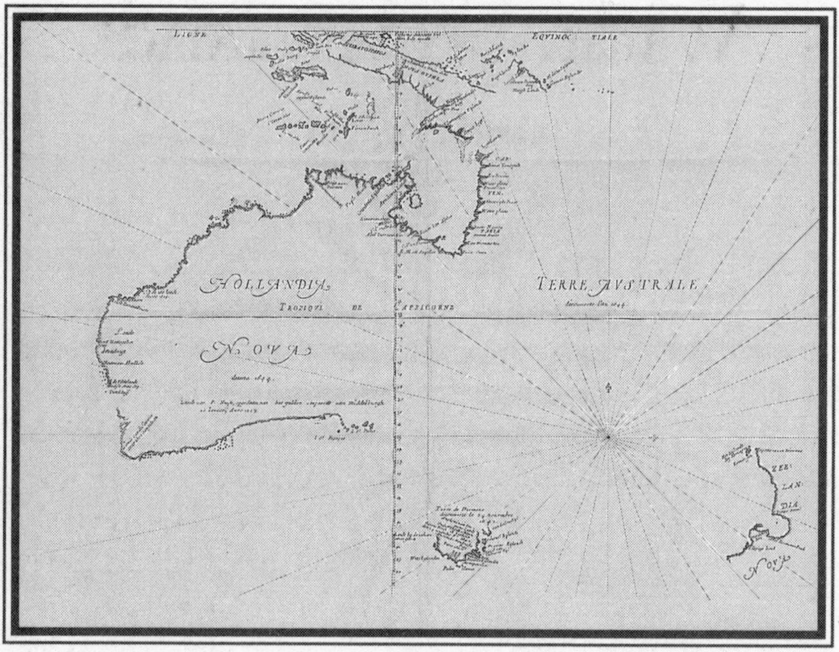
LIGNE
EQUINOC TIALE
HOLLANDIA
NOVA
TROPIQUE DE CAPRICORNE
TERRE AUSTRALE
ZEE
LAN
DIA
NOVA

1

Wide, brown land

The wide, brown land for me!
Dorothea Mackellar, 'My Country' (1908)

AT THE BASE of the great, wide treasure trove of Australian stories lies the land: the natural features, the environment, the people and places upon it and the things that have been done in those places. Indigenous stories are all about the land and the links between it, the ancestral creators, its plants and animals and the human beings who lived here for 50,000 years, perhaps longer. When visitors from other places began to arrive seeking trade and, later, settlement, they too needed to create an understanding of the land and to express it in their stories. Different though these stories are, they also tell of ways of living on and relating to the environment we all share.

Dorothea Mackellar's famous poem 'My Country' first appeared in a slightly different form in the English *Spectator* magazine in 1908 and was not published in Australia until 1911. Dorothea was only 22 at the time of writing and homesick for her home country while travelling in Britain. Her patriotic creation is often criticised as overly sentimental and unconscious of the Indigenous connection to country. On the other hand, it pointedly breaks with the British connection in its first verse, the fields and coppices the 'ordered woods and lanes' that 'I know but cannot share'.

The next verse begins with the lines best known to generations of schoolchildren: 'I love a sunburnt country'. The remainder is a highly emotional testament of love for the harsh environment: 'Core of my heart, my country'.

Ever since its first Australian publication, the poem—or 'verse' as Mackellar might have called it, refusing to be called a 'poet'—has been a touchstone for popular ideas of national identity and relationship to the land. But long before then, Aboriginal Australians were expressing their unique connections to the wide, brown land.

Eaglehawk and Crow

The wedge-tailed eagle or eaglehawk lives across the continent in considerable numbers. Not surprisingly, this fierce hunter appears frequently in traditional Aboriginal mythology. In Tiwi tradition (Melville and Bathurst islands, Northern Territory), Jurumu is the name for the wedge-tailed eagle, which, with Mudati the fork-tailed kite, made fire when they accidentally rubbed some sticks together. For the Wonnarua people of the Hunter Valley, Kawal is the wedge-tailed eagle, created by the great spirit Baiame (Byamee) to watch over them. In Victoria, Bunjil is the wedge-tailed eagle, the creator of the Kulin nation.

The eagle may also be associated with totems of one kind or another, and with the complex human and spiritual relationships in Aboriginal culture.

There are many wedge-tailed eagle stories, some involving Crow, who often represents the complementary darkness to the eagle or eaglehawk's light. Crow may also be a trickster figure and is frequently associated with fire. In some stories, the characters end up as stars in the night sky, as in traditions recorded along the Murray River. Here it was said that the earth was inhabited by a race of very wise black birds long before humans came to be there. The eaglehawk was the leader of this group and Crow was his deputy. The eagle's son was killed by Crow. In some versions, Eagle trapped Crow and killed him but the wily black bird came back to life and then disappeared. In this telling of the story, the argument between Crow and Eagle explains how crows come to be black.

One day, a crow and a hawk hunted together in the bush. After travelling together for some time, they decided to hunt in opposite directions, and, at the close of the day, to share whatever game they had caught. The crow travelled against the sun, and at noonday arrived at a broad lagoon which was the haunt of the wild ducks. The crow hid in the tall green reeds fringing the lagoon, and prepared to trap the ducks. First, he got some white clay, and, having softened it with water, placed two pieces in his nostrils. He then took a long piece of hollow reed through which he could breathe under water, and finally tied a net bag around his waist in which to place the ducks.

On the still surface of the lagoon, the tall gum trees were reflected like a miniature forest. The ducks, with their bronze plumage glistening in the sun, were swimming among the clumps of reeds, and only paused to dive for a tasty morsel hidden deep in the water weeds. The crow placed the reed in his mouth, and, without making any sound, waded into the water. He quickly submerged himself, and the only indication of his presence in the lagoon was a piece of dry reed which projected above the surface of the water, and through which the crow was breathing. When he reached the centre of the water-hole he remained perfectly still. He did not have to wait long for the ducks to swim above his head. Then, without making any sound or movement, he seized one by the leg, quickly pulled it beneath the water, killed it, and placed it in the net bag. By doing this, he did not frighten the other ducks, and, in a short time he had trapped a number of them. He then left the lagoon and continued on his way until he came to a river.

The crow was so pleased with his success at the waterhole that he determined to spear some fish before he returned to his camp. He left the bag of ducks on the bank of the river, and, taking his fish spear, he waded into the river until the water reached his waist. Then he stood very still, with the spear poised for throwing. A short distance from the spot where he was standing, a slight ripple disturbed the calm surface of the water. With the keen eye of the hunter, he saw the presence of fish, and, with a swift movement of his arm, he hurled the spear, and his unerring aim was rewarded with a big fish. The water was soon agitated by many fish, and the crow took advantage of this to spear many more. With this heavy load of game, he turned his face towards home.

The hawk was very unfortunate in his hunting. He stalked a kangaroo many miles, and then lost sight of it in the thickly wooded hills. He then decided to try the river for some fish, but the crow had made the water muddy and frightened the fish, so again he was unsuccessful. At last the hawk decided to return to his *gunyah* [shelter] with the hope that the crow would secure some food, which they had previously agreed to share. When the hawk arrived, he found that the crow had been there before him and had prepared and eaten his evening meal. He at once noticed that the crow had failed to leave a share for him. This annoyed the hawk, so he approached the crow and said: 'I see you have had a good hunt to-day. I walked many miles but could not catch even a lizard. I am tired and would be glad to have my share of food, as we agreed this morning.'

'You are too lazy,' the crow replied. 'You must have slept in the sun instead of hunting for food. Anyhow, I've eaten mine and cannot give you any.'

This made the hawk very angry, and he attacked the crow. For a long time they struggled around the dying embers of the camp fire, until the hawk seized the crow and rolled him in the black ashes.

When the crow recovered from the fight, he found that he could not wash the ashes off, and, since that time, crows have always been black. The crow was also punished for hiding the food which he could not eat by being condemned to live on putrid flesh.

Great floods

Indigenous tradition contains many stories of great floods. From Arnhem Land to coastal Queensland, in South Australia, Gippsland and into Western Australia, legends of catastrophic floods have been widely collected. Many of these stories seek to provide explanations or rationales for the way in which the natural world is organised. This one from southeastern Australia also involves Eaglehawk and Crow, as well as many other animals. Its theme is timeless and universal and could well speak to some modern Australian issues.

*T*he animals, birds, and reptiles became overpopulated and held a conference to determine what to do. The kangaroo, eaglehawk, and goanna were the chiefs of the three respective groups, and their advisors were koala, crow, and tiger-snake. They met on Blue Mountain.

Tiger-snake spoke first and proposed that the animals and birds, who could travel more readily, should relocate to another country. Kangaroo rose to introduce platypus, whose family far outnumbered any others, but the meeting was then adjourned for the day.

On the second day, while the conference proceeded with crow taunting koala for his inability to find a solution, the frilled lizards decided to act on their own. They possessed the knowledge of rain-making, and they spread the word to all of their family to perform the rain ceremony during the week before the new moon. Thus would they destroy the over-numerous platypus family.

They did their ceremonies repeatedly, and a great storm came, flooding the land. The frilled lizards had made shelters on mountains, and some animals managed to make their way there, but nearly all life was destroyed in the great flood.

When the flood ended and the sun shone again, the kangaroo called the animals together to discover how the platypus family had fared. But they could not find a single living platypus. Three years later, the cormorant told emu that he had seen a platypus beak impression along a river, but never saw a platypus.

Because of the flood, the platypuses had decided that the animals, birds, and reptiles were their enemies and only moved about at night. The animals organized a search party, and carpet-snake eventually found a platypus home and reported its location back to the others. Kangaroo summoned all the tribes together, even the insect tribe. Fringed lizard was ejected for doing mischief; he has turned ugly because of the hate he dwells upon. The animals and birds found they were both related to the platypus family; even the reptiles found some relationship; and everyone agreed that the platypuses were an old race.

Carpet-snake went to the platypus home and invited them to the assembly. They came and were met with great respect. Kangaroo offered platypus his choice of the daughter of any of them. Platypus learned that emu had changed its totem so that the platypus and emu families could marry. This made platypus decide it didn't want to be part of any of their families. Emu got angry, and kangaroo suggested the platypuses leave silently that night, which they did.

They met bandicoot along the way, who invited the platypuses to live with them. The platypuses married the bandicoot daughters and lived happily. Water-rats got jealous and fought them but were defeated. Platypuses have tried to be separate from the animal and bird tribes ever since, but not entirely successfully.

Firestick farming

When Europeans came to Australia they were surprised to find that much of the country had a park-like appearance. Many observers described the regular patterns of land management in terms of English gardens and grand estates. They saw carefully defined demarcations between bush, grassland and watercourses and wondered how people they usually considered to be 'savages' could have evolved and maintained such an advanced and effective system for managing their harsh environment and for surviving, even prospering, in it.

Those who took the time and trouble to look into this unexpected feature of the unknown south land soon discovered the Aboriginal skill with fire. One of the most perceptive and knowledgeable of all the European explorers was Ludwig Leichhardt. He disappeared during an attempt to cross the continent from east to west in 1848 and his fate remains a mystery today, but in the journals of his previous expeditions he recorded what he saw of 'firestick farming', as this method of environmental resource stewardship has become known. On his journey from Moreton Bay to Port Essington in 1844–45, a distance of almost 5000 kilometres, Leichhardt documented his firsthand experience of management by flame.

The natives seemed to have burned the grass systematically along every watercourse, and round every water-hole, in order to have them surrounded with young grass as soon as the rain sets in. These burnings were not connected with camping places, where the fire is liable to spread from the fire-places, and would clear the neighbouring ground. Long strips of lately burnt grass were frequently observed extending for many miles along the creeks. The banks of small isolated water-holes in the forest, were equally attended to, although water had not been in either for a considerable time. It is no doubt connected with a systematic management of their runs, to attract game to particular spots, in the same way that stockholders burn parts of theirs in proper seasons; at least those who are not influenced by the erroneous notion that burning the grass injures the richness and density of the natural turf. The natives, however, frequently burn the high and stiff grass, particularly along shady creeks, with the intention of driving the concealed game out of it; and we have frequently seen them watching anxiously, even for lizards, when other game was wanting.

~

Leichhardt was frustrated by those settlers who could not or would not see that this fire regime was the correct way to manage the country and wrote elsewhere: 'I longed to move those stupid enemies of fire onto such a plot of young grass to hear lectures alternately from horses, sheep, oxen and kangaroos about the advantages of burning the old grass.'

Leichhardt's concerns, as well as those of a few others, had little impact on the development of agriculture and land management. But the issue remains very much alive today as increasingly devastating bushfires roar across the land and we search for ways to minimise them.

'The landscape looked like a park'

In September 1853, squatter John G. Robertson of Wando Vale responded to an invitation from Governor La Trobe to detail his experiences on the new land. Robertson had arrived in Van Diemen's Land (VDL) in 1831 and 'like many of my countrymen, with a light purse—one half-crown and a sixpence was all my pocket contained'. By his own account he worked hard for three years and saved the considerable sum of 3000 pounds, which allowed him to set up as a farmer in Victoria. At the end of a very lengthy account, the tough squatter tells how his land has begun to change under the impact of agriculture.

*T*he few sheep at first made little impression on the face of the country for three or four years; the first great change was a severe frost, 11th November 1844, which killed nearly all the beautiful blackwood trees that studded the hills in every sheltered nook—some of them really noble, 20 or 30 years old; nearly all were killed in one night; the same night a beautiful shrub that was interspersed among the blackwoods (Sir Thomas Mitchell called it *acacia glutinosa*) was also killed. About three weeks after these trees and shrubs were all burnt, they now sought to recover as they would do after a fire.

This certainly was a sad chance; before this catastrophe all the landscape looked like a park with shade for sheep and cattle. Many of our herbaceous plants began to disappear from the pasture land; the silk-grass began to show itself in the edge of the bush track, and in patches here and there on the hill. The patches have grown larger every year; herbaceous plants and grasses give way for the silk-grass and the little annuals, beneath which are annual peas, and die in our deep clay soil with a few hot days in spring, and nothing returns to supply their place until later in the winter following. The consequence is that the long deep-rooted grasses that held our strong clay hill together have died out; the ground is now exposed to the sun, and it has cracked in all directions, and the clay hills are slipping in all directions; also the sides of precipitous creeks, long slips taking trees and all with them. When I first came here, I knew of but two landslips, both of which I went to see; now there are hundreds found within the last three years.

A rather strange thing is going on now. One day all the creeks and little watercourses were covered with a large tussocky grass, with other grasses and plants, to the middle of every watercourse but the Glenelg and Wannon, and in many places of these rivers, now that the only soil is getting trodden hard with stock, springs of salt water are bursting out in every hollow or watercourse, and as it trickles down the watercourse in summer, the strong tussocky grasses die before it, with nil others. The clay is left perfectly bare in summer.

The strong clay cracks; the winter rain washes out the clay; now mostly every little gully has a deep rut; when rain falls it runs off the hard ground, rushes down these ruts, runs into the larger creeks, and is carrying earth, trees, and all before it. Over Wannon country is now as difficult a ride as if it were fenced. Ruts, seven, eight, and ten feet deep, and as wide, are found for miles, where two years ago it was covered with tussocky grass like a land marsh.

I find from the rapid strides the silk-grass has made over my run, I will not be able to keep the number of sheep the run did three years ago, and as a cattle station it will be still worse; it requires no great prophetic knowledge to see that this part of the country will not carry the stock that is in it at present—I mean the open downs, and every year it will get worse, as it did in V.D.L.; and after all the experiments I worked with English grasses, I have never found any of them that will replace our native sward. The day the soil is turned up, that day the pasture is gone for ever as far as I know, for I had a paddock that was sown with English grasses, in squares each by itself, and mixed in every way. All was carried off by the grubs, and the paddock allowed to remain in native grass, which returned in eight years. Nothing but silk-grass grew year after year, and I suppose it would be so on to the end of time. Dutch clover will not grow on our clay soils; and for pastoral purposes the lands here are getting of less value every day, that is, with the kind of grass that is growing in them, and will carry less sheep and far less cattle. I now look forward to fencing my run in with wire, as the only chance of keeping up my stock on the land.

Captain Cook's Law

As well as the myths of creation and the ancestors, Aboriginal tradition includes more modern stories, or cycles of stories. One of these concerns Captain James Cook, still sometimes said to be the 'discoverer' of Australia. While Cook is a venerated figure in the history of navigation and maritime exploration, and rightly so, he has a much more negative image in Indigenous legend. In these stories, recorded from Aboriginal tellers around the country, Captain Cook arrives from the sea bringing disruption and violence.

In one version of the tale told in the Kimberley region, Cook uses gunpowder against Aboriginal people and then returns to his homeland claiming that the land is empty and can be settled. This is 'Cook's Law', by which the country is unfairly colonised and which is in direct contradiction to the traditional law and order of the original inhabitants.

In northern Queensland, Cook is depicted as a violent marauder who deceives the local people into showing him the place where they camp. This knowledge enables him to establish the cattle industry and also brings about massacres of Aboriginal people.

The Northern Territory story similarly revolves around Captain Cook stealing the land, violently oppressing the people and bringing a 'law' of dispossession. An Arnhem Land variation on this theme has two Captain Cooks arriving. The first is a good one who fights with an evil figure called Satan and wins. The victorious Cook returns to Sydney where he is rejected by his own people and dies. He is then followed by a whole lot more Captain Cooks who make war on the people.

The Indigenous people of the Bateman's Bay area in New South Wales tell simply of Cook coming with gifts of clothes and hard biscuits. He then sails away and the not so lucky receivers of his gifts cast them into the sea in disgust. Interestingly, this closely parallels the reactions of the Aborigines Cook did encounter during his voyage along the east coast: the newcomers' gifts were politely received but then discarded, as the Aboriginal people had no use for them.

Another Queensland tradition has it that Cook and his companions were seen not as intruders and murderers but as the returning spirits of the ancestors. These ghosts offered drugs, food and drink to the local people in the form of tobacco, beef, flour and tea. These were prepared in the European manner: the tobacco in a pipe, the beef salted and boiled, the flour baked and the tea in a kettle or billy. The Aboriginal people did not like the pipe, the tea or the bread. But the boiled beef was considered edible as long as the salt was washed away. Cook then took his men and sailed away to the north, leaving the Aboriginal people in dismay as the spirits of their ancestors disappeared.

The corners

There is a place where you can celebrate New Year three times. Called Poeppel or Poeppel's Corner, it is in the middle of nowhere, lying where the boundaries of Queensland, South Australia and the Northern Territory intersect—to be precise, at latitude 26 degrees S and longitude 138 degrees E.

In 1880, Augustus Poeppel identified this important point and drove a small tree trunk into the exact spot. Born in Germany, Poeppel had previously worked in a number of Australian colonies and in New Zealand. Later, his work in the outback led to him suffering from trachoma and the eventual loss of an eye. He was forced to retire and died in 1891 aged only 52. The original 'Poeppel's Peg' is now in the Migration Museum, South Australia, where it is known as 'Poeppel's Corner Post', a memento of the heroic feats of surveying undertaken in the colonial era and of their significance for the expansion of the Australian frontiers.

The vast expanse of land that lay beyond the western border of Queensland was almost totally unknown, an emptiness that swallowed the explorers Burke and Wills. When rescue parties went out to find them they stimulated interest in the region and settlement slowly began in the Barcoo, the Cooper, then Diamantina and the Channel country. By the 1870s it was necessary to draw some boundaries to prevent disputes between settlers, and the developing trade in the region also meant that customs barriers were needed, so the exact location of those borders had to be marked. Each colony set up its own customs departments to ensure collection of duties whenever their borders were crossed.

Poeppel and his team were in some of the continent's harshest land. They struggled across its hot, dry plains surviving on salt beef, damper and the kindness of Aboriginal people who showed them where to get water. They finally reached their goal late in 1880 and marked it with the timber post that came to be known as 'Poeppel's Peg'. It had to be moved later due to a slight measurement error and the original intention of establishing the corner between Queensland and South Australia failed, but Poeppel's accomplishment was hailed nevertheless as a great feat of surveying.

Poeppel's Corner has been the focus of an extended controversy, though. There has been a suggestion, based on evidence from the 1936 visitor Edmund Colson, that Poeppel tried to conceal his calculation error, committed because he was over-fond of the grog. The more or less official story goes that Poeppel's measuring tape somehow stretched, causing the error.

After the original survey party left, very few people went to Poeppel's Corner. There were visits in 1883, 1936 and again during the 1960s, but by then the post was rotten and termite-eaten and needed to be removed for conservation. In 1966, the Leyland brothers proved that the Simpson Desert could be accessed with four-wheel-drive vehicles and the area was subsequently opened up to tourism, and the corner is now quite frequently visited.

There are other 'corners' established by survey along many state borders. Surveyor-General's Corner lies on the intersection of the South Australian and Western Australian borders. Haddon's Corner is found where the northern boundary of South Australia turns south, and Cameron's Corner is on the same southerly line at the point where it joins the New South Wales and Queensland borders. These spots are also popular with four-wheel-drive tourists and are tangible memorials to the carving up of the continent.

2

Upon the fatal shore

The first day that we landed upon the fatal shore,
The planters came around us—there might be twenty score or more.
They ranked us up like horses and sold us out of hand,
They yoked us in a plough, brave boys, to plough Van Diemen's Land.
Street ballad

As SOON AS the news about founding a penal colony at Botany
Bay broke in 1787, the British press went into action. Articles,
pamphlets and street ballads appeared almost overnight. 'Botany
Bay: A New Song' was a tongue-in-cheek roll call of the English
underworld, the source of most of our first settlers. There were
'night-walking strumpets', 'lecherous whoremasters', 'proud dressy
fops' and 'monopolisers who add to their store/By cruel oppression
and squeezing the poor'. The second-last verse of this street
ballad expressed the popular view of the time:

The hulks and the jails have some thousands in store,
But out of the jails are ten thousand times more,
Who live by fraud, cheating, vile tricks and foul play,
They should all be sent over to Botany Bay.

This song also raised the possibility that the transports and their
keepers might 'become a new people at Botany Bay'. Of course

it did, though there were many unhappy moments along the path to nationhood, especially in the convict days. But mostly, convictism was about the personal trials, tragedies and triumphs of the 160,000 or so men and women transported to Australia between 1788 and 1868.

Leaden hearts

Transportation to the far ends of the earth, even for a relatively short term of seven years, meant the end of lives and loves for many convicts. Even before the settlement of Port Jackson, a custom grew in which convicts departing to penal colonies had coins filed smooth and an affectionate message engraved on both sides. These often handmade tokens—or 'leaden hearts'—were left with wives, families or lovers in the hope that they would not forget, even if the sentence were for life. Brief though these messages had to be, they hint at many poignant stories from the Australian experience of transportation.

Seventeen-year-old Charles Wilkinson stole a handkerchief and was transported for life in 1824. The crude carvings on his token read:

Your lover lives for you
CL
Only.
Til death

The reverse of his token told the story in a few terse words:

C Wilkinson
Lag[ged] for Life
Aged 17
1824

'C.L.' probably never saw Charles again. Wilkinson reoffended in Australia and did not receive a free pardon for twenty years. Like most convicts he probably remained here, unable to afford a passage home and after such a long absence perhaps not seeing much reason to return.

A Michael Williams (alias Flinn) was sentenced to death for stealing tea from the wharves in London. His token read:

M Flinn
Aged 25
Cast for death
September 16
1825

On the back:

A token of true love
when this you se[e]
remember me

Fortunately, his sentence was commuted to transportation for life.

Sometimes tokens expressed a degree of remorse and moralising. Joseph Kelf, aged twenty, was 'cast for death' after burgling a Norfolk home in 1833. His sentence commuted, he had a token made with the homily:

Honesty is the best policy

Many of these keepsakes were in verse, some elaborately so. John Waldon was given a fourteen-year stretch in 1832. His token reads:

17

No Pen can Write
No Tongue can Tell
The Aching Heart
That Bids Farewell.

Thomas Alsop, a Staffordshire sheep stealer, was 21 when transported for life in 1833. He could not write but had two fine tokens made, one for his 'dear mother':

The rose soon dupes and dies
The brier fades away
But my fond heart for you I love
Shall never fade away.

Convicted of murder in 1832, William Kennedy was lucky to have his sentence cut to a lifetime of labour in the colonies. He had the engraver inscribe his coin with a defiant verse:

When this you see
Remember me
And bear me in your mind.
Let all the world
Say what they will
Speak of me as you find.

Another 'When this you see think on me' token was made for Thomas Burbury of Coventry, who was convicted of rioting and machine breaking in 1832. Machine breakers, or 'Luddites', destroyed factories and mechanical weaving devices in the accurate belief that these devices would rob them of their employment as skilled handloom weavers working from their cottages. Sentences for these acts were severe and Burbury was sentenced to hang. But the local community, not considering such actions to be crimes, exerted enough pressure to have his sentence commuted to transportation for life.

He landed in Tasmania in 1832. Only a few months later, his wife and child also arrived, having been provided with a passage through public donations. Reunited with his family, Burbury began to buy land in his wife's name and became a valued assigned servant, helping to hunt down bushrangers. By 1837, he had his ticket of leave and a full pardon two years later. He went on to become a local council employee and a member of Oatlands local council, and died a respected local pioneer, as did many transported convicts.

The Ring

Almost as old a settlement as Port Jackson, Norfolk Island became known as one of the worse convict hellholes. A penal station was established on the island only a few months after the arrival of the First Fleet but was abandoned in 1814, and in 1825 a second penal colony was founded. There was a need for somewhere to put 'the worst description of convicts'; Norfolk was intended to be a place of no hope, where hard cases would be imprisoned and worked in irons until they died.

The island rapidly gained a reputation for horrifying brutality and sadistic oppression by a succession of military commanders and their squads of willing brutalisers. There was an unsuccessful revolt or mutiny in 1834 and when the Vicar General of Sydney, the Very Reverend William Ullathorne, arrived to tell the offenders who would live and who would die, he reported, 'As I mentioned the names of those men who were to die, they one after another, as their names were pronounced, dropped on their knees and thanked God that they were to be delivered from that horrible place, whilst the others remained standing mute, weeping. It was the most horrible scene I have ever witnessed.'

Despite these disturbing images, historical research suggests that while Norfolk Island was not a pleasant place to be, the more extreme images of brutality and degradation may be based on a selection of unusually brutal incidents and the amplifying effect of folk tradition. However, there are persistent tales of the terrors experienced on the island between 1825 and the penal station's final closure in 1856, largely in response to a number of damning reports.

An especially intriguing story involves an alleged secret society known as 'the Ring'. In Marcus Clarke's famous novel *For the Term of His Natural Life*, we first hear of the Ring when Rufus Dawes is sent to Norfolk Island and becomes its leader. In another Ring story, three convicts agree to drawing lots to decide which one will kill another, leaving the third as a witness against the murderer, ensuring that he will be hanged. This is based on a claim made in a British Select Committee of Parliament in 1838 by Colonel George Arthur: '. . . Two or three men murdered their fellow-prisoners, with the certainty of being detected and executed, apparently without malice and with very little excitement, stating that they knew that they should be hanged, but it was better than being where they were.'

In the writings of Clarke and Price Warung (William Astley), this relatively rare horror is transformed into a Ring custom. In *For the Term of His Natural Life*, Clarke has one of his characters note in his diary:

May 16th.—A sub-overseer, a man named Hankey, has been talking to me. He says that there are some forty of the oldest and worst prisoners who form what he calls the 'Ring', and that the members of this 'Ring' are bound by oath to support each other, and to avenge the punishment of any of their number. In proof of his assertions he instanced two cases of English prisoners who had refused to join in some crime, and had informed the

Commandant of the proceedings of the Ring. They were found in the morning strangled in their hammocks. An inquiry was held, but not a man out of the ninety in the ward would speak a word. I dread the task that is before me. How can I attempt to preach piety and morality to these men? How can I attempt even to save the less villainous?

In Warung's later short stories, said to be based on interviews with ex-convicts, we also read about an elaborately structured clandestine order existing within the prison system and effectively running it. Led by the One, the Ring is said to have been a hierarchy of 25 members. The lowest order consisted of nine members and was known as the Nine; the next were the seven members of the Seven; then the Fives and Threes. Only the Threes knew the identity of the One. Only the worst of the worst were invited to join at the bottom level and could work themselves up to the higher orders by even more evildoing. The Ring's rationale was complete denial of all penal authority. Any member who had any dealings with the gaolers was to be killed, and only then could a new recruit fill the gap. While the members of each order were known to each other, those of the other orders did not know them. Nor did anyone outside the Ring, convict or gaoler, know the identity of its initiates. But no one was in any doubt of its existence.

When the Ring decided to meet, word went through the prison that no non-member, including guards, should enter the prison yard. The One entered the yard first and faced a corner of the wall. He was followed by the Threes, Fives, Sevens and Nines, each arrayed in a semi-circle behind him. All were masked. Satanic prayers were intoned:

Is God an officer of the establishment?
And the response came solemnly clear, thrice repeated:

No, God is not an officer of the establishment.

He passed to the next question:

Is the Devil an officer of the establishment?

And received the answer—thrice:

Yes, the Devil is an officer of the establishment.

He continued:

Then do we obey God?

With clear-cut resonance came the negative—

No, we do not obey God!

He propounded the problem framed by souls that are not necessarily
corrupt:

Then whom do we obey?

And, thrice over, he received for reply the damning perjury which
yet was so true an answer:

The Devil—we obey our Lord the Devil!

And the dreaded Convict Oath was taken. It had eight verses
according to Warung:

Hand to hand,
On Earth, in Hell,
Sick or Well,
On Sea, on Land,
On the Square, ever.

It ended—the intervening verses dare not be quoted—

Stiff or in Breath,
Lag or Free,
You and Me,
In Life, in Death,
On the Cross, never.

They all then drank a cup of blood taken from the veins of each man.

After these rites were performed, the Ring would conduct their business, usually involving a trial and sentence of suspected collaborators among the convict population or of any of their gaolers who showed an inclination to be lenient to the prisoners.

At first look, the florid stories of the Ring seem more like a Masonic or occult order than a self-protection association of convicts on a remote Pacific island. Certainly Warung had a fertile imagination and colourful writing style. Historians have also pointed out that evidence for the existence of such an elaborate organisation depends on a single documented mention of Norfolk Island convicts defying their gaolers—not an uncommon event.

But despite the absence of historical evidence, the story of the Ring lives on, along with the darker suspicions about the depravity, degradation and despair of the Norfolk Island 'system'. While the secret order of the Ring and some of the more extreme events alleged to have occurred may be exaggerated, the remaining realities of Norfolk Island were horrifying enough to support the belief that an organisation like the Ring could have, and perhaps should have, existed.

The melancholy death of Captain Logan

Captain Patrick Logan was in charge of the Moreton Bay penal settlement on the Brisbane River from 1826. His tenure was notorious among convicts for its extreme cruelty, especially floggings while lashed to the 'triangle', a wooden structure designed to spreadeagle its victims to ensure maximum infliction of the lash across the back of the body.

In October 1830, Logan lost his life in an attack by 'natives', as Aborigines were invariably described in the nineteenth century. Captain Clunie of the 17th Regiment reported the details, as far as they could be ascertained, to the Colonial Secretary in Sydney on 6 November 1830. Logan was returning home from a mapping expedition near Mount Irwin when he became separated from his party. They went to find him a day or so later:

. . . we naturally concluded he had fallen into the hands of the natives, and hoped he might be a prisoner and alive, parties were sent out in every direction to endeavour to meet them; while, in the meantime, his servant and party found his saddle, with the stirrups cut off as if by a native's hatchet, about ten miles from the place where Captain Logan left them, in the direction of the Limestone station. Near to this place, also, were the marks of his horse having been tied to a tree, of his having himself slept upon some grass in a bark hut, and having apparently been roasting chestnuts, when he made some rapid strides towards his horse, as if surprised by natives. No further traces, however, could be discovered, and though the anxiety of his family and friends were most distressing, hopes were still entertained of his being alive till the 28th ultimo, when Mr Cowper, whose exertions on this occasion were very great, and for which I feel much indebted, discovered the dead horse sticking in a creek, and not far from it, at the top of the bank, the body of Captain Logan buried about a foot under ground. Near this also were found papers torn in pieces, his boots, and part of his waistcoat, stained with blood.

From all these circumstances it appears probable that while at this place, where he had stopped for the night, Captain Logan was suddenly surprised by natives; that he mounted his horse without saddle or bridle, and, being unable to manage him, the horse, pursued by the natives, got into the creek, where Captain Logan, endeavouring to extricate him, was overtaken and murdered.

❧

Logan's pregnant widow had his body shipped to Sydney for burial, mourning the loss of her husband as the captain's colleagues regretted the loss of an efficient commander. But the convicts reacted very differently.

Some time after Logan's death a new ballad began to circulate, and has done ever since. The song told the story of an Irish convict transported to Moreton Bay, where he meets another prisoner who tells him:

I've been a prisoner at Port Macquarie,
At Norfolk Island, and Emu Plains;
At Castle Hill and cursed Toongabbee—
At all those places I've worked in chains:
But of all the places of condemnation,
In each penal station of New South Wales,
To Moreton Bay I found no equal,
For excessive tyranny each day prevails.

Early in the morning when day is dawning,
To trace from heaven the morning dew,
Up we are started at a moment's warning,
Our daily labour to renew.
Our overseers and superintendents—
These tyrants' orders we must obey,
Or else at the triangles our flesh is mangled—
Such are our wages at Moreton Bay!

For three long years I've been beastly treated;
Heavy irons each day I wore;
My back from flogging has been lacerated,
And oftimes painted with crimson gore.
Like the Egyptians and ancient Hebrews,
We were oppressed under Logan's yoke,
Till kind Providence came to our assistance,
And gave this tyrant his mortal stroke.

The song ends with an expression of gratitude in the lines:

> My fellow-prisoners, be exhilarated,
> That all such monsters such a death may find:
> For it's when from bondage we are liberated,
> Our former sufferings will fade from mind.

The death of Logan was such a great moment in convict culture that its impact continued for another 50 years or more. The event was still very much alive in Ned Kelly's mind when he composed the Jerilderie Letter in the late 1870s:

> ... more was transported to Van Diemand's Land to pine their young lives away in starvation and misery among tyrants worse than the promised hell itself all of true blood bone and beauty, that was not murdered on their own soil, or had fled to America or other countries to bloom again another day, were doomed to Port Mcquarie Toweringabbie norfolk island and Emu plains and in those places of tyrany and condemnation many a blooming Irishman rather than subdue to the Saxon yoke Were flogged to death and bravely died in servile chains but true to the shamrock and a credit to Paddys land.

Before that, a convict known as Francis MacNamara would get the credit for composing the ballad of Logan's death. Whether he did or not, his story is another memorable tale of the convict era.

A Convict's Tour to Hell

Francis MacNamara—better known to his convict peers by the moniker of 'Frank the Poet'—may have penned the original version of the powerful lament of 'Moreton Bay', although he did not arrive in Australia until twelve years after Logan's death.

Arriving in Sydney in 1832 for the crime of breaking a shop window and stealing a 'piece of worsted plaid', MacNamara was one of the convict period's greatest characters. Like many of his Irish fellow convicts, he had a passionate hatred of the English and the convict system. Unlike most, he also had the ability to express his antagonism in witty and satirical verse. MacNamara's work was often more ambitious than the usual doggerel of the street ballads and included a parody of the literary versions of the mythic descent into the underworld theme, notable in the work of Dante and Swift. *A Convict's Tour to Hell* is a small masterpiece in which Frank dreams that he has died and, like Dante, must journey through the underworld to find his true resting place for all eternity. He visits Purgatory, which he finds full of priests and popes 'weeping wailing gnashing' and suffering the 'torments of the newest fashion'. He journeys on to Hell:

And having found the gloomy gate
Frank rapped aloud to know his fate
He louder knocked and louder still
When the Devil came, pray what's your will?
Alas cried the Poet I've come to dwell
With you and share your fate in Hell
Says Satan that can't be, I'm sure
For I detest and hate the poor
And none shall in my kingdom stand
Except the grandees of the land.
But Frank I think you are going astray
For convicts never come this way
But soar to Heaven in droves and legions
A place so called in the upper regions . . .

In Hell, Frank finds the overseers, floggers and gaolers of the convict system writhing in perpetual torture for the crimes they committed against poor convicts while alive on earth. Captain Cook, 'who discovered New South Wales', is here, along with dukes, mayors and lawyers. They are not alone.

> Here I beheld legions of traitors
> Hangmen gaolers and flagellators
> Commandants, Constables and Spies
> Informers and Overseers likewise
> In flames of brimstone they were toiling
> And lakes of sulphur round them boiling
> Hell did resound with their fierce yelling
> Alas how dismal was their dwelling . . .

One unfortunate seems to be suffering special torments so Frank asks:

> Who is that Sir in yonder blaze
> Who on fire and brimstone seems to graze?

Satan tells him that it is 'Captain Logan of Moreton Bay'.

While he witnesses this dreadful scene there is suddenly a great commotion in Hell. Drums are beaten, flags waved:

> And all the inhabitants of Hell
> With one consent rang the great bell
> Which never was heard to sound or ring
> Since Judas sold our Heavenly King
> Drums were beating flags were hoisting
> There never before was such rejoicing
> Dancing singing joy or mirth
> In Heaven above or on the earth
> Straightway to Lucifer I went
> To know what these rejoicings meant . . .

Satan is senseless with joy as the chief tormentor of all the convicts in New South Wales—Governor Darling—enters Hell. Satan's assistants have already chained him and prepared the brimstone in which he will writhe forever. Satisfied to have witnessed this wonderful sight, Frank travels on to 'that happy place/Where all the woes of mortals cease'. He knocks at the pearly gate and is met by St Peter, who asks him who in heaven he might know. Frank answers by naming bushrangers:

> Well I know Brave Donohue
> Young Troy and Jenkins too
> And many others whom floggers mangled
> And lastly were by Jack Ketch strangled ...

Then,

> Peter, says Jesus, let Frank in
> For he is thoroughly purged from sin
> And although in convict's habit dressed
> Here he shall be a welcome guest ...

A great celebration is then had by all the hosts in Heaven, 'Since Frank the Poet has come at last'. The poem ends with the lines:

> Thro' Heaven's Concave their rejoicings range
> And hymns of praise to God they sang
> And as they praised his glorious name
> I woke and found 'twas but a dream.

'Make it hours instead of days'

With a story like this, it is no surprise that Frank the Poet was still remembered into the twentieth century. In 1902, a rural newspaper published a memoir of Frank's life and times. The historical details are often wrong (Frank never actually met Captain Logan) but the spirit of the story and the respect for Frank's abilities is clear.

*F*rancis MacNamara was a man who came out to Botany Bay in the early days for the benefit of his country and the good of himself. He was one of those mixed up in the political intrigues of the 'Young Ireland Party,' and for the part he took in such with Smith O'Brien and others he was 'transported beyond the seas.' He was well educated, and gifted with a quick perception and ready wit. His aptitude in rhyming gained for him the appellation of 'Frank the Poet,' and many stories used to be told by old hands of his smartness in getting out of a difficulty.

During a time that he was under Captain Logan at Moreton Bay he was frequently in trouble. On one occasion he was called to account for some misdeed, and asked why he should not be imprisoned for fourteen days. He answered promptly—

'Captain Logan, if you plaze,
Make it hours instead of days.'

And the Captain did.

On another occasion he was brought before Logan for inciting the other inmates of his hut to refuse a bullock's head that was being served to them as rations. Captain Logan, in a severe tone, asked him what he meant by generating a mutinous feeling among his fellows.

'Please, sir. I didn't,' said Frank 'I only advised my mates not to accept it as rations because there was no meat on it.' 'Well MacNamara,' said the Captain, 'I am determined to check this insubordinate tendency in a way that I hope will be effective. At the same time, I am willing to hear anything you may have to say in defence before passing sentence on you.'

'Sure, Captain,' said Frank, 'I know you are just, and merciful as well. Kindly let the head be brought in, and you will see yourself that it is nothing but skin and bone, and ain't got enough flesh on it to make a feed for one man. I only said we won't be satisfied with it for our ration.' The Captain ordered the head to be brought, and when it was placed on the table he turned to Frank and said, 'There's the head. Now what about it?'

Frank advanced to the table, picked up a paper-cutter, and said to the Captain and those with him, 'Listen, your honours, to the "honey" ring it has,' and, tapping it with the paper knife, recited in a loud tone the following lines : —

'Oh, bullock, oh, bullock, thou wast brought here,
After working in a team for many a year,
Subjected to the lash, foul language and abuse
And now portioned as food for poor convicts' use.'

'Get out of my sight, you scoundrel,' roared Logan, 'and if you come before me again I'll send you to the triangle.' It is needless to say that Frank was quickly out of the room, chuckling to himself at his good luck. Some time after he was assigned to a squatter in New South Wales, and as was his wont, always in hot water. He was at last given a letter to take to the chief constable in the adjoining town.

Frank suspected the purport of the letter to be a punishment for himself, so he raked his brain in devising a means of escape. Having writing materials, and being an efficient penman, he addressed a couple of envelopes, and, putting them with the one he had received to give the officer, he started. On the outskirts of the town he met a former acquaintance, who was on 'a ticket of leave,' and a stranger to the district. Frank had known him elsewhere, and remembered him as a flogger: and on one occasion he had dropped the lash on himself.

31

Here was what Frank styled a heaven-sent chance, and it would be a sort of revenge for a past infliction if he succeeded in getting this fellow to deliver the letter. So he sat down and chatted for a while, and pulling out the three envelopes, regretted that they could not have a drink together. If his business was finished, they could; but his master, he said was a Tartar, and it wouldn't be safe to neglect it. So he would have to deliver the letters first. 'Perhaps I might be able to help you,' said the other. 'Blest if I know,' answered Frank, 'it would be all right so long as the cove didn't find it out.' 'Oh, chance it,' said the other, 'and we can have another hour together.'

Frank thought for a while, turning the letters about in his hands, and at last made up his mind to let the other assist him, so handed him the letter addressed to 'Mr. Snapem, Concordium.' They went on into town, and Frank, directing the ex-flogger, turned into a shop. Sneaking on a few minutes after, he heard enough to satisfy him that his surmise was correct, and he left.

On his return to the station, he was asked by the squatter if he had received any reply to the letter. 'Oh, yes,' answered he: 'a feeling reply, that I am likely to remember.' While having tea he appeared in such excellent humour that one of his mates asked the cause. 'Oh, nothing much,' said Frank, 'only circumstances to-day enabled me to pay a debt that I have owed for some years: and I am glad about it.'

Captain of the push

The newspaper also published another recollection of Frank's doings, this time in Sydney town with the forerunners of the larrikin 'pushes' or gangs who often terrorised the streets later in the nineteenth century: Frank had a great down on a 'push' in Sydney known as the 'Cabbage-Tree Mob', their symbol being the wearing of a cabbage-tree hat. Well, on one occasion they bailed up poor Frank, and asked him what he had to say that they should not inflict condign punishment on him. 'Well, boys,' he said,

'Here's three cheers for the Cabbage-tree Mob—
Too lazy to work; too frightened to rob.'

They made for Frank, but just then came along a policeman known as the 'Native Dog'; so Frank escaped that time.

The street gangs of Sydney and Melbourne are almost as old as the cities themselves. In Sydney, the 'Cabbage-Tree Mob' was frequently mentioned in negative terms in the local press: 'There are to be found all round the doors of the Sydney Theatre a sort of loafer known as the Cabbage-Tree Mob. The Cabbage-Tree Mob are always up for a 'spree' and some of their pastimes are so rough an order as to deserve to be repaid with bloody coxcombs.'

Probably not a coherent gang or 'push' so much as an occasional assembly of young working-class men, the mob was distinguished by the kind of headgear they favoured, a hat made from cabbage-tree fronds. Whatever their exact nature, the Cabbage-Tree Mob hung around theatres, race grounds and markets and specialised in catcalling and otherwise harassing the respectable middle classes. Some of them were ex-convicts; some were descended from convict stock.

By the 1870s, groups of this sort were being called 'larrikins'. Their favoured pastimes were a development of the earlier troublemakers and included disrupting Salvation Army meetings with volleys of rotten vegetables, rocks and the odd dead cat. The larrikins were also noted for dancing with young women friends, events often portrayed by journalists as 'orgies'. By the 1880s, observers began to speak of larrikin 'pushes' or gangs, also sometimes referred to as the 'talent'. These were usually associated with particular suburbs or areas; in Sydney there were the 'Haymarket Bummers', the 'Rocks push', the 'Cow Lane push' and the 'Woolloomooloo push'. In Melbourne it was the 'Fitzroy forties', the 'Stephen Street push' and the surely ironic 'Flying Angels', among others. The pushes were mostly male, young and with a strong loyalty ethic, each supporting the others when needed.

The larrikins revelled in fighting with police and resisting arrest, and there were notable pitched battles between them and large groups of police in the last decades of the nineteenth century. Despite, or because of, their criminality and antisocial behaviour, the crudely colourful larrikins soon became the objects of literary interest. Henry Lawson's 'The Captain of the Push' was an early rendering of the larrikin culture.

Based loosely on real events, 'The Captain of the Push' (also unprintably parodied as 'The Bastard from the Bush') begins:

As the night was falling slowly down on city, town and bush,
From a slum in Jones's Alley sloped the Captain of the Push;
And he scowled towards the North, and he scowled towards the South,
As he hooked his little finger in the corners of his mouth.
Then his whistle, loud and shrill, woke the echoes of the 'Rocks',
And a dozen ghouls came sloping round the corners of the blocks.

The ghouls, called the 'Gory Bleeders', 'spoke the gutter language' of the slums and brothels and swore fearsomely and fulsomely with every breath. Their 'captain' was:

. . . bottle-shouldered, pale and thin,
For he was the beau-ideal of a Sydney larrikin;
E'en his hat was most suggestive of the city where we live,
With a gallows-tilt that no one, save a larrikin, can give . . .

He wears the larrikin outfit of wide-mouthed trousers, elaborate boots, uncollared shirt and necktie. The gang encounters a stranger in the street, who turns out to be a man from the bush who wants to join the gang. He has read of their exploits in the *Weekly Gasbag* and, sitting alone in his bush humpy, decides that he

'. . . longed to share the dangers and the pleasures of the push!
'Gosh! I hate the swells and good 'uns—I could burn 'em in their beds;
'I am with you, if you'll have me, and I'll break their blazing heads.'

The larrikins demand to know if the bushman would match them in perfidy and violence. Would he punish an informer who breaks the code of loyalty?

'Would you lay him out and kick him to a jelly on the ground?' Would he 'smash a bleedin' bobby', 'break a swell or Chinkie' and 'have a "moll" to keep yer'? To all of which the stranger answers, 'My kerlonial oath! I would!' They test him practically by asking him to smash a window. The stranger is sworn in and becomes an exemplary larrikin, if a little over-zealous even for the Gory Bleeders.

One morning the captain wakes and finds the stranger gone:

Quickly going through the pockets of his 'bloomin' bags,' he learned
That the stranger had been through him for the stuff his 'moll'
    had earned;
And the language that he muttered I should scarcely like to tell.
(Stars! and notes of exclamation!! blank and dash will do as well).

The rest of the bleeders soon forget the bloke who briefly joined them and robbed their leader. But the captain 'Still is laying round in ballast, for the nameless from the bush.'

Louis Stone's flawed masterpiece, *Jonah*, presented a more realistic picture of the Sydney slum lifestyle that produced and nourished the larrikins. Its eponymous hero makes his own fortune by hard work and astute business sense, though forfeits his working-class roots, loses in love and fails as a decent human being in the process.

Probably taking his lead from this approach, C.J. Dennis began writing the verse that would eventually become the much-loved classics *The Songs of a Sentimental Bloke* and *The Moods of Ginger Mick*. These were highly romanticised and bore almost no resemblance to the realities of the street, with soft Bill 'the Bloke', his love for Doreen and friendship with street rabbit-seller Ginger Mick, and other characters who hung around Melbourne's 'Little Lon'. These verse novellas sold in great numbers, making Dennis a wealthy man and establishing the 'rough diamond' with a soft centre stereotype of the larrikin, recycled for decades in stage shows and the early Australian cinema. The image lives on still.

The Prince of Pickpockets

It is difficult to sift fact from folklore in the life of George Barrington (1755–1804). The Irish-born rogue of uncertain parentage was a colourful man-about-town in early nineteenth-century London, though his early life began in obscurity and crime.

His story begins with him stabbing a schoolmate and robbing his teacher. The sixteen-year-old ran away and joined a travelling theatre troupe where he gave himself the name George Barrington and learned the pickpocketing business. He then went to London where he affected the wealth and style of a gentleman, his eloquence assuring him of acceptance into even the highest circles. It became something of a social honour to have had one's pocket picked by the great thief. He notoriously relieved the Russian Count Orlov of a diamond-encrusted silver snuffbox said to be worth 30,000 pounds, an unimaginable sum for most people at the time. Barrington was caught and made to return his booty. Orlov refused to prosecute.

But the incorrigible Barrington was later arrested on another charge and sentenced to three years' hard labour. He was described at the time as 'the genteelest thief ever remembered seen at the Old Bailey', despite the fact that he lived in Charing Cross, then one of London's less respectable districts.

The Prince of Pickpockets was out after serving barely a year of his sentence. After his release he returned to his nefarious trade and was soon arrested again, this time going down for five years. He was freed through the influence of friends in high places on condition that he left the country. He did so briefly, but soon returned and was caught thieving yet again.

During his last appearance at the Old Bailey, Barrington made a lengthy and elaborate speech in his defence and argued against his hanging. This was quite unnecessary, as his crime was not a capital offence. Without delay the jury pronounced him guilty. Always wanting to have the last word, the eloquent cutpurse replied:

My Lord,

I had a few words to say, why sentence of death should not be passed upon me; I had much to say, though I shall say but little on the occasion. Notwithstanding I have the best opinion of your lordship's candour, and have no wish or pleasure in casting a reflection on any person whatever; but I cannot help observing that it is the strange lot of some persons through life, that with the best wishes, the best endeavours, and the best intentions, they are not able to escape the envenomed tooth of calumny: whatever they say or do is so twisted and perverted from the reality, that they will meet with censures and misfortunes, where perhaps they were entitled to success and praise. The world, my lord, has given me credit for much more abilities than I am conscious of possessing; but the world should also consider that the greatest abilities may be obstructed by the mercenary nature of some unfeeling minds, as to render them entirely useless to the possessor. Where was the generous and powerful man that would come forward and say, 'You have some abilities which might be of service to yourself and to others, but you have much to struggle with, I feel for your situation, and will place you in a condition to try the sincerity of your intentions; and as long as you act with diligence and fidelity, you shall not want for countenance and protection?' But, my lord, the die is cast! I am prepared to meet the sentence of the court, with respectful resignation, and the painful lot assigned me, I hope, with becoming resolution.

This was Barrington being brief! He was given seven years' transportation. Even his silver tongue could not save him from this fate.

By now the artful Barrington had become a celebrity criminal. His gentleman thief image, his clever tongue and ability to wriggle out of prison sentences made him a sensation of the London gossips and the press. The papers embroidered and invented exploits as outrageously as they do today. Even before he was transported to Botany Bay the papers reported his alleged attempt to escape Newgate wearing his female accomplice's dress. He was also reported to be lamenting that the great Barrington was to be banished to a land where the natives had no pockets for him to pick.

Little more than a year after his arrival in New South Wales, the pickpocket's talents and abilities saw him quickly freed, soon to become a superintendent of the convicts he had once laboured among and, later, chief constable of Parramatta. Governor Hunter granted him land and he purchased more, prospering as a farmer and more or less reformed character. Pensioned off the government service in 1800, Barrington's behaviour became increasingly erratic. He was declared insane and died in 1804.

But his legend lived on. Like many folk heroes, he was said by some to have lived to a ripe old age. His faked memoirs were frequently reprinted and he featured in newspapers even a century and a half after his death. Barrington was also, inaccurately, credited with some often-quoted lines that have passed into the traditions of transportation and convictism. At the opening of the colony's first theatre in 1796 he is supposed to have delivered this verse:

From distant climes o'er widespread seas we come,
Though not with much eclat or beat of drum.
True patriots all; for be it understood,
We left our country for our country's good.

Many other stories were told about him, not only in the raffish memoirs he allegedly penned but in folk tradition as well. One yarn had it that there was a party at the home of a wealthy Sydney merchant during Barrington's time in the colony. The gossip-worthy pickpocket came up as a topic during conversation. The merchant's wife and hostess of the event firmly proclaimed that she did not believe the outlandish yarns about the smooth-talking Barrington and his thieving skills.

A couple of days after the party a gentleman called asking to speak with the hostess's husband. He was away, so the hostess showed off her array of expensive jewels while they waited. But the husband did not return as expected and the man said he would try again another day. As he left, the debonair visitor put his hand in his coat and drew out the hostess's gold earrings and necklace. He bowed, saying, 'I think these are yours, madam. Kindly tell your husband that Mr Barrington called.'

3

Plains of promise

Our hearts they were willing, our bodies they were young
Upon the Plains of Promise we were broken by the sun.

From Anon., 'Plains of Promise'

THE EUROPEAN SETTLEMENT of Australia was a series of voyages from the old world to the new. It began with convicts and their gaolers but was soon followed by ships of free migrants searching for a better life, looking to make a fortune or even just planning to spend a few years in the colonies. The vast majority of those who came here before the 1950s were British, bringing their customs and traditions with them. A few of these thrived, many faded and others were adapted to form the basis of a national identity.

Promising though Australia was for many settlers, their voyages were often hard and tragic.

'I was not expected to survive'

Many were prepared to risk much, often all, in pursuit of the plains of promise. Ellen Moger arrived in Adelaide in January 1840. She wrote home to her parents after the voyage from England, 'four months to a day on the Great Deep':

*P*oor little Alfred was the first that died on the 30th of Oct, and on the 8th of Nov, dear Fanny went and three days after, on the 11th, the dead babe was taken from me. I scarcely know how I sustained the shock, though I was certain they could not recover, yet when poor Fanny went it over-powered me and from the weakness of my frame, reduced me to such a low nervous state that, for many weeks, I was not expected to survive. It seems I gave much trouble but knew nothing about it and, though I was quite conscious that the dear baby and Fanny were thrown overboard, I would still persist that the water could not retain them and that they were with me in the berth. I took strange fancies into my head and thought that Mother had said I should have her nice easy chair to sit up in and, if they would only lift me into it, I would soon get well. I had that chair of Mother's in my 'mind's eye' for many weeks and was continually talking about it.

Later in the letter she discusses the health of her surviving daughter:

My dear Emily now seems more precious to us than ever, and I feel very thankful I did not leave her in England. Her health is not as good as formerly, having something Scurvy, the effects of Salt diet. She is also troubled with weak eyes, a complaint exceedingly common in this town, from the great degree of heat, light and dust.

Ellen Moger's tragedy was not unique. The poorer assisted-passage emigrants shipped in steerage class, herded together for many months in crowded and often unsanitary conditions, ideal for the incubation and spread of frequently fatal diseases including scarlet fever, measles, typhus and even cholera on some ships. Illness struck children and adults alike, but it was the infants who died in the greatest numbers, often from the less exotic but equally lethal cases of severe diarrhoea.

In 1839, Sarah Brunskill watched her infant son die of convulsions following acute diarrhoea. Twenty-four hours later, her two-year-old daughter died in an agonising fever so hot that her mother found it painful to touch her.

'She, like her brother, was thrown into the deep about the same time on the Thursday. The Union Jack was thrown over them, and the burial service Performed.' Sarah thought that they were like 'two little angels, they looked so beautiful in death'.

Multiple deaths from disease were not uncommon in the early decades of sailing ship migration. From the 1850s, sanitation and health care improved and mortality rates dropped considerably. Deaths aboard migrant ships fell to a level equal to, or even less than, those on land for adults and older children, though infants remained at great peril. Sarah Brunskill and her husband were among the better-off passengers, though this factor did not spare their children.

The shipboard experience of some migrants was sometimes as bad as the worst of the convict ships. In some ways it was even more despairing. At least the transports looked forward to little, while the migrants left home full of hope for a new and better life for themselves and their children.

The town that drowned

They called it the 'valley of hope'. The mainly German migrants who came to South Australia from the 1830s wanted land to grow their crops and a place to practise their religious beliefs unhindered. Early arrivals soon found the Barossa region and other suitable places and were followed by families and single men of Lutheran beliefs, establishing settlements and using the housing and agricultural styles that were familiar to them. Of course, they also built churches as the single most important structures in each settlement.

In 1847–48, the village of Hoffnungsthal was founded. Its settlers included Christian Menzel and Maria Richter with their ten children, the Huf family of six, the Beinkes and the Seelanders, among others. By 1848 they had nearly 400 acres under cultivation and began building a church and looking for a pastor.

Each year they celebrated the leaving of their homelands and their settling at Hoffnungsthal.

They were happy people, those dwellers in old Hoffnungsthal. To them this new country looked like the Land of Canaan, for it flowed with milk and honey. In the great old gums the bees had their hives and in very warm weather, the combs overflowed and the honey dropped to the ground. And if anyone was lucky enough to possess a cow or two, he also had milk. So abundant was the feed for the cows, that often, too, these could not retain their milk, and like the honey, it flowed to the ground. There were no fences in those days, the country was open in all directions and the cows were free to wander and seek for themselves the most succulent grasses. In the gullies of the Barossa Ranges, the pasture was sweet and the water in the creeks as clear as crystal.

For the farmers and tradesmen and their families, this was as close to paradise as they were likely to get this side of the grave. They took to their new country with enthusiasm and the same intensity as they brought to their religious values, growing wheat, barley, oats, peas, beans, lentils and potatoes from the seeds they had carefully brought with them. They brought their distinctive dress with them, too, including the black suits the men wore to church and perhaps other religious occasions. They made 'coffee' with rye and milk and their cottage gardens supplied many of their wants, along with the bounty of the countryside: wild ducks, white cockatoos and kangaroo. It was reported that the local Aboriginal people were greatly impressed with the efficiency of the German firearms in downing wildlife.

In other things they followed the ways of their homeland, apparently unaware that they had built on dangerous country. The Peramangk people of the area called the place Yertalla-ngga, meaning 'flooding land'. Their story is that one of their men, known as Jemmie, warned the newcomers against building in their valley of hope because it was prone to serious flooding. Biblically, they ignored this good advice and after a few years of this happy life:

*L*arge tracts of bush country had been cleared and the good people were beginning to feel settled and comfortable. But the happiest conditions of life may come to an end very suddenly. It was about the year 1853 in the month of October when the disaster came. It rained heavily and continuously. For a day and a night the rain came down like a deluge. One family had to leave its house during the night and seek refuge beneath a huge boulder on the side of the hill. In the morning a scene of desolation met the gaze of the people as they emerged from their cottages. All the farms and gardens were submerged. The water was already entering the homes and was rising rapidly. In great haste they had to open pens and yards for pigs and cattle to escape. Then was there much weeping among mothers and children and many were asking why the hand of the Lord had thus descended upon them. Had they done anything to offend God? With a little reflection they had to admit that they themselves were to blame for the disaster that had overwhelmed them. The old blacks had warned them that sometimes much water would flow together there where they had built their village, although possibly they had not understood the warning. They had not had much experience of the vagaries of the Australian climate. It was hardly to be expected that God would alter the laws of nature on their account. Their work of clearing the land of timber and brush had made the progress of the flood waters all the more rapid. Before the creeks and gullies had finished emptying out their waters Old Hoffnungsthal was submerged beneath some eight feet of water.

~

The valley of hope had become a lake of lapping waters, and there was no way to economically drain it. There was nothing else for the people of Hoffnungsthal to do but to leave their homes, hopes and memories behind and move on to start again. Some founded a new settlement, which they called Neu Hoffnungsthal. Some moved to Victoria, where they established Hochkirch (now Tarrington). Some were so disillusioned that they left Australia altogether and voyaged to America.

Although the town was no more, the area retained some settlers and gained new ones. Roads, bridges and other improvements still needed to be maintained and developed for the overall infrastructure of the area. In 1883 there were more floods, though with minimal damage. The town's name was changed to Karrawirra in World War I due to anti-German prejudice, but was restored in 1975.

Little now remains of old Hoffnungsthal: one or two buildings and the sturdy church, built high on a hill to be closer to God. Over the years, this gradually decayed and its stones were salvaged for other buildings around the region. Today there is not much to see but a few stone heaps.

Wine and witches

The sunny Barossa Valley winelands are an unlikely setting for dark mutterings from the age of witchcraft, but tales of occult beliefs and practices lingered there for a very long time. It all began with the migration of the early German settlers. Many of these people were Lutherans or members of other sects with a strong belief in good and evil, which could lead to superstitious behaviour. Locals used to guard against witchcraft by wearing red ribbons around their necks or putting their clothes on inside out, using magic to fight magic.

The story of the devil coming to the Barossa's largest hill, Kaiserstuhl, stems from an incident in the very early years of settlement. A group led by Pastor Kavel concluded that this would happen on a certain night. They had a blacksmith forge a mighty chain that would last for 1000 years, and took the chain to the hill with the intention of capturing the devil and locking him away from the world so he could do no more evil. As far as anyone knows, the devil did not make an appearance, but one night the same pastor took a group of his followers to a spot outside Tanunda, where they intended to wait out the end of the world, an event that would destroy what they saw as the debauchery of the settlement. While Tanunda burned, Kavel and his people would enter into paradise in a state of natural grace. Instead, it rained, and the end-of-days enthusiasts had to return home drenched to their beds.

It is also whispered in local tradition that the occult text known as the *Sixth and Seventh Books of Moses*, or known more popularly as *The Witches' Bible*, was circulating in the valley, perhaps as early as 1842. Although banned by the Lutheran Church, copies of this work were known to have been secreted by some and also handed on from generation to generation in the belief that anyone who owned this book would never be able to die unless it was given to another. If that were not possible, the book might be laid in the coffin along with its last owner. The coffin then had to be dropped to the ground three times in a ritual of farewell and finality.

This book is said to have contained spells for all manner of magical operations, including hexes. One story has it that a farmer and his wife had an argument one morning. He stamped out to plough and she went huffily off to market to sell the vegetables, hexing him as he went. When she returned at the end of the day, her husband was still standing at the plough, just as he had been when she had left in the morning. The story does not say whether his wife had calmed down enough to release the farmer from the plough.

Barossa legend is full of tales about wheels falling off or locking up on wagons passing particular houses, cows suddenly losing their milk or hens failing to lay eggs. There were reported incidents of witchcraft in the Barossa as late as 2007 and local landmarks such as The Sanctuary, a grassed rectangle of land with a group of stones at one end, are said to have occult associations.

Phantoms of the landfall light

Born in the wake of a maritime tragedy and said to be haunted by several ghosts, the Cape Otway Lighthouse has an intriguing history. The powerful beacon is known as a 'landfall light', meaning the first coastal light to be seen by ships at sea. After Bass Strait was opened up as a shorter passage to Victoria in the early nineteenth century, the lighthouse was the first sight that many migrants had of Australia after their long voyage away from home.

Only the second lighthouse to be built on the mainland, its light first flashed out in 1848. Although there had long been plans to build a light on the Cape, the difficulty of access and cost of construction held the project back until the *Cataraqui* was wrecked off King Island in September 1845, with the loss of more than 350 lives and a handful of survivors. This was not the first and far from the last tragedy in the hazardous Bass Strait. Public dismay and outrage stirred the government into finally tackling the challenging building project. Even with the help of local Aborigines and plenty of resources, it took the Port Phillip District Superintendent C.J. La Trobe three attempts and a whole year to reach the Cape by land. Then they had to map and build a road. Then they had to build a very large structure, together with buildings to house its keepers. After mammoth efforts by land and sea, the lighthouse was completed and equipped with the latest optical technology in 1848. Every 50 seconds the sperm oil-powered reflectors lit the night sky for three seconds, heralding the arrival of another ship of migrants and making the remainder of their journey as safe as possible.

The isolation of the Otway light meant that the keepers and their families could receive supplies by boat only twice a year. The little community needed to do everything themselves, including giving birth. Catherine Evans, wife of Assistant Light Keeper William Evans, lost two children at birth during their 22 years at the light. Born in 1867 and 1868, the children's graves are among the earliest still to be found in the local cemetery.

This is only one of many sad stories that provide the lighthouse with the right atmosphere for some supernatural traditions. According to another story, the wife of Assistant Light Keeper Richens was driven to mental instability by the isolation and harshness of the life and had to be institutionalised until her death in the 1930s. Her ghost is said to trouble the building in which she once lived, nowadays the café. Known as 'the Lady in Grey', she is said to simply appear and join groups of visitors. Some have heard her singing lullabies, together with other physical manifestations of a presence.

Another tradition concerns a four-year-old girl who died at the telegraph station adjacent to the lighthouse during the 1870s. The coolest place to keep the body until the medical examiner could make the long trek was a cupboard, so she was locked in there. No evidence for this happening has ever been found, but now some women entering the station experience unexplained sadness, cameras mysteriously fail and dogs refuse to enter the building. Mediums also claim to have been distressed at hearing a little girl's voice during their paranormal investigations.

After many upgrades, the Cape Otway light was decommissioned in 1994 and is now the focus of a busy local tourism industry, trading in part on its ghosts. There is certainly a folkloric basis for these stories, mostly unfounded in documentation. Now a guide at the light, Malcolm Brack, the son of a keeper, lived there for many years, and recalls that the keepers believed the signal station was haunted.

Ongoing inquiries by local historians and paranormal investigators may reveal further folklore and facts about the history of the lighthouse. Whether they do or not, the landfall light will always have the honour of having shown thousands of migrants the way to their new lives and to have saved the lives of uncounted mariners.

Tragedy on Lizard Island

Hard times forced the Oxnam family, like so many others, to leave the Cornish town of Truro in 1877. They sailed to Queensland, where their seventeen-year-old daughter Mary found work as a governess and also set up a private school in Cooktown. Mary was reportedly 'reserved, nervous and delicate', though her skills at the piano made her popular. She married Captain Robert Watson, part owner of the Lizard Island *bêche-de-mer* (sea cucumber) station, in 1880 and the following year gave birth to their son, whom they named Ferrier.

Towards the end of 1881, Captain Watson was away from the island on other business. Mary and Ferrier, accompanied only by Ah Leong, the gardener, and a houseboy named Ah Sam, were attacked by Aboriginal men from the mainland. Unwittingly, the factory and household had been set up on ground important to the local Aboriginal people, probably related to its being the home of the sand goanna, *manuya*. According to Mary's diary, Ah Sam noticed smoke from the Aborigines' camp on 27 September. Two days later Ah Leong was speared to death at the farm, not far from the cottage. At seven the following evening, Mary drove a group of Aborigines off the beach with her revolver. The next day Ah Sam was speared seven times, though he survived. There was nothing else to do but leave by sea with the wounded Ah Sam and baby Ferrier. Mary recorded their desperate voyage on a few pencilled pages:

*L*eft Lizard Island October 2nd 1881, (Sunday afternoon) in tank (or pot in which beche de mer is boiled). Got about three or four miles from the Lizards.

October 4 Made for the sand bank off the Lizards, but could not reach it. Got on a reef.

October 5 Remained on the reef all day on the look out for a boat, but saw none.

October 6 Very calm morning. Able to pull the tank up to an island with three small mountains on it. Ah Sam went ashore to try to get water as ours was done. There were natives camped there, so we were afraid to go far away. We had to wait return of tide. Anchored under the mangroves; got on the reef. Very calm.

October 7 Made for another island four or five miles from the one spoken of yesterday. Ashore, but could not find any water. Cooked some rice and clam-fish. Moderate S.E. breeze. Stayed here all night. Saw a steamer bound north. Hoisted Ferrier's pink and white wrap but did not answer us.

October 8 Changed anchorage of boat as the wind was freshening. Went down to a kind of little lake on the same island (this done last night). Remained here all day looking out for a boat; did not see any; very cold night; blowing very hard. No water.

October 9 Brought the tank ashore as far as possible with this morning's tide. Made camp all day under the trees. Blowing very hard. No water. Gave Ferrier a dip in the sea; he is showing symptoms of thirst, and I took a dip myself. Ah Sam and self very parched with thirst. Ferrier is showing symptoms.

October 10 Ferrier very bad with inflammation; very much alarmed. No fresh water, and no more milk, but condensed. Self very weak; really thought I would have died last night (Sunday).

October 11 Still all alive. Ferrier very much better this morning. Self feeling very weak. I think it will rain to-day; clouds very heavy; wind not quite so hard. No rain. Morning fine weather. Ah Sam preparing to die, have not seen him since 9th. Ferrier more cheerful. Self not feeling at all well. Have not seen any boat of any description. No water. Nearly dead with thirst.

That was the final entry in Mary's sea-stained journal. Searchers found it three months later, along with the remains of the three and Mary's Bible.

Outrage, fear and hatred gripped the settlers in the area, fanned by inaccurate newspaper reports relying on prejudice and fear rather than the facts. Retribution against the perpetrators, actual and assumed, came swiftly. Men, women and children of the local Aboriginal groups were slaughtered, many of those massacred seemingly not of the same group that had attacked Mary's household. And so one tragedy was made even greater.

The bodies of Mary, Ferrier and Ah Sam were buried in

Cooktown, and in 1886 the citizens raised an impressive memorial fountain. The Mary Watson fountain is inscribed:

In MEMORIAM
MRS WATSON The Heroine of Lizard Island, Cooktown,
North Queensland, A.D. 1881

Erected 1886 Edward D`Arcy, Mayor 1885.

Five fearful days beneath the scorching glare
Her babe she nursed God knows the pangs that woman
had to bear
Whose last sad entry showed a Mother's care
Then—'Near dead with thirst.'

Who was Billy Barlow?

With migrants arriving in more or less steady streams in the colonial period, 'new chums' became a popular stereotype. Colonial folksong and literature is full of disparaging references to newcomers who were not properly dressed or equipped, or emotionally prepared for the rigours of pioneer life. It was even suggested that they should be shipped back to where they came from when they failed to measure up:

When shearing comes lay down your drums
And step to the board, you brand new chums
With a row-dum, row-dum, rubba-dub-dub
We'll send 'em home in a limejuice tub

The song makes fun of the unskilled and unhardened British recruits to the backbreaking shearer's trade and profoundly masculine lifestyle. It ends by suggesting that the new chum would be better off going back home in a 'limejuice tub', a British sailing ship—than 'humping your drum in this country'. Eventually the new chums either went home with their tails between their legs or became 'old hands' themselves, adopting the attitudes of their detractors and subjecting newcomers to the same treatment in their turn. So prevalent was the new chum that he came to be represented by a mythical figure named 'Billy Barlow', ridiculed in song and on stages across the country.

The earliest reference to Billy Barlow popped up in the 1840s, though the earliest song seems to date from an American minstrel song of a decade or so earlier. The newspaper review of an amateur theatrical production one 1843 evening noted, 'Several songs were sung, and the following, which was written expressly for the occasion by a gentleman in Maitland, was received with unbounded applause.'

In this version of the story, poor Billy is left a thousand pounds by his old aunt and decides to further his fortunes in Australia. By the second verse he has already been taken down:

When to Sydney I got, there a merchant I met,
Who said he would teach me a fortune to get;
He'd cattle and sheep past the colony's bounds,
Which he sold with the station for my thousand pounds.
Oh dear, lackaday, oh,
He gammon'd the cash out of Billy Barlow.

Things go from bad to worse; as Billy goes 'up the country' he is bailed up by bushrangers and left for dead tied to a tree. Eventually freeing himself, he is arrested because his belongings have been stolen and so he cannot identify himself. Taken to Sydney, he is eventually identified and released but on returning to his station discovers Aborigines have speared his cattle. Even nature conspires against the hapless new chum:

And for nine months before no rain there had been,
So the devil a blade of grass could be seen;
And one-third of my wethers the scab they had got,
And the other two-thirds had just died of the rot.
Oh dear, lackaday, oh,
'I shall soon be a settler,' said Billy Barlow.

Deep in debt, Billy is reduced to poverty and hunger—'as thin as a lath got poor Billy Barlow'. He is arrested and imprisoned for debt back in Sydney again and listed as an insolvent, or bankrupt:

Then once more I got free, but in poverty's toil;
I've no 'cattle for salting,' no 'sheep for to boil';
I can't get a job—though to any I'd stoop,
If it was only the making of 'portable soup'.
Oh dear, lackaday, oh,
Pray give some employment to Billy Barlow.

Despite his tragi-comic trials, Billy Barlow is not totally ground down and still contemplates repairing his fortunes in the final verse:

But there's still a 'spec' left may set me on my stumps,
If a wife I could get with a few of the dumps;
So if any lass here has 'ten thousand' or so,
She can just drop a line addressed 'Mr. Barlow'.
Oh dear, lackaday, oh,
The dear angel shall be 'Mrs. William Barlow'.

So popular and pervasive was the contempt for the new chum that 'Billy Barlow' became a stock character of popular entertainment for decades. He assumed all sorts of guises, including rat catcher, London street clown, butcher, clerk and gold-digger, as well as the know-nothing tenderfoot of Australian tradition. Although now long forgotten, we still don't know who Billy Barlow was, or if he ever existed outside ballads and the popular theatre of Britain, Canada, America, South Africa and colonial Australia.

The temple of skulls

On 25 July 1836, Charles Morgan Lewis and his crew were razing the Torres Strait island of Aureed to smoking oblivion. Searching for any survivors of the *Charles Eaton* wrecked in those parts a few years earlier, they had found what they were looking for and they did not like what they saw.

Bound for Canton (now known as Guangzhou) under Captain Morley, the barque *Charles Eaton* was wrecked in the little-known Torres Strait in mid-August 1834. The passengers and crew were thrown into several groups in their desperate efforts to survive. Some escaped to the Netherlands East Indies on the ship's cutter, and one group of six managed to build a makeshift raft. Among the group were the first officer, Mr Clear; the second officer; a crewman; and three ship's boys, one named John Ireland. After drifting through the shallow waters for several days and nights they encountered a group of islanders in canoes. The islanders demonstrated that they were unarmed and signalled the Europeans to join them in their craft. After some discussion, the castaways got into the canoes. They were paddled to a cay where they searched for food accompanied by the islanders, but it was not long before the survivors of the *Charles Eaton* sank onto the ground in exhaustion. Their rescuers now began to laugh and gesture in an unfriendly way and the survivors realised they intended to kill them. The first officer, a minister's son, calmly led the little group in prayer and resignation to their fate. Completely fatigued and despite their peril, the survivors fell asleep.

Young John Ireland awoke to the sound and sight of his

companions having their brains beaten out with islander clubs. Only he and another boy named Sexton were spared. Both the boys fought back; although wounded, their resistance and their youth probably saved them. Nearby, the islanders celebrated their victory dancing around a large fire, and in the flickering light Ireland saw the decapitated heads of his companions and the remains of their bodies floating in the surf.

The islanders took the boys to Pullan Island in the Torres Strait, where they met the remnants of another group of *Charles Eaton* survivors who had suffered much the same fate. Their severed heads, still recognisable, were also on the island. After a few months, Ireland and an infant survivor of the second group named William D'Oyley were taken on a lengthy voyage by their captors. Eventually the two passed into the care of a Mer (Murray) Islander named Duppar, who purchased them for two bunches of bananas. Duppar treated Ireland kindly, effectively adopting him, while D'Oyley was entrusted to the care of another Mer Islander named Oby.

While these terrifying events were taking place at the northern extremity of Australia, efforts were being made in England to mount a search and, hopefully, a rescue mission. The crewmen who had escaped in the cutter were eventually rescued and gave their version of events, and there were rumours that others had also escaped. Although many of these accounts and speculations were contradictory and vague, there was some reason to hope that at least some passengers and crew of the *Charles Eaton* were still alive somewhere. Eventually there would be several expeditions, but it was one mounted from Sydney under Charles Lewis on the *Isabella* that finally solved the mystery.

On 19 June, *Isabella* anchored off Mer. Among a large group of islanders on the beach, Lewis saw a European man. Four large outrigger canoes came alongside the *Isabella*, indicating a desire to trade for axes and knives. After some difficult negotiations, the islanders accepted an array of these items in return for freeing their European captive. Although he could now barely speak English, Lewis soon confirmed that the boy was the missing John Ireland.

Further negotiations and a show of strength from the armed crew of the *Isabella* eventually produced William D'Oyley, but the youngster did not want to leave Oby and clung crying to his adoptive father. Lewis showered gifts on Duppar and Oby in recognition of their kindness to the boys and wisely followed this up with more gifts to the other Mer Islanders. The *Isabella* departed a few days later, the best of friends with the local people.

Lewis had achieved a part of his goal in rescuing the two boys. But what of the other survivors? As Ireland gradually regained his English, he was able to tell Lewis more of the gruesome story and direct him to where the other survivors might be. After conversations with Darnley Islanders, it was confirmed that the second group of survivors had been murdered and their heads were kept on Aureed Island, a ritual centre for local beliefs. The Darnley people also told Lewis that the killers had eaten the eyes and cheeks of the dead, forcing their children to do the same, in accordance with the belief that this would make them strong warriors.

Lewis made for Aureed. By the time he arrived the island was deserted, as word of his coming had travelled ahead. Following a red shell-lined avenue, in the islander village he entered a low thatched hut, where he found a grisly icon of tortoiseshell, feathers and shells, in the form of a mask about five feet long by two and a half feet high. Around the edges were many skulls, held to the mask with ships' rope. Many of the skulls were battered and cracked but in some cases could be identified as those of women and children. Lewis had found the remains of the murdered group.

Taking the ritual figure to his ship, the disgusted Lewis angrily gave orders for his men to torch the 'temple of skulls', as it would later be dubbed, along with any other structures. Soon the entire island was ablaze. While cutting down the remaining coconut trees, they found two more scorched skulls to add to those on the mask. Lewis renamed the place 'Skull Island'.

The *Isabella* returned to Sydney on 12 October, having been away for almost twenty weeks. There was a dispute over the reward for the rescue and Lewis was denied his money. Eventually he went mad and by 1845 was totally destitute. With support from his friends he was finally awarded a significant gratuity of 300 pounds.

In 1844, a British navy ship revisited Mer and inquired after Duppar. An elderly man with grey beard and swollen limbs identified himself as the boys' saviour. He was presented with a large ceremonial axe in gratitude for helping John Ireland and William D'Oyley.

And what of the skulls? Governor Bourke had them detached from the mask and buried beneath a large altar stone in the cemetery then at Devonshire Street. As for the mask, long thought to have been destroyed by fire, it has recently been suggested that it has lain hidden among artefacts gifted to the National Museum of Denmark in the 1860s, incorrectly labelled through a series of museum clerical errors.

In 2011, Britain's famous Natural History Museum announced that it would repatriate the remains of 138 Torres Strait Islanders souvenired, traded or otherwise acquired during the period of colonisation. Many of these items were skulls.

Chimney Sweeps' Day

Most traditional British customs failed to make the transition from one side of the world to the other, but one May Day custom that did persist for some time in Australia was known as Chimney Sweeps' Day. Adapted from earlier customs involving the soliciting of money on their annual holiday, chimney sweeps in larger towns and cities developed the custom of parading a roughly two-metre-high flower- and leaf-covered, bell-shaped 'Jack-in-the-Green'. This was originally a simple floral decoration traditional to May Day celebrations. Over many years the garland expanded to the point where it completely covered the wearer. The person carrying this device danced along the street, usually accompanied by an appropriately dressed 'Lord' and 'Lady', sometimes by a 'wife' known as Judy, and beribboned sweeps, crashing their brooms and shovels together to create 'rough music'. Sometimes there was more formal musical accompaniment of whistle, fiddle and tabor (a small drum). The group processed through the streets, soliciting donations from passers-by. In some cases, these activities would be kept up for some days after 1 May, or even begun a day or two earlier. No doubt there was a fair bit of drinking as well.

The custom appeared in Hobart in the early 1840s and seems to have been observed there, and in Launceston, until at least the 1870s. Chimney Sweeps' Day was also recorded in Sydney during the 1840s. However, the dramatic seasonal and other differences took a heavy toll on this British custom as the nineteenth century progressed. Newspaper descriptions of the Sweeps' Day in Tasmania from the 1840s to the 1870s reveal an almost annual shrinking of numbers, gaiety and enthusiasm, as the antipodean seasons, public opinion and, it seems, a declining need for chimney sweeping combined to render the celebration pointless.

But there may have been additional reasons for the demise of Jack-in-the-Green. May Day, later Labour Day, celebrations have long had a clear political–industrial agenda, deriving from the struggle for the eight-hour working day that occupied Australian industrial relations for decades through the nineteenth century. The earlier craft guild May Day observation of Jack-in-the-Green could also be associated with pointed political comment and activity. In 1857, a poem titled 'Reflections by a Chimney Sweep', or 'chummy' as they were known, was specifically critical of politicians and the political system. It began:

I'm glad I'm not an M.L.A.
Least ways in Hobart Town;
I'd rather much a chummy be,
And earn an honest crown.

The poem continued:

If we were sent to parliament
We wouldn't mop and mow,
Like apes and other animals
I've seen at Wombwell's show.

Later, it criticises the Tasmanian attorney-general by name. Two years before this poem was published, the 'King of the Hobart Sweeps', John Gordon, upset many citizens by taking part in the Jack-in-the-Green procession with his ribbons the colours of a candidate in the local elections.

Other imported customs also gradually faded with the century. The merrymaking Whitsuntide customs associated with the Christian feast of Pentecost, still featured throughout Britain today, seem to have ceased in Australia by the 1890s, while May Day was only rescued from oblivion and school dancing classes by its association with the trade union movement. In many cases, as in Britain and elsewhere in Europe, the spirit of the times was against the old customs, often considered backwards, silly and uncomfortably superstitious by the Victorian middle-class mind. After welcoming the Jack-in-the-Green custom in Hobart during the 1840s, by the 1860s the local newspapers were hoping that this 'foolish custom' was quickly dying out.

The dragon of Big Gold Mountain

They came in their thousands: Chinese gold-diggers drawn by the hope of striking it rich in the rushes that began in 1851. The Chinese called the Victorian diggings Dai Gum San, meaning Big Gold Mountain, and by the middle of the 1850s there were around 4000 on the Bendigo fields, many having walked overland from the port of Robe in South Australia, a distance of almost 500 kilometres.

Fearful of Chinese competition and also of the 'yellow peril', the Victorian government imposed a restrictive entry tax on Chinese hopefuls, although there were no such restrictions in the colony of South Australia. The Chinese were industrious and successful in their gold mining, attracting prejudice as well as economic jealousy from the predominantly European goldfields population. There was violence, discrimination and numerous attempts to stop or restrict Chinese gold-seekers.

But there was a brighter side. The riches of the gold rushes soon generated prosperous communities in Ballarat and Bendigo and in 1869 (some sources say 1870), a fair and procession were established as an Easter celebration and to raise funds for charity. The Chinese joined the parade a couple of years later and within ten years had become the major feature of the Bendigo Easter Fair, as it became known. Australia had seen nothing like it before. Traditional costumes, flags and decorations of all kinds were imported from China in large quantities and displayed during the parade. In 1892 the longest dragon in the world arrived, a fearsome five-clawed beast known as *loong*, the Chinese word for 'dragon'. *Loong* has continued to be the major feature of the fair, along with other Chinese customs, some of which no longer exist in China.

As well as the Chinese contribution, the early fairs were extravaganzas of wild animal shows, theatrical performances, magicians, singing, art displays, dancing booths, fairground rides and a sideshow alley, as well as the inevitable hucksters. Police had to remove a three-card-trick shyster at the 1874 fair. That year there were 20,000 paid admissions, with plenty to drink and plenty of legal gambling in the form of lotteries. The opening ceremony and grand procession were gala events, with orchestras, a Chinese band, representatives of various friendly societies and masonic lodges, a wild man, and 'lady' cricketers 'in their gay blue and pink uniforms, in three vehicles, forming a galaxy of beauty that attracted all eyes'. Following the fire brigade there was a presumably spoof 'His Celestial Majesty Jam Je Bu-ic-ker':

> . . . preceded by six retainers, all in gorgeous attire. His Majesty was dressed in loose trousers and Chinese jumper of rich blue satin magnificently worked with flowers and dragons in different colors. Around his neck was a yellow silk scarf beautifully worked with flowers, a black cap with rosette of peacocks' feathers adding to the effect. He carried an umbrella of novel pattern, there being one large oval of yellow silk, fringed with blue, while on the top of that was a small parasol of red silk fringed with yellow. The dress was a gorgeous one. A fine tail 4 feet long, completed the outfit. The dresses of his retainers were of richly flowered chintz robe with blue trousers, with black stripes, while on their backs and breasts were rosettes of peacocks' feathers.

At night, even more people seemed to crowd the scene. The grounds were lit up with multi-coloured Chinese lanterns strung between the trees, 'giving a most fairy-like and enchanting appearance to the scene'. The night finished with a fireworks display watched and applauded by thousands and, 'It was not until a late hour that the grounds were cleared.'

Sun Loong first appeared at the 1892 procession and was an immediate hit:

The Chinese made a magnificent display nearly a thousand of them marching, and their brilliant raiment, queer musical instruments, and quaint battle weapons created much interest. A novel feature of the procession was a huge dragon. This was 200ft long supported by 80 Chinamen, and consisted of [a] wire framework, covered with gorgeous silk. The dragon was made to sway about, whilst its rolling eyes, lolling tongue, and generally ferocious appearance were sources of great wonderment and consternation to the children. The dragon was preceded by copious discharges of fireworks and revolving balls, which were symbolical of stars that the dragon was seeking to devour.

Today, the celebration remains a major local, state and national event known as the Bendigo Easter Festival. Still organised by the descendants of the original Bendigo Easter Fair Society, it is the oldest continually running festival of its kind in the country.

4

A fair go

Do you call this a fair go?

Shearers' strike leaders being arrested by police, 1891

ONE OF AUSTRALIA's most powerful beliefs is the idea expressed in the phrase 'a fair go'. Convicts, swagmen and workers of all kinds, as well as Indigenous people, have felt compelled to express their discontent and ask for a fair go in stories that go to the heart of the Australian sense of national identity.

In 2006, a survey showed that 91 per cent of Australians put 'a fair go' at the top of their list of values. This is nothing new, of course. The idea that it is important for everyone in the country to have equal opportunity goes back to the earliest years of modern Australia, closely associated with the enforced levelling of convict society, with pioneering and with the creed of mateship.

Black Mary

Armed with a musket and a brace of pistols, she became known to history and legend as 'Black Mary'. But the name she went by in colonial Tasmania was Mary Cockerell. Like many Indigenous Tasmanian women of the time, Mary worked as a servant for a settler family named Cockerell, taking that name as her own. She became the lover of Michael Howe, joined his bushranging gang and became an effective accomplice until the gang was attacked by soldiers. During this attack, Howe allegedly wounded the heavily pregnant Mary in order to facilitate his own escape. An early Tasmanian settler recalled the events many years later when the layers of folklore had settled over the facts:

*H*owe and the girl, Mary, were traced and pursued near Jericho by a party of soldiers, and being hard pressed, Howe, to facilitate his own escape, fired at the poor black girl, who was wounded and captured. Her injuries proved but slight, and the treatment received from Howe led to her turning against her former associates, and she subsequently became of great assistance to the military as a female 'black tracker'.

Howe wrote to the Governor offering to give himself up and furnish important information about his former associates and their haunts, and the offer was accepted, Howe arriving in Hobart on 29th April, 1817. He underwent various examinations, but little information was obtained from him, and at length, on the plea that confinement was impairing his health, Howe was allowed to go about with a constable, an indulgence he repaid by escaping in July.

Watts, who had once been a companion of Howe, now determined to save his own neck by capturing Howe, and communicated with the authorities. With the assistance of Black Mary and a stockkeeper named Drewe, Howe was run down and taken while asleep. They bound him, and were marching him to Hobart, Watts being in front with a loaded gun, and Drewe, who was unarmed, following Howe, when Howe disengaged his hands, and drawing a concealed knife, with a sudden spring stabbed Watts in the back. As Watts fell Howe seized his gun and shot Drewe dead. Black Mary escaped into the bush, while Howe was swearing he would shoot Watts as soon as he loaded his gun. Watts managed to crawl into the bush, when Mary returned with assistance, and Howe made his escape. Watts was removed to Hobart, but died three days after his arrival.

Howe was not heard of for some time, but necessity compelled him to commit robberies on distant stockkeepers. After his daring exploit none dare venture it [sic] personal attack upon him, but Black Mary was continually on his heels, guiding the military.

⌒

Howe had been transported for highway robbery in 1811, escaped two years later and quickly became a scourge of the settlers, attacking their properties, stealing their stock and mistreating many of those he took captive. It was also rumoured that many were in mutually beneficial relationships with the outlaw in order to protect their lives and property.

After his own lucky escape from the wrath of Black Mary, Howe disappeared for some time. He began styling himself 'lieutenant governor of the woods' in dark contrast to the official lieutenant governor of the colony. During this period he had a substantial 100-guinea reward placed on his head, later doubled, with any convict who caught him guaranteed a pardon and free passage home.

Howe was tracked by an Aboriginal convict from New South Wales known as Musquito, who had been captured in 1805 and took up the hunt to gain a passage back to his country. Then, towards the end of 1818:

A soldier named Pugh, of the 48th Regiment, and a stockkeeper named Worrall determined to capture Howe. They entered into a league with a kangaroo hunter named Warburton, who agreed to join them. Howe had to meet Warburton, who had agreed to let him have some ammunition if he would come to his (Warburton's) hut. Howe, after great hesitation, ventured into the hut, where Pugh and Worrall were concealed. As soon as Howe entered he cocked his gun, and Pugh fired at him, but missed. Howe retreated a few paces and then returned the fire, but also missed, and Worrall fired, but with no better effect. Howe then retired, loading his gun as he retreated backwards, and was followed by the other men. Howe fired at Warburton and fatally wounded him, and was then rushed by the two others, a desperate encounter taking place. Howe fought long and died hard, dangerously wounding Pugh, but was overpowered, his head being battered to pieces. They then cut off Howe's head, which was taken to Hobart, the body being buried near the scene . . .

On their way back to Hobart, the bounty hunters met the prominent settler Dr Ross and his travelling companions, who asked them what they had in the bloodstained blue bag they carried. The men 'good-naturedly opening the bag, showed them a human head'. Then:

*T*aking it by the hair, he held it up to our view, with the greatest exultation imaginable, and for a moment we thought we had indeed got amongst murderers, pondering between resistance and the chance of succour or escape, when we were agreeably relieved by the information that the bleeding head had belonged two days ago to the body of the notorious bushranger, Michael Howe, for whom, dead or alive, very large rewards had been offered. He had been caught at a remote solitary hut on the banks of the River Shannon, and in his attempt to break away from the soldiers who apprehended him, had been shot through the back, so that the painful disseverment of the head and trunk, the result of which we now witnessed, had been only a postmortem operation.

Howe's severed head was then displayed in Hobart town as proof of the rule of law. It was a popular display with the colonists.

While these events were playing out, Mary had been sent to Sydney to prevent her returning to Howe's side. Now that he was dead, she was allowed back to Hobart. While Worrall and Pugh were rewarded for the death of Howe, Mary's only reward for her service to the Crown was free victuals from the government stores. Nor did they have to hand these out for long. She died, probably of tuberculosis, the following winter. Musquito received no reward at all and went on to become a threat to colonial order in his own right, partly as a result of the failure of the government to honour the promise of repatriation. He was captured, tried and hanged on dubious legal grounds in 1825.

The Tambaroora line

When the goldfields towns of Hill End, Sofala and Tambaroora started growing from the early 1850s, they needed transport links with Bathurst and beyond. In those days it was only a coach and horse to transport people and goods from place to place, and there were carriers of all kinds, none more colourful than Bill Maloney.

Small operators like Maloney were threatened when Cobb & Co. began in the 1860s. Not only could the new competition boast better and faster coaches, but they were organised along corporate lines that gave them an extra edge. According to legend, Bill Maloney took this in his stride. The only way to hold his own against the rivals was to drive faster and along shorter but more dangerous routes. Bill was skilled at this, but whenever he did encounter or pass a Cobb & Co. coach on the road, he bawled out a special ditty he had composed to the tune of a popular bush song:

> Now look here, Cobb & Co.,
> A lesson take from me,
> If you meet me on the road
> Don't you make too free,
> For if you do you'll surely rue . . .
> You think you do it fine,

But I'm a tip-and-slasher
Of the Tambaroora line.

Then into the boastful chorus:

I can hold them, steer them
And drive them to and fro,
With ribbons well in hand, me boys,
I can make 'em go.
With me foot well on the brake, lads,
I'm bound to make them shine,
For I'm a tip-and-slasher
Of the Tambaroora line.

This went on for years. Cobb & Co. tried to buy Hill out but he would not budge. Although Cobb & Co. could offer a better service, most of Bill's customers admired his spirit and travelled with him whenever they could. And eventually, Bill won. Cobb & Co. decided to suspend its Bathurst operation. Shortly before closing down, the managing director of Cobb & Co., James Rutherford (see Chapter 11), invited his tenacious local rival to the factory where the company built its cutting-edge coaches. They walked through the works until they came to an especially well-built and -equipped coach painted out in the same colours that Bill used for his own coaches.

'What do you think of this one, then, Bill?' asked Rutherford.

Despite himself, Bill was impressed and said so, wishing that he could afford such a fine piece of equipment. Rutherford then handed Bill the reins and said he was gifting it to him for being such a worthy competitor.

Maloney received this magnanimous gift with gratitude and used it for many successful years on the Tambaroora line, later succeeded by his son.

Mates

Australia's tradition of mateship can be traced from the rough necessity of convict survival, through the tribulations of pioneering, the excitement of the gold rushes and the formation of trade unions from the 1890s, and finding its most evocative location on the ridges of Gallipoli and the trenches of the Western Front during World War I. Along the way, a number of outstanding examples of men's loyalty to each other include Ned Kelly returning to the fight at Glenrowan to help his mates and the story of Simpson and his donkey, among many others. C.E.W. Bean, a major influence on the Anzac legend, wrote that the typical Australian was rarely religious and:

> So far as he held a prevailing creed, it was a romantic one inherited from the gold-miner and the bushman, of which the chief article was that a man should at all times and at any cost stand by his mate. That was and is the one law, which the good Australian must never break. It is bred in the child and stays with him through life . . .

At the shining end of this spectrum, mateship is an admirable quality. At its darker extremes it can exhibit shades of misogyny. This is why the topic has always been controversial. Even mateship's greatest singer recognised its realities: many of Henry Lawson's stories and poems celebrate mateship, if with a jaundiced eye. In one titled *A Sketch of Mateship*, Lawson tells it like it probably was:

Bill and Jim, professional shearers, were coming into Bourke from the Queensland side. They were horsemen and had two packhorses. At the last camp before Bourke Jim's packhorse got disgusted and home-sick during the night and started back for the place where he was foaled. Jim was little more than a new-chum jackeroo; he was no bushman and generally got lost when he went down the next gully. Bill was a bushman, so it was decided that he should go back to look for the horse.

Now Bill was going to sell his packhorse, a well-bred mare, in Bourke, and he was anxious to get her into the yards before the horse sales were over; this was to be the last day of the sales. Jim was the best 'barracker' of the two; he had great imagination; he was a very entertaining story-teller and conversationalist in social life, and a glib and a most impressive liar in business, so it was decided that he should hurry on into Bourke with the mare and sell her for Bill. Seven pounds, reserve.

Next day Bill turned up with the missing horse and saw Jim standing against a veranda-post of the Carriers' Arms, with his hat down over his eyes, and thoughtfully spitting in the dust. Bill rode over to him.

'Ullo, Jim.'

'Ullo, Bill. I see you got him.'

'Yes, I got him.' Pause.

'Where'd yer find him?'

''Bout ten mile back. Near Ford's Bridge. He was just feedin' along.' Pause. Jim shifted his feet and spat in the dust.

'Well,' said Bill at last. 'How did you get on, Jim?'

'Oh, all right,' said Jim. 'I sold the mare.'

'That's right,' said Bill. 'How much did she fetch?'

'Eight quid;' then, rousing himself a little and showing some emotion, 'An' I could 'a' got ten quid for her if I hadn't been a dam' fool.'

'Oh, that's good enough,' said Bill.

'I could 'a' got ten quid if I'd 'a' waited.'

'Well, it's no use cryin'. Eight quid is good enough. Did you get the stuff?'

'Oh, yes. They parted all right. If I hadn't been such a dam' fool an' rushed it, there was a feller that would 'a' given ten quid for that mare.'

'Well, don't break yer back about it,' said Bill. 'Eight is good enough.'

'Yes. But I could 'a' got ten,' said Jim, languidly, putting his hand in his pocket.

Pause. Bill sat waiting for him to hand over the money; but Jim withdrew his hand empty, stretched, and said: 'Ah, well, Bill, I done it in. Lend us a couple o' notes.'

Jim had been drinking and gambling all night and he'd lost the eight pounds as well as his own money.

Bill didn't explode. What was the use? He should have known that Jim wasn't to be trusted with money in town. It was he who had been the fool. He sighed and lent Jim a pound, and they went in to have a drink.

Now it strikes me that if this had happened in a civilized country (like England) Bill would have had Jim arrested and jailed for larceny as a bailee, or embezzlement, or whatever it was. And would Bill or Jim or the world have been any better for it?

⌒

Henry Lawson was realistic enough to recognise that mateship was often something that grew in the glow of a drink or three, once stating: 'The greatest pleasure I have ever known is when my eyes meet the eyes of a mate over the top of two foaming glasses of beer.'

Mateship is most frequently linked with another Australian characteristic, usually known as anti-authoritarianism, though more flowingly expressed in the phrase 'Jack's as good as his master', sometimes followed with 'if not better'. Again, the origins of this attitude can be traced to the convict era, through the relationships between bosses and workers in the bush, in factories, on building sites and wharves, as well as a dislike of uniformed authority in particular and regulation in general. Most famously we find it in the reluctance of Australian volunteer soldiers in World War I and after to salute their officers, the subject of endless digger yarns. Again like mateship, this idea is sometimes considered to be a myth.

A glorious spree

Australia's long love affair with the grog begins with the 'Rum Corps' in colonial New South Wales and extends to the present. Along the way have been told many beery tales of mammoth sprees and monumental hangovers. The balladry of the bush overflows with references to alcohol, much of it 'sly' or illegal. The 'hocussed' or adulterated shanty grog took down many a shearer's cheque. A famous example occurs in the traditional song 'On the Road to Gundagai', where a bloke named Bill and his mate make the mistake of camping at Lazy Harry's sly grog tent on their way to Sydney with the season's shearing wages.

> In a week the spree was over and our cheque was all knocked down
> So we shouldered our Matildas and we turned our backs on town.
> And the girls they stood a nobbler as we sadly said goodbye,
> And we tramped from Lazy Harry's on the road to Gundagai.

In vain did the forces of law and order try to police and control the sly grog trade. Colonists mostly insisted on their right to a drink and the grog quickly became an element of the 'fair go' ethos, as events at Pakenham demonstrated in 1879:

*A*n interesting raid was made by the revenue officers of the Shire of Berwick, on Wednesday last, on a number of unlicensed shanty-keepers, who for some time past have been carrying on an illicit traffic in liquor in the neighbourhood of a large quarry near the Gippsland railway, about seven miles from Berwick, from which metal has been obtained for the Oakleigh end of the line. At this place a large camp of quarry men and stonebreakers has been formed consisting of about 100 tents and shanties of all kinds and descriptions, and as there are no public houses in the locality sly grog-selling is carried on to a great extent.

It came to the knowledge of the Revenue officers a few days ago that a large quantity of spirituous liquor had been sent up to the camp and having determined to take some action to put a stop to this illicit traffic, the revenue inspector, Mr. Robinson, visited the place on Wednesday last, accompanied by the inspector of licensed premises, Mr A. Cartledge, and three mounted constables, and made a sudden descent on the camp before the casks and cases containing the liquor could be removed or secreted by their owners. At the first place which was visited, that of Mr. R. Stout's, about a dray load of stock was seized and placed in a dray which had been provided for the occasion.

In the meantime a large number of the navvies had assembled, and seeing the state of affairs commenced looting the shanties and grogshops in spite of the efforts of the police, who endeavoured to roll back the casks into the tents as the mob took them out, but of course were outnumbered, and the result was that casks of bottled beer and cases of brandy, whisky, &c. were smashed open and rifled. By this time the mob had increased to about 100 persons, and an assault was made on the police by a party armed with pickhandles, sticks and other weapons, and the police were rather severely handled—so much so that they had to produce their revolvers, and the revenue officer's party took advantage of the tranquilising effect which this manoeuvre produced to retire from the camp.

The scene that ensued baffles description; yelling and screaming the mob either stoved in the ends of the casks and opened the cases and removed their contents for immediate consumption, or took them away into the bush for a future occasion. It is estimated that about £30 of spirituous liquor was taken or destroyed by the mob, including the dray load, which the inspector had seized.

Not surprisingly, the police were planning to summon the known rioters to court.

The Greenhide Push waltzes Matilda

Our unofficial national anthem had humble origins as a ditty knocked up by 'Banjo' Paterson and Christina Macpherson at Dagwood Station near Winton in 1895. In those days, people entertained themselves and the opportunity to sing a new song around the piano was highly appreciated, especially when it was such a rousing lyric and tune as that of 'Waltzing Matilda'. Almost as soon as the song was composed it flew off into oral tradition around northeast Queensland. It was sung with gusto in that part of the country long before it was the popular piece it has since become.

Just how popular the song was—in at least one of its different versions—is conveyed in an account of events at Hughenden race time in April 1902. All the young bloods in town organised a procession along the main street. They called themselves 'the Greenhide Push' and they were armed with the then-new hit, assisted by the local newspaper, which had thoughtfully printed up the lyrics on flyers and had them posted around town. Old Queensland hand Fred Archer was there and recalled the scene over forty years later:

They got the Salvation Army's big drum, some cornets and tambourines and the black boys' gum leaves. The streets were crowded with people. The drum boomed, wild notes came from the cornets, tambourines clashed—all in the theme song, 'Waltzing Matilda'.

The crowds on the footpath took it up, horses started to buck and throw their riders, the black boys thumbed their mounts and beat them with their wide-brimmed hats. They yelled and so did everyone else. The drummer was down but couldn't care less, he still continued whacking the drum—boom-boom. Bucking horses were everywhere. Finally, the procession reached the Great Western-Hughenden Hotels and such horses as were under control were tied to hitching posts.

Tall, lean men in white Canton riding trousers, red shirts, riding boots and long-necked spurs were among the crowds that milled through the hotels, thumped the pianos, roared 'Waltzing Matilda' from beginning to end, over and over again, in parlour, bar and verandah, while excited horsemen rode into the middle of the singers and took up the chorus . . .

And so the party went on for hours. The following day the makeshift band was placed on a wagon and dragged around the town to play the song wherever they stopped. In the evening mounted men galloped through town firing guns in time with the music: 'This they kept up till they reached the police station, yelled out for troopers 1, 2, 3, then laid whips to their horses and bolted . . .' Not surprisingly, the local police were unimpressed with this larrikinism. Such roistering scenes are difficult to imagine today, especially with the inspiration being a song. It was an age when the sung and spoken word was still a powerful form of conviviality and communication, assisted in this case by high spirits, grog and the irresistible urge of the Greenhide Push to call out the police using the anti-authoritarian lines of the song.

The Bunuba resistance

On the morning of April Fool's Day 1897, the outlaw Jandamarra was shot dead outside his cave hideout at Tunnel Creek. The man who shot this feared scourge of the settlers was another Aborigine known as 'Micki', a police tracker. Jandamarra had led the remnants of his people in a prolonged resistance through the rugged region of Western Australia's northwest.

Australia's vast and mostly arid northwest had been largely ignored until the 1880s, when its almost infinite acres attracted sheep and cattle farming and its seas an embryonic pearling industry. As settlement increased, the newcomers increasingly encroached on the traditional lands of the many Indigenous groups in what would become known as the Kimberley region. Some of these groups resisted; others seemed to fade away as the frontier pushed relentlessly north and east. The Bunuba were not inclined to simply walk off their land and nurtured an ongoing resistance that eventually produced their hero.

Jandamarra was already approaching initiation age when his country became the object of commercial and political interest. At around eleven years of age he was taken into employment on a local station to be trained as a stockman. Jandamarra appeared to be the ideal type for such conversions, quickly excelling at the necessary skills and eventually also becoming a crack rifle shot. Although he was unusually short for a Bunuba man—they were typically six foot or more—he had great speed and agility, leading to the settlers nicknaming him 'Pigeon'. Working and living in the company of the settlers caused Jandamarra to grow up without being initiated into the spiritual secrets that would rightly have belonged to a Bunuba man, so although Jandamarra would come to know his country, its gullies, hills, trails and caves intimately, he was never fully a man in Bunuba society.

None of these matters worried Jandamarra, it seems. He was content to work for the settlers and even to become a blacktracker or adjunct member of the police force and take part in tracking down other Aboriginal men and women wanted by the law.

Meanwhile, resistance to settlement continued. Stock was speared, supplies stolen and whites attacked by one or usually small groups of Aborigines. The settlers reacted with violence based on fear as much as racism, and attack led to counterattack as Aborigines sought to stem the unstoppable advances of the settlers and the settlers sought to 'disperse' the Aborigines so their stock could graze the grassland and drink from the waterholes.

A noted Bunuba warrior of the time was a man named Ellemarra. Through the late 1880s he offered fierce and ongoing resistance to the settlers, often being arrested but usually escaping again. So dangerous did Ellemarra become that the settlers called for 'the whole tribe of natives inhabiting the Napier Range to be outlawed'. Ellemarra was among the most wanted of the resisters and Jandamarra, caught between the worlds of white and black, formed part of a police party sent out to bring him in, effectively going against his own people. Ellemarra was flogged and imprisoned. He eventually escaped again but was recaptured and chained with a group of other Aboriginal prisoners. But again, possibly with the help of Jandamarra, Ellemarra managed to break his chains and escape.

Now Jandamarra had to again take part in tracking down Ellemarra, under the command of a policeman named Richardson. Jandamarra led the policeman to his countrymen and they were captured in late October 1894, the largest haul of resisters the police had yet netted. Richardson delayed returning with them in order to gain a greater allowance for being on active duty. It was a fatal mistake. The Bunuba men naturally placed pressure on Jandamarra to let them go and acknowledge his true Bunuba identity. Eventually Jandamarra accepted their argument, released Ellemarra and shot Richardson dead while he slept. The two men then released their comrades, took the guns and ammunition and disappeared into the bush. They soon raised a large group of Bunuba and engaged in a large-scale battle with police sent to track them down for the murders of a number of settlers in November. Ellemarra and a number of Bunuba women were killed in the shooting and Jandamarra seriously wounded. He managed to escape, evading the pursuit through his unparalleled knowledge of the country. An undeclared war was in progress, which would make Jandamarra a great hero to his people and their struggle.

While Jandamarra was in hiding, recovering from his wounds, the government sent police reinforcements to the Kimberley as quickly as was possible at the time.

The police had almost convinced themselves that the Bunuba resistance was broken when rumours of Jandamarra's survival were confirmed in May 1895. Jandamarra and the Bunuba now conducted a guerrilla war; police continually came across the outlaws' tracks, only to lose them in the rocks and ravines.

The Bunuba people also employed the characteristic tactic of using outlaw sympathisers. Misleading the police with false information was effective and had the advantage of making the police look like fools, further demoralising them in their futile hunt for Jandamarra and his now small, mobile band.

In October 1895, Jandamarra became over-confident and failed to post a guard around his camp, and the police surprised him and his band. Employing his legendary agility, Jandamarra disappeared into a convenient cave, but most of his band was captured.

Over the following months Jandamarra concentrated on harassing and demoralising police and settlers by demonstrating his mastery of the country and of stealth. He robbed storehouses, visited police camps at night and shadowed police patrols, always ensuring they knew he had been among them. Jandamarra, the uninitiated man, now came to be seen by his own people as a lawman, an individual with great spiritual authority and great magical powers. He was said to be able to turn himself into a bird and fly away from the police. He was also said to be invulnerable because his real spirit was hidden at his hideout, and it was only his animated body that crossed his country to taunt the police and the settlers.

This went on for many months, including the besieging of the police outpost at Lillimooroola station, immediately below the limestone cliffs that marked the easily defended edge of Bunuba country. Towards the end of 1896 the settlers began forcing their cattle deep into Bunuba land, effectively going behind Jandamarra's front line. The Bunuba resistance went back into action with psychological warfare and attacks on settlers. The police cranked up their attempts to end the conflict, committing more atrocities against the Bunuba, but had no more success than in their previous attempts.

But within the police ranks was a secret weapon. An Aboriginal member of the force named Micki was from far outside Bunuba country and had no loyalty towards Jandamarra's fight. The Aborigines also considered him to have magical powers. On 23 March 1897, Micki was solely responsible for capturing five of Jandamarra's band. Jandamarra attempted to free his comrades but was badly wounded. He was pursued through the ranges as he struggled towards his hideout cave at Tunnel Creek, 30 miles east. He made it back inside the cave through one of its many secret entrances, but Micki was waiting for him outside the cave's main entrance. The two lawmen faced each other with Winchester rifles. Jandamarra missed and Micki's shot sent him hurtling down a 100-foot cliff. The police reached the scene, confirmed the body was that of their feared foe and then chopped the head from the torso with a tomahawk. It was reportedly despatched to adorn the trophy wall of a British arms manufacturer.

The Bunuba resistance was finally broken with Jandamarra's death, but his legend lived on, becoming a powerful oral tradition in the Kimberley. It has also been the subject of several books and is being turned into a feature film.

The bagman's gazette

The 'bagman's gazette' was a term for the efficient word-of-mouth network on the track. News, rumour and gossip were carried along this unofficial route with amazing speed. Under the title 'Bagman's Gazette', 'The Organiser' began his column for the *Darwin Northern Standard* in the Depression year of 1931 with a quotation from Lewis Carroll's famous nonsense poem 'The Walrus and The Carpenter'. The article was about wages and politics, suggesting that not much had changed since the strikes of forty years before:

'The time has come,' the Walrus said,
'To talk of many things;
Of shoes—and ships—and sealing wax—
Of cabbages—and kings—'

*B*agmen discussing politics at a recent session around the Camp fire touched on the so-called necessity for equal sacrifice taking it for granted that all sections would be required by this to dub up in proportion so as to save the country from financial chaos. After disposing of the theory that lower wages would increase employment and quoting their experiences in search of employment in the pastoral industry in Queensland, where wages are as low as 15/- a week, one bagman quoted the proposed British Budget as a sample of equal sacrifice. It is proposed to save Britain by reducing the unemployment dole by £66,500,000 and education grants, and teachers' salaries by £13,000,000. This makes a total of £79,500,000 out of £96,500,000 it is proposed to save. The workers even contribute a big part of the remaining £17,000,000.

Now if this equal sacrifice were a real thing and if those who have no income can contribute £66,500,000 to the national income, how much can those who do not work, never have worked, never will work, and have huge incomes, contribute in this 'equal sacrifice' humbug? Then again in Australia if a worker on five quid a week can sacrifice 20 per cent of that for the national good, a judge or a politician or a bondholder should be able to sacrifice all the income he or she gets above five quid. They would then still be 20 per cent above the poor plugger that works for his bit and it is more questionable whether they are worth 20 per cent more.

The bagmen were unanimous that the only patriot expected (in war time or peace) to sacrifice everything for his Country is the toiler and they furthermore thought that it is time the Workers of Australia put up a fight against this 'equal sacrifice' humbug and wage reduction campaign of the super patriots, but they are only bagmen.

Homes of hope

As the Great Depression rolled over the lives and hopes of millions, an Anglican minister came up with a plan to house some of the families evicted from their homes, often with no means of financial support. Robert Hammond was archdeacon at St Barnabas' Anglican church in Sydney's Broadway. Wondering what he could do to alleviate the suffering he saw all around, he invited married men to a meeting in February 1932. His idea was what he called a 'consolidated settlement', a residential development on new land where the families of unemployed would help themselves and each other to build, rent and eventually purchase their own homes. Each would use their skills to help others and after around seven years would have paid sufficient rent to own their houses outright.

To qualify for the scheme a married couple needed to be unemployed, have at least three children and possess a skill useful to the community. They had to show that they had been recently evicted and make a commitment to joining the community in growing its own food. Rents were very reasonable and did not need to be paid by those who continued to be unemployed.

The 'Pioneer Homes' scheme, as it was originally known, received 800 applications and began with 13 acres near Liverpool. Although the initiative received little official support, donations from the public enabled it to expand and by the end of the next year 26 homes were completed. Another 40 homes were built the following year, and another 150 acres were purchased with a generous individual donation. By 1937, 110 homes were housing families. Hammondville, as it came to be called after its visionary founder, had a church, post office, general store and school by 1940. A senior citizens' facility was developed in later years and Hammondville continued to thrive.

The community grew further during the war, and many of the men served in the armed forces. By the end of the war in 1945, most families had already paid off their properties and now owned them along with the acre of land on which they stood.

Hammondville tradition is full of stories about individuals who made great contributions to a unique community. They include Constance Jewell and her 'Depression recipe' cakes, so popular at dances and fundraisers. Shopkeeper Alf Morley was known as the 'Mayor of Hammondville' because of his popularity. Alf opened the town's first shop with a 100-pound loan from the founder and provided generous terms of payment as well as free ice-creams for the kids.

Other notable people from the community include property developer Jim Masterson and politician John Hatton. Reverend Bernard Judd and his wife, Ida, had a long connection with Hammondville and were prime movers in establishing various local institutions, including the Girl Guides and the Senior Citizens' Home.

Robert Hammond's vision and energy were recognised in 1937 when he was awarded an OBE. He died in 1946, almost 76 years of age.

5

How we travel the land

With a ragged old swag on their shoulder,
And a billy quart-pot in their hands,
I tell you they'll 'stonish the new chums,
When they see how we travel the land.

'The Springtime it Brings on the Shearing'

MOVEMENT ACROSS THE vast distances of the continent is one of
the deepest and most persistent themes of Australian tradition.
Aboriginal creation myths speak of ancestral beings travelling
far across the country to make the rivers, mountains and plains.
Aboriginal peoples moved constantly around their countries,
following the seasons and acknowledging the sacred sites that
lay along their 'songlines', preserving this ancient knowledge in
a rich culture of song, dance, art and story.

When Europeans arrived, they explored and opened up new
lands for agriculture and the pastoral industries that largely made
the nation in the nineteenth century. The lore of the bush is full
of overlanders, bullockies and swagmen who rode or walked across
the country. Even that enigmatic figure, the bushranger, 'ranges'
the country in search of sustenance and plunder, trying to keep
a few steps ahead of the mounted troopers close behind, often
assisted by deadly efficient blacktrackers.

When horses began to give way to motor vehicles, it was still a common sight to see swagmen 'humping their bluey' along isolated bush tracks. Many had to take up this itinerant way of life during the Depression of the 1930s. Sometimes the railways might assist them, if they were clever enough to 'hook a rattler' and get off it again without being caught by the police. Spending a night or two in the cells for vagrancy—sometimes after a beating—was a topic sung about in the country ballads of that era.

Today, the familiar sight of 'grey nomads' on a campervan or caravan pilgrimage around the country is perhaps an updated expression of this ancient Australian need to travel the land.

Rangers and rouseabouts

The ballads of the bush began to describe and celebrate the roaming necessities from early times. The famous chorus of 'The Wild Colonial Boy' is all about movement and freedom:

So come along my hearties, we'll roam the mountains high,
Together we will plunder, together we will die.
We'll gallop across the mountains and scour across the plains
And scorn to live in slavery, bound down in iron chains.

The development of sheep and cattle production created new groups of travellers. This time they were either working or in search of work, rather than plunder. The 'overlanders' were a flamboyant group of men who carried out some legendary feats of droving across usually harsh terrain, celebrated in many ballads and in the popular literature of the time.

There's a trade you all know well, it's bringing cattle over
On every track to the Gulf and back, men know the Queensland
    drover.

So, pass the billy 'round, boys, don't let the pint-pot stand there
For tonight we'll drink the health of every overlander.

And so it went on, bragging about the deeds of the Queensland drovers. Another ballad on the same themes, 'Brisbane Ladies', told of their exploits.

We'll rant and we'll roar, like true Queensland drovers,
We'll rant and we'll roar as onward we push
Until we return to the Augathella station,
For it's bloody dry going in the old Queensland bush.

The wool industry produced another swag of now-iconic songs about shearers and rouseabouts, all spreading out across the land to clip the fleeces that, for a long time, provided the backbone of the Australian economy. One of many was 'The Springtime it Brings on the Shearing':

Oh, the springtime it brings on the shearing,
And then you will see them in droves,
To the west country stations all steering,
Seeking a job off the coves.

With a ragged old swag on their shoulder,
And a billy quart-pot in their hands,
I tell you they'll 'stonish the new chums,
When they see how we travel the land.

The 'coves' mentioned in 'The Springtime it Brings on the Shearing' were the bosses, the owners or managers of the sheep stations. There was strong tension between the shearers and their employers, a troubled relationship that was an important element in the formation of the trade union movement in the late nineteenth century. The tension was reflected in 'Banjo' Paterson's poem 'A Bushman's Song'. The continual movement of the song's main character to 'the stations further out' captures the necessity for, but also the freedom to be had from, the travelling life.

'A Bushman's Song', usually known in its bush ballad form as 'Travelling Down the Castlereagh' or 'The Old Jig-Jog', hymns the freedom of the wandering life and tells the story of a station hand travelling down the Castlereagh River 'handy with a roping pole and handy with a brand'. He is always moving further away from the settled regions further out:

> So it was shift, boys, shift, there wasn't the slightest doubt
> I had to make a shift for the stations further out
> Saddle up my horses and whistle up my dog
> And it's off across the country at the old jig-jog.

He gets a job with his brother on the Illawarra but finds that he has to 'ask the landlord's leave before he lifts his arm', which doesn't suit him at all. He then takes a job at shearing 'along the Marthaguy' but finds they shear non-union—'I call it scab, says I'. Finally, the station hand decides to go 'where they drink artesian water from a thousand foot below'. Here he meets the overlanders and their mobs, where they 'work a while and make a pile, then have a spree in town'.

'A Bushman's Song' captures the independence and dream of freedom that pioneering life promised for many men at that time. The hero of the song is fortunate enough to travel the land on horseback; many others went on foot, often called 'swagmen'.

The swagman's union

Folklore has it that there was such a thing as a 'swagman's union', and according to this account there was such an organisation.

Formed in the 1870s, this association had some interesting rules by which its members were allegedly regulated.

*T*he old-time swagman is fast disappearing, but to-day my thoughts go back to some of the real old-time 'whalers' of the Murrumbidgee and other Southern watercourses (writes 'Bill Bowyang'). The genuine 'whaler' in the halcyon days of yore was a feature of the Murrumbidgee tracks and along the routes fringing some of the Western Queensland rivers.

Those who carried the swag on the Lachlan were known as the 'Lachlan Cruisers' but there were also the 'Darling Whisperers', the 'Murray Sundowners' and the 'Bogan Bummers'. Each member cherished an unbounding pride in his clan, and there were at times fierce fights under the big river gums when some favored fishing hole was usurped by an interloper from an alien band.

Scanning an old scrap book recently I came across an interesting record of an occurrence that at the time created a great stir in swag-men circles throughout the West. It tells of a meeting that was held to bring about a combination of the scattered units of swaggydom in a society known as the 'Amalgamated Swagmen of Australia'. This first union was formed in a bend of the Lachlan, near Forbes, in 1877, and a conference of delegates from far and wide gathered for the occasion. They were a motley crew, frowsy dead beats, loony-hatters, and aggressive cadgers.

By the fitful flames of yarran and myall fires, officers were elected, branches formed, and rules drawn up. Sir William Wallaby was the first President, and Sir John Bluey, secretary; T. Billy Esq., is named as treasurer, and Dr. Johnny Cake medical adviser. The well-known firm of Walker and Tucker were solicitors. The rules were as follows:

1. No member to be over 100 years old.
2. Each member to pay one pannikin of flour entrance fee. Members who don't care about paying will be admitted free.

3. No member to carry swags weighing over ten pounds.

4. Each member to possess three complete sets of tucker bags, each set to consist of nine bags.

5. No member to pass any station, farm, boundary rider's hut, camp, or private house without 'tapping' and obtaining rations or hand-outs.

6. Each member to allow himself to be bitten by a sheep. If a sheep bites a member he must immediately turn it into mutton.

7. Members who defame a 'good' cook, or pay a fine when run in, shall not be allowed to enter the Kingdom of Heaven. Amen.

8. No members allowed to hum baking powder, tea, flour, sugar, or tobacco from a fellow unionist.

9. Non-smoking members must 'whisper' for tobacco on every possible occasion, the same as smokers.

10. At general or branch meetings non-smoking hums must give up their whispered tobacco to be distributed amongst the officers of the society.

11. Any member found without at least two sets of bags filled with tucker will be fined.

12. No member to own more than one creek, river, or billabong bend. To sell bends for old boots or sinkers is prohibited.

13. No member to look for or accept work of any description. Members found willing will be at once expelled.

14. No member to walk more than five miles per day if rations can be hummed.

15. No member to tramp on Sundays at any price.

This union is many years defunct and its original members as widely scattered as the ashes of their long-dimmed camp-fires, yet the spirit and the rules are adhered to sacredly, even in these days, by those who hump the swag. Par chance these rules extend to Paradise, and the sturdy beggars still tramp through eternity with Matilda up.

Amongst the old time 'whalers' Scotty the Wrinkler was perhaps the most famous. A garrulous Scotch man of scholarly attainments, he had, perhaps, less need to cadge than any other. Scotty I always recognised as somewhat of a poseur. His habits were so settled that he dwelt most of the year in a huge hollow log on the banks of the Murrumbidgee, near Narrandera, and he even acquired his name from the original holder, who was a Darling River Whisperer.

The oozlum bird

The oozlum bird is an Australian version of a mythical creature also found in British and American traditions. 'Ouzel' is a name given to a variety of bird species in the British Isles, most commonly, it seems, the blackbird. In Ireland the water ouzel is associated with the danger of malignant disease, while the blackbird is the carrier of numerous superstitions, as in English folklore. The ouzel also appears in Welsh mythology and in that of the Ainu, the aboriginal inhabitants of what is now Japan. Intriguingly, in this belief system, the ouzel is associated with improved sight, perhaps echoed in the Australian version's capabilities, or lack of them.

Our oozlum bird flies backwards, either because it wishes to gaze admiringly at its own tail feathers or to keep the dust out of its eyes. Or it could be because it likes to know where it has been because it does not know where it is going. It can be large enough for a human to ride upon. If startled, the oozlum bird may fly in smaller and smaller circles until it eventually disappears into its own fundamental orifice—sometimes in a puff of blue smoke.

Around 1897, the journalist and poet W.T. Goodge penned a few verses featuring the oozlum bird, also helpfully explaining how the town of Birdsville got its name. The poem begins by introducing 'Ginger Joe' of the Diamantina:

He was old and he was ugly,
He was dirty, he was low.

Joe was also a noted teller of tall tales, and the best anyone ever heard him tell was about Jock McPherson's trip to Sydney on the famously speedy oozlum bird. According to Joe, this is just how it happened:

You can talk about yer racehorse
And the pace as he can go,
But it just amounts to crawlin',
'Nothink else!' said Ginger Joe.
And these cycle blokes with pacers,
You can take my bloomin' word,
They're a funeral procession
To the blinded Oozlum Bird!

Do yez know Marengo station?
It's away beyond the Peak,
Over sixty miles from Birdsville
As you go to Cooper's Creek,
Which the blacks call Kallokoopah,
And they tell you that Lake Eyre
Was one time an inland ocean.
Well, the Oozlum Bird is there!

Bet yer boots it ain't no chicken,
It's as big and wide across
As the bird what beats the steamships,
What's it called? The albatross!
That's the bird! And old King Mulga
Used to tell the boys and me
They were there when Central 'Stralia
Was a roarin' inland sea!

I was cook at old Marengo
When McTavish had the run,

And his missus died and left him
With a boy—the only one.
Jock McPherson was his nephew,
Lately came from Scotland, too,
Been sent out to get 'experience'
As a kind of Jackeroo!

Well, this kid of old McTavish
Was a daisy. Strike me blue!
There was nothing, that was mischief,
That the kiddy wouldn't do!
But he was a kindly kinchen
And a reg'lar little brick,
And we all felt mighty sorry
When we heard that he was sick!

But, McTavish! Well, I reckon
I am something on the swear,
But I never heard sich language
As McTavish uttered there;
For he cursed the blessed country,
And the cattle and the sheep,
And the station-hands and shearers
Till yer blinded flesh would creep.

It was something like a fever
That the little bloke had got,
And McTavish he remembered
(When he'd cursed and swore a lot),
That a chemist down in Sydney
Had a special kind of stuff
Which would cure the kiddy's fever
In a jiffy, right enough!

So he sends me into Birdsville
On the fastest horse we had,
And I has to wire to Sydney
For the medsin for the lad.
They would send it by the railway,
And by special pack from Bourke;
It would take a week to do it
And be mighty slippery work.

Well, I gallops into Birdsville
And I sends the wire all right;
And I looks around the township,
Meanin' stopping for the night.
I was waitin' in the bar-room—
This same bar-room—for a drink
When a wire comes from McPherson,
And from Sydney! Strike me pink!

I had left him at Marengo
On the morning of that day!
He was talking to McTavish
At the time I came away!
And yet here's a wire from Sydney!
And it says: 'Got here all right.
Got the medsin. Am just leaving.
Will be home again to-night!'

Well, I thought I had the jim-jams,
Yes, I did; for, spare me days!
How in thunder had McPherson
Got to Sydney, anyways?
But he'd got there, that was certain,
For the wire was plain and clear.

I could never guess conundrums,
So I had another beer.

In the morning, bright and early,
I was out and saddled up,
And away to break the record
Of old Carbine for the Cup.
And I made that cuddy gallop
As he'd never done before;
And, so-help-me-bob, McPherson
Was there waiting at the door!

And the kid was right as ninepence,
Sleepin' peaceful in his bunk,
And McTavish that delighted
He'd made everybody drunk!
And McPherson says: 'Well, Ginger,
You did pretty well, I heard;
But you must admit you're beaten,
Joe—I rode the Oozlum Bird!'

Said he'd often studied science
Long before he'd came out here,
And he'd struck a sort of notion,
Which you'll think is mighty queer—
That the earth rolls round to eastward
And that birds, by rising high,
Might just stop and travel westward,
While the earth was rolling by!

So he saddled up the Oozlum,
Rose some miles above the plain,
Let the Earth turn underneath him
Till he spotted the Domain!

Then came down, and walked up George-street,
Got the stuff and wired to me;
Rose again and reached Marengo
Just as easy as could be!

'But,' says I, 'if you went westward
Just as simple as you say,
How did you get back?' He answered:
'Oh, I came the other way!'
So in six-and-twenty hours,
Take the yarn for what it's worth,
Jock McPherson and the Oozlum
Had been all around the earth!

It's a curious bird, the Oozlum,
And a bird that's mighty wise,
For it always flies tail-first to
Keep the dust out of its eyes!
And I heard that since McPherson
Did that famous record ride,
They won't let a man get near 'em,
Couldn't catch one if you tried!

If you don't believe the story,
And some people don't, yer know;
Why the blinded map'll prove it,
'Strike me fat!' said Ginger Joe.
'Look along the Queensland border,
On the South Australian side,
There's this township! christened Birdsville,
'Cause of Jock McPherson's ride!'

Another variation exists in the United States military, where an 'Oozlefinch' has been the official mascot of the Air Defense Artillery since the early twentieth century. As befits an air force mascot, the featherless Oozlefinch flies at the incredibly fast pace that sped Jock McPherson to Sydney and back, but has the additional military advantage of tearing enemy aircraft from the skies. Like our own species, the Oozlefinch flies backwards, but is not thought to perform the same unique vanishing act when alarmed.

The Tea and Sugar Train

The world's longest stretch of straight railway line runs for 478 kilometres along the track that tethers Port Augusta to Kalgoorlie, forming part of the Trans-Australian Railway. It was a condition of Federation that the 'Trans' be built across the Nullarbor Plain to link up the east and west coasts. When the rails were finally connected in 1917 it was possible to travel across the continent by rail for the first time—as long as passengers did not mind frequent stops and transfers to the different rail gauges that were then a feature of the railway system. As the visiting American humourist Mark Twain remarked after experiencing this irritation in the 1890s—'Now comes a singular thing, the oddest thing, the strangest thing, the unaccountable marvel that Australia can show, namely the break of gauge at Albury. Think of the paralysis of intellect that gave that idea birth.'

During the gruelling seven years of surveying and building the nearly 1700 kilometres of the Trans, workers had to be supplied by trains coming from the South Australian and the Western Australian ends of the line. At an indeterminate time during and after the construction of the line, the regular service that came to be known as the 'Tea and Sugar Train' appeared. No one knows just when it started running, but the 'Tea and Sugar', as it was affectionately known, was well established by 1917. At this stage, the train consisted of a fruit and vegetable carriage, a butcher's shop and a general supply van. Because there was no refrigeration at that time, the butcher's van had to carry live sheep, slaughtering them as they went. The train was gradually improved, though it was still lacking a stove in 1919. Staff had to jump off the train when it stopped, light a fire and boil their billy beside the line. It was not unusual for the train to leave before they could brew a cup of tea.

Because the line was so long and crossed some very tough terrain, maintenance was—and is—a big issue. A number of settlements of railway workers and their families grew up along the track, including a number named after prime ministers and other notable Australians, as well as Boonderoo, 913 Mile, Rawlinna and Ooldea. Somehow, these tiny settlements had to be supplied with the necessities of life—including water—and the Tea and Sugar was the only way to do it. The needs of these communities were stored in a vast warehouse in Port Augusta, from where the Tea and Sugar would roll out for the four-day trip to a few miles outside Kalgoorlie. The journey took 57 hours, though the train travelled only by day, stopping at night to take orders for the next trip.

In 1925, life was still a frontier experience for the people living along the Trans:

Sometimes the scene is picturesque. Bush men mounted on horses, mules or camels may rub shoulders with uniformed railway employees and their women folk and children and it is not unusual for scantily clad aboriginals to patronise the moving stores. The train-shopkeepers are smartly clad in the regulation garb of their particular trade. Mr. K.A. Richardson, who for many years prior to the coming of the East-West train, carried mails from Port Augusta to Tarcoola, has seen wild natives hovering about the train. That was in the early days of the line, and most of the natives are now semi-civilised.

Conditions for those living and working on the line were extreme, as an observer related in 1928:

Here and there along the railway line are little settlements mostly composed of railway workers. The huts that these workers live in are of the two-compartment shanty type or one room. At least, you can hardly call them rooms. In the hot summer sun (the temperature is 116 degrees in the shade) the workers and their wives suffer and stew, and the little children cry for a cool drink. Meanwhile, in the trans train, the toff-class enjoy themselves to the limit.

The highlight of the year for the children of the Trans was Christmas. The anxiously awaited Tea and Sugar would arrive with a special load of seasonal treats, otherwise impossible to come by in the emptiness of the Nullarbor Plain.

The importance of this lifeline was highlighted during World War II, when shortages prevented the Tea and Sugar running. After two to three weeks without bread, meat and other supplies, the workers along the line threatened to stop work. The Australian Workers Union had to step in to get the train running once again.

By 1955, the pioneering efforts of Dr Eleanor (or Rita, as she was known) Stang (1894–1978) saw an infant health and mother-care 'oasis' attached to the Tea and Sugar, bringing much-needed medical care and advice to the isolated mothers along the line. In the 1970s, general medical services were also sometimes available through the train.

The Tea and Sugar Train continued to bring food and comforts to the families along the line until 1996. By then it boasted air conditioning and a conversion to a rolling supermarket through which buyers walked and selected their needs from rows of shelving. The Tea and Sugar is still fondly remembered by many.

The black stump

Where is it? How did it originate? What does it mean? That iconic Australian expression 'beyond the black stump' or 'not this side of the black stump' refers to any location considered to be far away from the speaker, usually well beyond the rural urban fringe, in the bush or in the outback. No one is quite sure where the outback begins and ends, but we all know that it's a long way away and very big. So important is the black stump that it has evolved its own considerable body of lore and legend to explain its existence.

Some stories rely on what the dictionary makers call etymology, the history of a word from its origins—at least as far as these can be determined—and its appearance in books, newspapers and other documentary sources. There are various tantalising allusions to the black stump in nineteenth-century sources of this kind, but nothing very conclusive; we have to wait until the twentieth century to find references. Before that, so the story goes, the term originated among rural carriers who used fire-blackened tree stumps as way finders; for example, 'Turn left at the third black stump after the river.' Needless to say, there is absolutely no evidence for this belief, which, of course, does not mean it is wrong, just unsubstantiated.

A number of bush towns claim the honour of being the location of the original black stump. As in all good folklore, each has an elaborate tale to justify its claim. In Coolah, New South Wales, it is said that one of the early 'limits of location' involved the boundary of a property known as the 'Black Stump Run'. Later, in the 1860s, an inn was built in the area and named The Black Stump Inn. This establishment was an important stop for travellers and so 'beyond the black stump' came into use as a reference to going beyond the boundaries of settlement. Variations on this theme include the suggestion that blackened stumps functioned as unofficial markers for property boundaries.

A colourful legend underlies the Riverina village of Merriwagga's claim to be the location of the original blackened stump. In 1886, the wife of a passing carrier, Barbara Blain, was burned to death when her dress caught alight in the flames of the camp fire. It is said that in describing the body, her husband said it resembled a black stump. A local waterhole is named Black Stump Tank.

Not to be outdone by New South Wales, the Queensland town of Blackall has a scientific legend to bolster its claim. A surveying party visited the area in the late 1880s and established a site for observing longitude and latitude. Theodolites mounted on tree stumps were used for this work, a number of which were fire-blackened. The remote country beyond this site was considered to be 'beyond the black stump'.

Just how remote and isolated the black stump and beyond could be is highlighted in at least one traditional yarn.

Some time in the 1930s a boundary rider is well out beyond the black stump. He comes across an old prospector who asks him how the war is going. Taken aback, the boundary rider tells him that the 1914–18 war has been over for years.

'Really!' exclaims the prospector. 'Can you tell me who won it?'

'Our mob won, of course.'

The prospector cackled. 'I expect Queen Vic is happy then, she never liked the bloody Boers.'

It has also been said that the term originated in an Aboriginal story. A giant Aboriginal man once threw an enormous spear high into the sky. When it eventually returned to earth most of the wooden spear had been burned away, leaving only the blackened stump in the ground where it fell. Apparently, the legend does not say exactly where the spear fell, which is the whole point (ouch!) of the story.

There are also outrageous assertions that New Zealand actually originated the phrase. The Kiwis might use it, but of course they got it from us!

Whatever we might think of these passionately held claims to the first black stump, they do not explain those other essentials of bush geography like Oodnagallabie, Woop Woop, Bullamakanka or simply 'out to buggery'. Where are these places?

The rise and fall of Cobb & Co.

The legendary coaching line known as Cobb & Co. has a special place in Australian history. The company, in one or another of its various forms, was an integral element of everyday life from the 1850s to the early twentieth century (for more on Cobb & Co., see Chapter 4).

The company saw off its many rivals over that time, basing its success on its ability to provide a faster and, sometimes, more comfortable means of getting from place to place. Then, as now, time was money, and the men who established and ran Cobb & Co. profited handsomely from their ability to exploit this reality.

Cobb & Co. was established during the Victorian gold rush era by expatriate Americans Freeman Cobb and three others. The company imported 'Concord coaches' from the United States, a sturdy design well suited to the difficulties and distances of Australian roads and tracks. One of its features was a suspension system of leather straps supposed to make the ride a more comfortable experience for the passengers, which gave Cobb & Co. a competitive edge over their many rivals.

Freeman Cobb sold out after a few years and returned to America, leaving the company in the hands of a consortium, the main figure in which turned out to be another American. James Rutherford was a chronic over-worker, almost continually on the roads, railways and coaching routes from before dawn until after dark. He kept up a punishing schedule of surprise visits on the company's employees, deal making and generally powering the enterprise that would make a modern CEO wilt.

A secret of Cobb & Co.'s success was its ability to win government mail contracts. And when they could not win them, there were always competitor companies holding such contracts to be bought out and closed down. Almost continual expansion and agglomeration were key features of the business model.

As the enterprise expanded into different colonies, it split into different businesses, though all retained the valuable asset of the Cobb & Co. name. It is arguable that Cobb & Co. was Australia's first iconic brand name, so widespread, influential and recognised did it become.

From the mid-1860s, the success of the business allowed its owners to branch into other areas of opportunity, including extensive pastoral properties and minerals development. Success also allowed the continual improvement of the vehicles and their horses, though coach travel always remained the ordeal it had been in 1860 when a visiting Englishwoman described her experience of travelling 'up the country':

But oh! The crushing misery. The suffocation of these public conveyances . . . These vehicles are licensed to carry far too many passengers—from forty or fifty, including those outside. Inside they hold twelve to fifteen. I do not know how many inches are allotted to each passenger; I fancied that only about fifteen fell to my share . . . I know that I was condensed to a smaller compass than I could have imagined possible.

She went on to describe the closeness of those beside her and those opposite her 'keeping from us the pure air'. Just as she felt that she would faint, the woman sitting beside her did so.

Despite these discomforts, by the mid-1860s it was possible to travel on the Cobb & Co. brand from Cape York, down the eastern seaboard and into South Australia. The coaching company's mileage was probably the world's most extensive, larger even than that of the American Wells Fargo.

The main threat to Cobb & Co. was the railways. Rather than try to compete head-on, the coaching men worked with the railways to provide transport to and from railheads and important stations. This strategy served the company well until they were tempted to have a try at railway-line building. While this might otherwise have been a smart move, the company's inexperience in building transport routes as opposed to developing and running them was an expensive financial disaster.

It is likely that this experience contributed to the decline of the company in later years. But so complex and diverse were the incomes and expenditures of Cobb & Co.'s interlocking business interests that it is impossible to tell. Perhaps it was just the passing of time.

As the business aged, so did its operators. Although Rutherford lived well into his eighties, his mental health deteriorated along with his grasp of the business. The company failed to perceive the value of the motor vehicle, resisting motorisation until it was already providing smaller competitors with the essential edge, and was in receivership by 1911. The last horse-drawn coach ran in 1924.

A vintage British and Australian television series called *Whiplash* was loosely based on the Cobb & Co. story, filmed during 1959–60 and first reaching Australian screens in 1961. The 'Australian western' series starred the American actor Peter Graves in the lead role of Freeman Cobb, though the rest of the cast were locals, including Leonard Teale, Chips Rafferty, Lionel Long and Robert Tudawali. Although a rather painful, sometimes jarring representation of colonial life, the series did help the developing Australian industry move towards more realistic depictions of its history in shows like *Rush*, *Cash and Company* and *Against the Wind*.

The Long Paddock

The Long Paddock is the unofficial name for Travelling Stock Routes, or TSRs. Mostly originating in the nineteenth century, these are official routes for droving livestock from place to distant place, with wide strips of grass at each side to allow the passing sheep or cattle to graze. Water points are available at regular intervals, although these can easily fail in times of drought. Many Long Paddocks are famous in Australian tradition, including the Canning Stock Route (established 1906–10) between Wiluna and Halls Creek; the Birdsville Track (1880s), 520 kilometres from Birdsville in Queensland to Maree in South Australia; and the Tanami Track, between Halls Creek and the MacDonnell Ranges in the Northern Territory. Many of these TSRs have colourful tales to tell.

The Strzelecki Track runs through South Australia and was established by the bushranger Harry Redford, or 'Starlight', who drove 1000 stolen cattle from Queensland to Blanchewater (South Australia) in 1870, selling them for a large amount of money but later apprehended for the crime. He was tried but found not guilty by a jury impressed with his outstanding journey and unintended contribution to rural infrastructure.

One of the deadliest tracks is known as the 'Ghost Road of the Drovers'. It's only 230 kilometres long, but the Murranji Track runs through dense scrub from Newcastle Waters to Old Top Springs and is a shortcut between the Kimberley and markets in

Queensland. Formed in 1885 and taking its last mob in 1967, the track was notorious for its difficulty of access and the frequent failure of its water supply. At least eleven bodies are said to lie at Murranji Bore and Waterhole, which is also a sacred site to the Mudburra people. In 1942, Billy Miller passed on his recollections of the track in its early days.

*I*n 1886 . . . Nat Buchanan first crossed what is now the Murranji Track, going through from Newcastle Waters to Victoria River. Beginning at Newcastle Waters, the Track follows the Four Mile Creek for twenty-five miles until it reaches a waterhole, called by the drovers The Bucket. Here the Track leaves the creek and goes west, crossing a plain for about fifteen miles, after which it enters thick scrub of hedgewood and lance-wood. Thirty-five miles further on it reaches the Murranji Waterhole, which is surrounded by old box trees. This is the loneliest place I have seen in all 'the Outback' of the north.

Thirty-five miles west from here the Track reaches an aboriginal 'mickeree' (native well). The aborigines dug these wells so that they could walk down to the water. They had a crude but effective way of timbering them. The earth dug out in making or deepening them is not piled up at the edges, but scattered about the surrounding land; the idea being not to make the wells conspicuous. Aborigines never make camp close to the water—always over a mile away in some thick patch of scrub. In walking to the water to fill their coolamons, they avoid going the same way twice, thus making no pad that would lead strangers to the mickerees.

A further fifteen miles brings the Track to the Yellow Waterholes (native, 'Bin-kook-wee-charra'). Nine miles west from here it reaches the Jump Up. On the 109 miles from The Bucket Waterhole to the Jump Up there were only two surface waters—that is, in the old days—which explains the aborigines' need to guard their mickerees. To-day there is a cut line through the dense scrub, and there are bores with large tanks and pumping plants also. It is no trouble now to cross the Murranji Track.

In 1894, when I was stockkeeping on Newcastle Waters cattle station, the blacks about the Yellow Waterholes were very hostile. Some packers from the Cook Town country were going out to Halls Creek, I recall, and, at night, when they were camped, blacks threw spears into their mosquito nets, but luckily did not kill anyone.

In 1900, 'Mulga Jim' McDonald and Hardcastle were camped at the Yellow Waterholes, and, in the night the blacks attacked their camp also. A spear struck Hardcastle in the chest, but, as it was a cold night, he had two rugs and a camp sheet over him, and these stopped the point from penetrating deeply. However, the spear wound caused his death two years later.

On Armstrong's Creek about twenty miles west of the Yellow Waterholes, Jim Campbell and I were camped one night, when the natives let go a shower of spears at our mosquito net. The spears hit our packsaddles, but missed us! They missed because, having learned from experience, we anticipated the raid and, rigging our nets as usual, slept a little way off in the grass. That tricked them!

Thirty-eight years ago I was working on a newly-formed station called Illawarra. The leased country held by the owners was from Top Springs to the Yellow Waterholes, so that cattle travelling the Murranji Track would traverse the station for 40 miles.

When Ben Martin, Jim Campbell and Mick Fleming took the country up, cleanskin cattle were plentiful and very wild. We were moonlighting and running them in to 'coachers' and throwing and tying. Eventually we pulled a fair-sized herd together.

Wave Hill Station was sending bullocks away, some to Queensland and some to Oodnadatta. Victoria River was also sending two mobs of cows to Kidman's Annandale Station on the Lower Georgina. I had to pick up each mob at Top Springs and go with them through the Illawarra country to the Yellow Waterholes, a distance of 40 miles. And I had to keep our station cattle from boxing with the travelling mobs!

With me were two blacks about 17 years of age, who, only three years previously, had been living a stone-age life and had never seen a white man. Now they were top-notch riders. They could take their place 'moonlighting' and could throw and tie up a beast as well as the best of us.

The first mob I picked up was with Blake Miller, a contract drover. He had 1,000 head of cows from Victoria River Downs. After seeing him through to the Yellow Waterholes I returned to Top Springs and picked up Steve and Harry Lewis, who had 1,000 head of Wave Hill bullocks for Oodnadatta.

Bringing down the next mob I was with 'Jumbo' Smith ('Brown of the Bulls' in 'We of the Never Never'). Suddenly, in the darkness, the cattle rushed off the night camp. I heard the stampede, jumped out of bed, and picked up my bridle and whip. My horse was close at hand. I jumped on bare-back and raced for the lead. I put the stockwhip into the leaders and had them blocked, when one of my black boys came up. Then 'Jumbo' Smith (he weighed 18 stone) arrived on the scene. We put the cattle back onto camp, and at day-light 'Jumbo' counted them. He found that we were only two short!

The next lot to be pushed through was a mob of 1,500 head of Wave Hill bullocks, with Jack Dick Skuethorp contract drover. Following him was Oswald Skuethorp, who had 1,250 head of Wave Hill bullocks.

On the second day Oswald asked me to take charge of his bullocks as he wanted to stay with his waggonette to help the cook, who was also the driver. The road was rough limestone in places and very difficult for a vehicle. A wheel of the waggonette broke, as Oswald feared it might, and, worse still, as they were fixing it up the horses strayed away. They did not get them together until late. Putting some cooked tucker on the horses, Oswald started on in the night, hoping to pick up the cattle. However, he did not turn up. In the darkness he had mistaken a cattle pad for the road and 'gone bush'.

The food for the cattlemen was with the waggonette. I had my horses and packs with me, so I knocked up some johnny cakes, boiled some corned beef, and fed the men. I put two of my horses and my two black boys to help with the night watch. The next day we went on but by nightfall there was still no sign of the waggonette, the boss, or the cook. The following day we went up the Jump Up and on to the Yellow Waterholes. We had watered the bullocks and they were feeding on the small plain close to the water when we saw Oswald Skuethorp coming up with the horses and waggonette. We were right glad to see them, as the food supply was exhausted.

⌒

It used to be assumed that pioneers developed these vital transport corridors from scratch, but recent research suggests that while this was so in some cases, many follow traditional pathways. While the TSRs are little used for droving these days, there are calls to preserve them as important elements of the environment as well as for their heritage value.

A final surprising fact about the Long Paddock: the Bradfield Highway that crosses Sydney Harbour Bridge is officially designated as a Travelling Stock Route.

The real Red Dog

The earliest European visitors to the continent often commented on the many dogs they saw accompanying Aboriginal groups. When the new settlers came they soon realised the value of canine companions, and dogs became as much a part of the working stock of the land as horses, bullocks, sheep and cows. They accompanied drovers overland, keeping mobs of cattle and flocks of sheep in order. They hunted, retrieved, protected and became an inseparable part of many families. Dogs also featured in songs, stories, art and even in early silent movies, where they often appeared in the chase scenes, well beyond directorial control and simply enjoying the thrill of it all.

Lawson wrote of the dog loaded with a stick of explosive. The famous song about whatever the dog did on—or in—the tucker box at Gundagai entered folklore, as did the wild native dog, the dingo. Dogs were often mascots in military units, the best known being Horrie, the war dog of the 1939–45 conflict, though he was only one of many fighting hounds. Dogs were an indispensible element of Australian life and are still with us as family pets, sporting beasts and the cargo in the back of country utes.

One of the most famous dogs of recent times was known simply as 'Red Dog'. Red Dog was a crossed Kelpie–cattle dog born in Paraburdoo in 1971, known as 'Tally' or 'Blue' in some areas of the vast distances he is said to have covered in his travels. Red Dog became a well-known, if smelly, wanderer throughout the Pilbara region. Many tales were and are told of his amazingly long and arduous journeys and gargantuan appetite, not only for food but for lady dogs as well. He was a generally loved character in the region, frequently being given lifts by passing vehicles as he made his way from one favourite feeding place to another. He even made a trip as far south as Perth.

Not everyone liked Red Dog, though. He took, and was probably given, a strychnine bait in Karratha on 10 November 1979 and died ten days later. Red Dog was buried between Roebourne and Cossack and commemorated in a statue at Dampier, in verse, as well as in a number of books and especially in Pilbara folklore.

In 1998, the writer Louis de Bernières travelled to the Pilbara and saw the locally famous statue. He became fascinated by the story and returned a few months later to collect Red Dog yarns still being told by the locals, turning these anecdotes into a bestselling book published in 2001. Being a writer, de Bernières naturally made an even better tale out of the legends and it is now even more difficult to tell where truth ends and fiction begins. Not that it matters. Assisted by the hit movie based on the book in 2011, Red Dog is now a household name throughout Australia, having made the leap from local legend to national hero.

What a hound! Perhaps Red Dog could only have become such a figure in Australia with its long and strong canine tradition. The movie was a great hit here, but did not do so well overseas. But those with a commercial interest in this venture are not too worried. To date, *Red Dog* is the eighth-highest grossing Australian film and plans are said to be well in hand for *Red Dog the Musical*.

6

Doing it tough

'The banks are all broken,' they said,
'Times will be hard and rough.
There's relief for the poor
At the dole-office door
But you'll have to keep doing it tough.'

Anonymous

ALTHOUGH AUSTRALIA HAS often proved a bountiful place for many, it also has a long history of hard times. The image of the battler is a well-known one and a term that is still often heard today in relation to people who, for whatever reason, are forced to do it tough just to scrape by.

The free selectors of the post-gold rush years lived notoriously basic lives, often subsisting on 'pumpkin and bear' and little else. People had to fend for themselves as far as their health was concerned and in just about every other aspect of life, work and leisure. When the Great Depression hit Australia in the 1930s, very many people who had previously held decent jobs and rented or were purchasing homes were thrown out of work and often onto the street. They coped by adopting some of the strategies of earlier generations who knew what doing it tough meant.

Depending on the harvest

In April 1880, a journalist for the *Argus* newspaper travelled through northeast Victoria interviewing hard-pressed selectors 'where hopefulness was coupled with rough living and plenty of work'. This is what he found.

*T*he husband was out ploughing, behind a pair of horses, and the wife was occupied in 'burning off' which meant hauling small logs and boughs to the heaps of dead timber, and keeping several fires in a state of activity. The children, too small to be of any use, were amusing themselves picking up sticks, and following their mother about. They were very poorly clad all of them and had evidently not worn new clothes for several seasons. The husband was very glad to leave off ploughing to have a consultation with his friend and adviser the bailiff. He took up 320 acres in February, 1877, beginning with a capital of £200. He had fenced all the land in, and was now getting 70 acres ready for sowing. Last season the crop was good, but the season before he did not gather in a single bushel.

Nothing looked better in the summer of 1878–9 than the standing corn but owing to the rust the grain never formed in the ear. He was depending on the harvest of 1879 for the means of clearing off liabilities and did not realise a penny. In this instance the selector had bought a stripper, on bills, in anticipation of the harvest. Having no means of meeting the bills he had to make arrangements with his storekeeper for an advance. In 1878 the account against him stood at £64 and though he sent £154 worth of corn to his storekeeper in January last, there was still a heavy balance against him in the books. The storekeeper was dealing very fairly with him, charging 12 per cent on the bills, which were renewed from time to time and threatening no pressure. The lease was due, but the selector could not take it up until he paid £96 in rent—ie £64 arrears under the licence, £16 under the lease, and £16 more coming due. Should the harvest of 1881 turn out a good one, he would be able to clear off his debts and raise enough money on the lease to carry him on for the future. Just now he was in doubt how to act. Having only paid £32 (one year's rent), ought he to forfeit the amount, as some advised, and start afresh under the Act of 1878 paying only £16 a year instead of £32?

So long as he was without the lease, no one except the Crown could dislodge him; but he saw no hopes of being able to pay rent, or any of his other obligations, before next February. The horses and plant were covered by bill of sale, and there was nothing on which he could just now raise any money. He bought 100 sheep on credit for £44 some time ago, but they got out through the fences, and 80 had been lost. It was likely when a muster took place at the station that most of them would be recovered. The man he bought the sheep off would take them back, and if they fetched within £10 of what was due on them probably he would be satisfied. Sheep had fallen in price since the purchase of this flock. He had two horses before beginning to plough but one took ill and he was obliged to borrow £5 to buy another.

This was the case of a man absolutely destitute of ready cash, with 10 borrowed months before him, no means of raising any funds, and carrying on only by the forbearance of the storekeeper, whose long bill was produced for our inspection. The first half of the account was contained in one line—'account rendered', and the remainder filled two pages of foolscap. No item in it looked unreasonable, and the goods supplied consisted chiefly of requisites for earning on farming. The family lived in a bark hut, divided into two apartments by a partition. The inner room, where all the family slept, was not lighted by any window. Indeed, but for two doors the whole place would have been dark. A mud floor worn into holes and dusty walls with a few paper decorations, some sacks of wheat kept for seed, a wide fireplace, a kettle swinging over the fire, a table, and a piece of dried meat hanging in a smoky place—these were the only noticeable features of the interior. In the old gold-digging times rough men would have been contented with similar lodging but it could not be said that the place was a suitable one for bringing up three children, shortly to be increased to four.

The children, being under six, were too young for school but in a year or two it would be safe to let them walk by themselves across the bush to the schoolhouse. It cannot be said that selectors in distress have failed for want of industry. Here was this one, out first thing every morning with his horses ploughing, preparing the ground for a harvest 10 months distant, and his wife (who would not be equal to field work long) helping him in the afternoons at 'burning off'. Everything in this instance was depending on the results of the harvest of 1881, and favourable weather in the meantime—on a fall of rain at proper intervals, dry days at ripening time, a good yield, assistance in money from the storekeeper at reaping and threading (for the harvest labourers must be paid in cash) and a good market when the grain is ready for sale—a good market depending on the state of affairs in Europe as well as on the condition of things here. And when the corn is being threshed out, the storekeeper will be standing by to make sure of the bags of grain. Until his account is squared up there will be nothing available for the payment of arrears of rent or for the purposes of another season's preparations. If anything, the facts of this case have been understated.

'Women of the West'

George Essex Evans was an English-born Australian balladist and writer whose work was very popular during his short life. He died in 1909 at the age of 46 after a varied life as a failed settler, journalist and public servant. The work he is best remembered for is 'The Women of the West'. Although the poem speaks of the collective story, it sums up the experience of many women along the 'frontiers of the Nation' and 'the camps of man's unrest'. Many people at the time and since have found this poem well captures the often forgotten experiences of the wives, mothers, daughters and sisters of the 'men who made Australia', celebrated by Henry Lawson in his poem of that name, written a few years earlier.

They left the vine-wreathed cottage and the mansion on the hill,
The houses in the busy streets where life is never still,
The pleasures of the city, and the friends they cherished best:
For love they faced the wilderness—the Women of the West.

The roar, and rush, and fever of the city died away,
And the old-time joys and faces—they were gone for many a day;
In their place the lurching coach-wheel, or the creaking bullock
    chains,
O'er the everlasting sameness of the never-ending plains.

In the slab-built, zinc-roofed homestead of some lately-taken run,
In the tent beside the bankment of a railway just begun,
In the huts on new selections, in the camps of man's unrest,
On the frontiers of the Nation, live the Women of the West.

The red sun robs their beauty, and, in weariness and pain,
The slow years steal the nameless grace that never comes again;
And there are hours men cannot soothe, and words men cannot say—
The nearest woman's face may be a hundred miles away.

The wide Bush holds the secrets of their longings and desires,
When the white stars in reverence light their holy altar-fires,
And silence, like the touch of God, sinks deep into the breast—
Perchance He hears and understands the Women of the West.

For them no trumpet sounds the call, no poet plies his arts—
They only hear the beating of their gallant, loving hearts.

But they have sung with silent lives the song all songs above—
The holiness of sacrifice, the dignity of love.

Well have we held our fathers' creed. No call has passed us by.
We faced and fought the wilderness, we sent our sons to die.
And we have hearts to do and dare, and yet, o'er all the rest,
The hearts that made the Nation were the Women of the West.

Cures!

Hard times seem to bring out the make-do spirit in Australians. Clearing land on the frontier, surviving in war, or coping with the hardships of the Great Depression were experiences that have inspired inventions of all kinds. As well as inventing new things, Australians have continually recycled and repurposed sugar bags, furniture, clothing, bedding and anything else deemed useful for an application other than its original purpose. This inventiveness and resilience is a feature of Australian identity and can be seen in some of our favourite character types, including the digger, the bushman and especially the battler.

Making do also involves looking after the health of families far from professional—or even unprofessional—medical assistance. Usually by necessity, medicine was often homemade as well.

Constipation, colds, hiccups, head lice and the panoply of family ailments were treated with medicines sometimes efficacious, sometimes calamitous! Favourites were molasses, perhaps a herbal poultice or brew of some kind, cod liver oil and castor oil, applied in liberal quantities to cure everything from constipation to skin irritations. Kerosene was good for cuts, as was tar if you could get it. Spider webs were also used to treat wounds. Piles could be treated with a preparation of copper sulphate known as 'Bluestone', which was added to a bucket of boiling water over which the luckless sufferer squatted.

Ginger was good for arthritis, while tennis balls sewn into pyjamas would reduce snoring. Honey helped hay fever and dandelion helped kidney stones. Colds might yield to garlic and rum or six drops of kero on a teaspoon of sugar. Sore throats were treated with iodine, painted on the throat with a chook feather, or by tea leaves wrapped in a tea towel and wrapped around the neck—especially good for tonsillitis.

In German tradition, potato water was good for frostbite. So was urinating on your hands in the unlikely event that you suffered that problem in most parts of Australia. Upset tums were said to surrender to flat lemonade, Coca-Cola, plain toast or, more enjoyably, port wine and brandy. Boils were susceptible to a dose of shotgun cartridge powder or a poultice of sulphur and molasses. And of course that old standby for insect bites and stings, a bag of Blue, once a common detergent.

The notion that chicken soup and hot lemon juice are good for colds is old and pervasive, and folk wisdom even provided helpful medical advice, such as 'feed a cold, starve a fever'. These cures and nostrums could even extend into the realms of magic, with wearing red flannel scarves to supposedly protect against a sore throat and removing warts by rubbing them with meat, burying the meat and waiting for it to rot. The wart would allegedly decay in magical sympathy with the meat.

Around Condobolin the Kooris swear by the bush medicine known as 'old man's weed'. It will cure anything.

Aboriginal bush medicine could perform some remarkable cures, according to many bush observers. Retired prospector Jock Dingwall recalled seeing a fight between some Aboriginal men, somewhere at the back of Kuranda. The fight ended with one man speared in the stomach, one with a broken arm and a third with a battered skull. The wounds were treated with a mysterious white substance, not unlike chewing gum, found growing in a seam across the river. The broken head was coated in the white substance and bound up with vines. After returning the broken arm bones to their proper location, the jagged wounds were plastered with the bush medicine. The man with the spear wound had his stomach covered in swamp weed and the magical white salve. All three recovered in a month or so.

Jock's experience of Aboriginal bush medicine was recorded in 1972, by which time he'd tried many times to locate the site of the fight and of the magical natural medicine. He reckoned it would be valuable, although he could never find it.

As well as making home remedies essential, the lack of doctors left a wide field for the purveyors of commercial cures and potions. These were advertised widely, often through verse. Even Henry Lawson, always in need of a bob, knocked out one of these for the cough medicine known as 'Heenzo'. Henry called it 'The Tragedy—A Dirge'.

Oh, I never felt so wretched, and things never looked so blue,
Since the days I gulped the physic that my Granny used to brew;
For a friend in whom I trusted, entering my room last night,
Stole a bottleful of Heenzo from the desk whereon I write.

I am certain sure he did it (though he never would let on),
For he had a cold all last week, and to-day his cough is gone:
Now I'm sick and sore and sorry, and I'm sad for friendship's sake
(It was better than the cough-cure that our Granny used to make).

Oh, he might have pinched my whisky, and he might have pinched
    my beer;
Or all the fame or money that I make while writing here—
Oh, he might have shook the blankets and I'd not have made a row,
If he'd only left my Heenzo till the morning, anyhow.

So I've lost my faith in Mateship, which was all I had to lose
Since I lost my faith in Russia and myself and got the blues;

And so trust turns to suspicion, and so friendship turns to hate,
Even Kaiser Bill would never pinch his Heenzo from a mate.

A seasonal guide to weather and wives

Do-it-yourself weather forecasting has long been a favourite
activity, especially among farmers. Before the era of scientific
weather forecasting, farmers and anyone else needing to know
if it would rain or not used traditional methods to decide when
to plant or when to take an umbrella. In practice, this meant
knowing a great many seemingly trivial pieces of information
about the relationship between plants, animals and the seasons.

In springtime, if you saw a rainbow round the moon it would
rain in two days. Black cockatoos calling meant that rain was on
the way. If ants built their nests high, a lot of rain was on the
way. If the currawongs called to each other, a southerly change
was coming. If the sky was yellow at sunset, there would be wind
tomorrow. The other seasons had their traditional forecasts, all
equally reliable.

SUMMER

If it rains on a full moon, it's going to be a wet month.

Herringbone sky, neither too wet nor too dry.

When the kookaburras call, the rain will fall.

Spider webs in the grass in the morning mean it will not rain that day.

If there is heavy dew, it will not rain.

When flies are hanging around the doors and windows, it is a sign
of rain.

Cows lying down are good indication of rain.

A ring of clouds around the moon means it will rain within a day.

When the ants build nests in summer, rain is one week away.

If flying ants are about, rain is only six hours away.

AUTUMN

If the moon is tilted sideways or upside down, it will rain.

Mackerel sky, mackerel sky—never long wet, never long dry.

If flies land on you and bite, it is going to rain.

Croaking frogs mean rain is coming.

If it rains on the new moon, it will either rain again a week later,
     or rain for a full week, or the month will be generally wet.

Moss dry, sunny sky, moss wet, rain we will get.

WINTER

A ring around the moon means rain in five days.

Rain before seven, clear by eleven.

Winter is not over until you see new buds on a pecan tree.

When the fog goes up the hill it takes the water from the mill.

When the fog comes down the hill, it brings the water to the mill.

Herringbone sky, won't keep the earth 24 hours dry.

If anthills are high in July, winter will be snowy.

If ants build in winter, rain is one day away.

A lot of this information was handed down through the
generations and a lot of it also turned up in almanacs and farmers'
guides. These were full of useful information about planting times,
dates, seasons and all manner of things necessary for agriculture.
They also carried other items that could just turn out to be useful
for the man on the land. If he needed to determine the nature
of a potential wife, he could turn to folklore for an indication of
what married life might be like. All he needed to know was the
birth month of his wife-to-be:

A January bride will be a prudent housewife and sweet of temper.

A February bride will be an affectionate wife and a loving mother.

A March bride will be a frivolous chattermag, given to quarrelling.

An April bride is inconsistent, not over wise, and only fairly good
looking.

A May bride is fair of face, sweet tempered and contented.

A June bride is impetuous and open-handed.

A July bride is handsome but quick of temper.

An August bride is sweet-tempered and active.

A September bride is discreet and forthcoming, beloved of all.

An October bride is fair of face, affectionate but jealous.

A November bride is open-handed, kind-hearted, but inclined to
be lawless.

A December bride is graceful in person, fond of novelty, fascinating,
but a spendthrift.

Backyard brainwaves

The great urge to invent things has long been an Australian
characteristic. The need to adapt to a strange and usually harsh
environment inspired some earlier inventions such as the stump-
jump plough. Long before then, Indigenous Australians had been
creating new tools such as the boomerang and the woomera, or
spear thrower. A characteristic of these devices was that they
were often multipurpose. Not only was a boomerang efficient
in bringing down game, but it could also be used as a musical
instrument to beat out a rhythm. Similarly, the woomera could
be used as a digging tool. Aboriginal people were also quick to
adopt items they found useful from Europeans. The first known
Europeans to set foot on Australia came with Willem Jansz in
1606. Because they were seeking exploitable riches, the Dutch
brought various trade items with them, including glass and metal
objects, and the Aborigines they met quickly saw the cutting value
of a glass shard and the hardness of metal.

Famous agricultural inventions from the time of European
settlement include the grain stripper devised by John Bull and

John Ridley in 1843, followed by the stump-jump plough in 1876, which, as the name suggests, did exactly that, allowing for faster and more efficient clearing of land for agriculture. Another agricultural invention was the Sunshine header harvester, an improvement on an 1880s invention of the stripper harvester by Hugh McKay. While this was a useful device, it could not cope with crops laid flat by wind or rain. Headlie Taylor taught himself the essentials of mechanics and built his first header harvester in 1914, which solved the flattened crop problem and caused less damage to the harvested heads of wheat.

The need to preserve food was especially important in the bush, particularly where there was a little water and a lot of heat. In the 1890s, the goldfields town of Coolgardie saw Arthur McCormick, an amateur handyman, use his observation and wits to construct the first fridge, the Coolgardie Safe. He made a wooden box covered with a hessian bag draped with strips of flannel, put a metal tray on top, and filled it with water twice daily. The water flowed slowly down the strips, keeping the bag wet and the contents inside the 'meat safe', as these devices were often later known, nice and cool. (The famous bushman's hessian water bag works on the same principle.) While this ingenious arrangement of evaporation largely solved the problem of keeping food cool, it didn't stop the ants crawling into the food. A homemade remedy for this was to place a tin can full of kerosene at the bottom of each leg of the safe, which the ants would not cross.

McCormick was a keen gardener and noted amateur athlete who later became mayor of the goldfields town of Narrogin from 1927 to 1930. He does not seem to have made any money from his useful invention.

The sea has been another important focus of Australian inventiveness. The familiar reels used by surf lifesavers to control their safety lines were thought up by Lester Ormsby and first used in 1906 at Bondi. Speedo swimming costumes, 'togs', 'bathers' or 'budgie-smugglers' first appeared in the late 1920s.

At Gallipoli, Australian soldiers invented the periscope rifle, an ingenious device that allowed a sniper to fire at a target observed through a series of lenses mounted in a wooden box with complete safety, as the device could be fired by pulling on a string attached to the trigger and ending well below the top of the trench. It was especially handy for use at short range, the minimal distance between the Turkish and Anzac trenches being sometimes less than 50 metres. Credit for this idea is due to Lance Corporal William Beach, who came up with it in May 1915. A makeshift assembly line was set up on the beach to satisfy the demand for periscope rifles throughout the campaign.

Another innovation was the jam tin bomb. Not unique to Gallipoli, but a characteristically spontaneous element of the fighting, this simply involved filling empty jam tins with spent cartridge cases, bits of Turkish barbed wire and explosive. They were used like an old-fashioned grenade, with a fuse protruding from the top. This had to be lit before throwing, so timing was crucial: if the bomb were thrown too early, the enemy had time to pick it up and lob it back. If it was held too long there was a danger of it exploding in the thrower's hand. A citation for Lance Corporal Leonard Keysor's VC won at Lone Pine gives a graphic insight into the use of grenades in hand-to-hand combat:

*O*n the morning of 7 August, as the Turks developed their counter-attacks, a great bombing duel developed at the positions held by the 1st and 2nd Battalions. As pressure mounted on the forward posts, the Colonel of the 2nd Battalion was killed and junior officers badly wounded.

It was now that Keysor's bravery and skill was fully demonstrated. Using little cover, he flung dozens of bombs, returned some Turkish ones and smothered others with sandbags. At times, much to the amazement of his comrades, he was seen to catch incoming bombs in flight and throw them straight back. In all, he was an inspiration to the weary defenders.

Despite the efforts of Keysor and others they were forced gradually back and positions had to be given up. Rallying behind new barricades, Keysor continued his bomb throwing despite being twice wounded. Indeed, he kept up his efforts for over 50 hours until the 1st Battalion was relieved by the 7th on the afternoon of 8 August, so ending what was described as 'one of the most spectacular individual feats of the war'.

⁓

This make-do approach was also in evidence when the Anzacs departed Gallipoli in December 1915. Normal rifles were often set up with water-dripping or candle-burning arrangements so that they would fire automatically, giving the Turks the impression that the Anzacs were still in their positions.

Another fertile ground for spontaneous wizardry has been the backyard. Various forms of clothes line were developed to dry the washing of Australia's families, ranging from a handy tree limb or bush to lengths of twine held up by forked poles or similar supports. A rotary clothes hoist was first developed in the 1920s but it was the Hills Hoist that became the iconic backyard feature. In 1945, returned digger Lance Hill's wife was unhappy about the way the traditional pole and rope line interfered with the garden plan. Lance went off and improvised the first of his hoists out of some metal tubing and bits of wire, then invented a cast aluminium winding mechanism to wind the hoist up and down. Adopted enthusiastically, the Hills Hoist was known as the 'gut buster' because of the tendency of its early versions to suddenly wind down without warning, giving the luckless clothes hanger an unwelcome thump in the stomach.

That other essential of the backyard, the Victa lawnmower, also attained a folk name early on: developed in the 1950s by Mervin Victor Richardson, it was known as the 'toe-cutter', for obviously painful reasons. Later models greatly improved the safety of the machine. It was not the first rotary blade mower, but it was lighter and more powerful than its predecessors, and ideal for the tough backyards of the fibro frontier springing up across the country as the post-World War II baby boom encouraged people to throw up suburban houses in the hundreds of thousands. Mervyn knocked out the early models in his garage and sold them locally; people soon heard about them, and the rest is history.

Sugar bag nation

The sugar bag or chaff bag was used for carrying all sorts of loose dry goods in colonial Australia, and for long after. Made of hessian or burlap, they were cheap and could simply be thrown away after use, then becoming handy carrying bags for those who could not afford better, such as swagmen and battlers. During the Great Depression the sugar bag could be seen all over the country as people did it tough and made do to get by as best they could. The humble sugar bag was used for carrying feed for livestock, as mats, as blankets often in the form of the 'Wagga rug', as curtains, beds, hammocks and whatever else human need could contrive for them.

The Great Depression is usually said to have started with the Wall Street stock market crash of 1929. British and American bankers called in the loans they had made to the rest of the world, including Australia, and began the long, grinding process of unemployment and despair that, for many, lasted throughout the 1930s. For many working Australians and their families, life became a constant struggle to survive, as Isy Wyner recalled in 1999:

. . . you'd line up there and walk past these cubicles with your sugar bag, and they'd throw a hunk of meat at you and stick it in the bag—and a couple of loaves of bread and a pound of tea, and you'd figure, well, you'd then have to hump that home.

Many Australians felt that the Depression did not really end for them until the outbreak of World War II in 1939. By then the nation had endured a decade of misery, deprivation and social dislocation so profound that the folk memory of the time was transmitted down the generations.

In New South Wales, the Labor government of Premier Jack Lang repudiated the state's debts to the British banks and defied Canberra's economic strictures derived from the prescriptions of a visiting banker, Sir Otto Niemeyer. Niemeyer insisted that the Australian government cut spending, exactly the wrong response to the drying up of money and credit and one that made the Depression harder and longer than it needed to be. In the streets, they sang to the tune of 'Titwillow':

What Rot-o
Sir Otto
Niemeyer

In the crisis that followed, the Governor, Sir Phillip Game, dissolved the New South Wales Parliament, effectively ending Lang's government. While these events played out in the maelstrom of political and financial power, many lost their livelihoods, their homes and their families.

The Great Depression polarised political points of view and strong parties emerged at both ends of the political spectrum, the proto-fascist New Guard on the right, and various socialist and workers' groups on the left, most notably the Australian Communist Party. In 1999, the 90-year-old Jock Burns, still an active member of the Communist Party, rendered a Depression ditty to the tune of a popular song of the era, 'I'm Forever Blowing Bubbles':

> I'm forever striking trouble,
> Striking trouble everywhere,
> The landlord came, the landlord went,
> I said I've no work, no rent,
> The butcher wants his money,
> Baker, grocer too,
> I sent all the bills to Jack Lang,
> 'Cause he said he'd pull us through.

Jock added: 'Which he never!'

Jack Lang, demonised as a dangerous radical, attracted both support and censure. To the tune of 'Advance Australia Fair' his supporters sang:

> Now Premier Lang for us will fight
> We've got to see it through
> His motto clear is 'Lang is right'
> We've got to see it through
> He's blotting out our enemies
> His courage never fails
> So give three cheers for Premier Lang and good old New South Wales
> So sing and let your voices ring for Lang and New South Wales.

His opponents had their own song to the tune of an Irish song known as 'The Stone Outside Dan Murphy's Door', an indication of the ethnic background of many working-class people of the time:

> The songs that we sang were about old Jack Lang
> On the steps of the dole-office door

He closed up the banks, it was one of his pranks
And he sent us to the dole-office door

We molested the police, 'till they gave us relief
On the steps of the dole-office door
Yes, the songs that we sang were about old Jack Lang
On the steps of the dole-office door

Many returned soldiers from World War I could not get work during the 1920s, a period when Australian society and politics were fragmented and conflicted. It was not uncommon to see men dressed in the remains of their uniforms, sometimes maimed, begging in the street or selling self-penned and -published collections of verse and yarns door to door. For such people, and for many in the country, the onset of the Depression in the 1930s was hardly noticed, so impoverished had their lives become. As a bush worker remembered:

Depression! There's always been a depression in Australia as far back as I can remember. I was walking the country looking for work from the end of the First World War until the start of the Second, till 1939!

On a similar theme, but with more direct bitterness at the way in which returned soldiers had been treated, was 'Soup', to the tune of 'My Bonnie Lies Over the Ocean':

We're spending our nights in the doss-house
We're spending our days on the streets
We're looking for work but we find none
Won't someone give us something to eat?

Soup, soup, soup, soup,
They gave us a big plate of loop-the-loop.

Soup, soup, soup, soup,
They gave us a big plate of soup.

We went and we fought for our country
We went out to bleed and to die
We thought that our country would help us
But this was our country's reply:

Soup, soup, soup, soup . . .

While governments—state and federal as well as local—were considering what to do, people simply had to get on with living as best they could. They coped, as always, by laughing at their circumstances. They parodied popular songs to make light of their lot:

When your hair has turned to silver we will still be on the dole
We'll live in Happy Valley where the Reds have got control
We'll draw the weekly ration and the child endowment too
And when we get the old age pension I will leave the rest to you.

As unemployment increased, those affected found it difficult to keep up with mortgage or rent payments. Many landlords decided to evict families who could no longer pay, an action that caused a number of violent eviction riots. Among the most notorious were those in Newtown and Bankstown in 1931:

For we met them at the door,
And we knocked them on the floor,
At Bankstown and Newtown,
We made the cops feel sore,
They outnumbered us ten to one,
And were armed with stick and gun,

But we fought well, we gave them hell,
When we met them at the door.

The Great Depression didn't so much end as fade into World War II. After a decade of hard times things had started to improve and with the need for soldiers, industry and other war supplies, the unemployed were soaked up. Soon there would not be enough people to do the work and even women would have to be drafted as factory workers, transport drivers and food producers.

Happy Valley

One of the darkest years of the Depression was 1933. It had been going for years and for many, poverty had become a way of life. All over the country shantytowns known as 'Happy Valley' grew up on wasteland. Those in Sydney were typical of hundreds more 'unemployed camps' in other states.

*O*n the left of the tramline at La Perouse two of these colonies can be seen. They are easily distinguishable. Made for the most part of scraps, usually galvanised iron, they are not a pleasant sight. The roofs are all of iron, old and rusty. A few lengths of stove or some other piping may serve for a chimney. Doors may be real or a piece of sacking hung from the frame. Stones may keep the roof on. There may be an open square for a window, or it may have glass. The hut may be of one room, or it may consist of three or four. It may be ugly and have canvas walls. Still, home—home for somebody.

A few have a show of making an 'appearance'—really comfortable little homes built in house style, but small. One or two are weatherboard; perhaps there is a tiny verandah. Fences of odd sticks, bits of wire, brushwood, and other materials are around the garden plots, and the vegetable growth in the sand is astonishing. Occasionally one comes on a bed of bright, cheerful flowers. Apparently a man erects a hut at a place which suits his ideas, puts some plants or seeds in the ground, and fences the plots. They are in no way regularised allotments. The settlements are on a haphazard plan, facing every and any way. But from the outside the general appearance is one of dilapidation and squat ugliness, the low roofs and the rusty iron dominating the landscape. Water at the settlement at Long Bay is obtained from 'soaks'—spots to which the moisture seeps down the hillsides, filtering through the white sand. There are about 50 or 60 camp dwellings in the settlement near Long Bay on the Commonwealth ground, on which are the rifle ranges.

Near the tram terminus at La Perouse the line skirts a gully in the sandhills lying to the left. The verdure is profuse, and the huts are scattered in it, about the hillsides, and along the ravine towards the ocean. Several of them have taken on the air of permanent dwellings, with an occasional coat of paint. There are glass windows with curtains, and some brick chimneys. Most have their tiny gardens. Children are everywhere. Dogs abound—happy dogs and happy children, un-touched by the cares of a distressing economic situation. There are no hard paths, no lighted roadways, no electric supply. There is no rent to pay, no municipal rates, no income returns to bother about. Clothes do not matter. Nobody wears boots. The beaches are close. Down the gully is the ocean. Over the hill is the bay. Trams pass every quarter of an hour. A water pipe runs through the settlement, with taps at intervals. This is what has been dubbed Happy Valley, and it looks as though life might be happy enough if it was not for the curse of idleness.

'I've been here three years,' said a young man with a snug-looking shanty behind a small garden. 'Three wasted years of life!' The bachelor abode can be distinguished from the one sheltering a family. It needs only one room. The real stringency of circumstances is to be detected in the ragged tent, or the hessian-sided hut, where the late-comers are establishing themselves.

'How do you like living this way?' a reporter asked a woman with three lusty, bare-footed youngsters playing about. She said it was 'Good-o'. The children probably never think it anything else. Even the dogs—well fed, somehow or other—seemed to find it the same. There is work now and again. The relief work gives a little cash, and child endowment will also provide some income. About 150 dwellings are in the gully and on the hillsides.

Over on the other side of the neck of land, which ends at Bare Island, and between La Perouse and the Bunnerong Powerhouse, are probably some hundreds of huts on the sandhills. They have in general the rusty scrap iron appearance, but a few have an air of substantiality. There is more space available and no crowding. In several a wireless mast and lead-in wire indicate some degree of comfort, and generally there is evidence that one must not altogether judge by exteriors, as quite good furniture is in some of the dwellings. At Yarra Bay, which is in Botany Bay, the hills on which they stand slope gently, and the windows or open doors look out over the shimmering blue water. Rockdale has about 150 scattered along the foreshores at Brighton-le-sands, all of the same character as the others. An occasional business sign is to be seen where an artisan is ready for customers. After the manner of human proclivities in the gathering together of people with a common interest, there is an 'Unemployed Campers Association'. At Clontarf, in the Manly Municipality, there are about 40 or 60 camps on a pleasant area close to the silvery sands and the crystal clear water of Middle Harbour.

The municipalities are perturbed about the growth of a new class of citizenry—these new suburbanites, who pay no rent, ask for no leases, and put up my kind of a habitation. The hitherto inviolate rules that have pressed a little hardly in requirements on the residents are broken. Ejection seems impossible, for if deprived of their shelter the campers must be provided for in some way. They are treated sympathetically. Rockdale sends them fruit, vegetables, firewood, and other things, attends to the sanitary necessities, and provides water.

A tram guard on the La Perouse line deposits daily a can of milk by the wayside. It is given by a company. And so on. It is the cheapest way of living for those who would otherwise be thrown on the hands of the authorities. They are on Crown lands, and not encroaching on private property, but the householders in the vicinity, who have undergone considerable expenditure and pay heavily towards the peace, order, and good government systems under which they live, look perplexedly at the deteriorative effects of the invasion of shanties, and wonder what is to be the end of it.

The Rockdale Council gave notice to a number of campers some time ago that they would have to move to make way for a relief work, about 20 being affected. The Manly Council, alarmed at the growth of the claim to permanence on the Clontarf reserve, gave notice that the camps would have to be vacated and demolished by the end of December, but representations were made, and delay has been granted until a further investigation is made.

The matter of these camps having become so important, it was put before the Government some time ago, and consideration is being given to it.

Sergeant Small

A notorious figure during the Great Depression was a burly Queensland policeman known to every bagman as 'Sergeant Small'. The sergeant seemingly took it upon himself to make the lives of those hopping freight trains in search of usually non-existent work even more desperate than they needed to be. His favourite trick was to disguise himself as a swaggie and clamber aboard a rail truck carrying an illegal fare. When he was close enough to collar his prey, the sergeant dropped his fake swag and arrested the unfortunate. The victim would suffer a pummelling from the Sergeant's fists, then spend the night or even longer in the local gaol on a vagrancy charge. Sergeant Small was, not surprisingly, a deeply unpopular man whose name became a byword for ill-treatment of this kind.

Country singer Tex Morton, himself no stranger to the travelling life and the odd brush with the law, wrote a song about the Sergeant. The song told the story of a bagman or 'hobo', as Morton sang, riding on a timber train and being hoodwinked by the Sergeant who 'dropped his billy and his roll and socked me on the chin'. The prisoner was taken to the police station where five policemen beat him up. Morton wished he was 'fourteen stone and I was six feet six feet tall' so he could take the train back north again just 'to beat up Sergeant Small'.

Morton recorded the song in 1938 but it was allegedly banned from the airwaves of the then fledgling Australian radio because it was considered to be potentially subversive with its strong anti-police theme. This did not stop it being a popular item in Morton's famous travelling shows and, in a reworked version, the song remains popular today, having been recorded by numerous folk and country artists.

What of the sergeant? Well, despite research by a number of people, there does not seem to have been a Sergeant Small working for the Queensland Police at the relevant time and place. He may well be a figure of folklore—the surname 'Small' for such a big bloke is perhaps a hint. But even if he is a myth, the uniformed authority figure wielding power in an excessive way is a common feature of Australian tradition. In this case, the story and characters are set in the Great Depression and represent an unpleasant experience suffered by many travellers searching for work during what were, for many, if not all, 'the hungry years'.

The farmer's will

Life on the land has always been tough, but dying on it can be even harder, as the maker of this will suggests:

I've left my soul to me banker—he's got the mortgage on it anyway.

I've left my conversion calculator to the Metrification Board. Maybe they'll be able to make sense of it.

I have a couple of last requests. The first one is to the weatherman: I want rain, hail and sleet for the funeral. No sense in finally giving me good weather just because I'm dead.

And last, but not least, don't bother to bury me—the hole I'm in now is big enough. Just cremate me and send me ashes to the Taxation Office with this note: 'Here you are, you bastards, now you've got the lot.'

A Farmer

7

Home of the weird

And the sun sank again on the grand Australian bush—the
nurse and tutor of eccentric minds, the home of the weird,
and of much that is different from things in other lands.

Henry Lawson, 'The Bush Undertaker'

FOR ALL THE gritty realities of colonial life, Australia has its fair
share of unexplained discoveries, odd events and mysteries of
all kinds. The continent had existed in myth for so long before
its actual discovery, charting and eventual European settlement,
that peculiarities appeared very early on. By the time Lawson
wrote his conclusion to his short story 'The Bush Undertaker',
the bush—meaning anywhere outside a city, quite an area—was
well known as a place of mystery as well as hardship.

Curious discoveries

In January 1838, an ambitious soldier named George Grey led
an exploration party into the completely unknown northwest of
Australia. Grey would go on to an astounding career in politics
and government in two Australian colonies, in New Zealand and
South Africa, and eventually would be knighted for his sometimes
controversial actions and approaches. But now he was still in his
mid-twenties and keen to make his name as an explorer. He was

totally inexperienced in Australian conditions, as were most of the others in his party. Nevertheless, Grey's military background and iron will kept the expedition going through unexplored terrain, battles with the local inhabitants and many other hardships recounted in his journals.

Grey and his men were the first Europeans known to have seen the Wandjina paintings and other ancient rock art of the Kimberley region. But they also made some even more enigmatic discoveries that continue to puzzle us today. In his journal, Grey describes his discovery of the cave containing the carved, or 'intaglio' head:

*A*fter proceeding some distance we found a cave larger than the one seen this morning; of its actual size however I have no idea, for being pressed for time I did not attempt to explore it, having merely ascertained that it contained no paintings . . .

I was moving on when we observed the profile of a human face and head cut out in a sandstone rock which fronted the cave; this rock was so hard that to have removed such a large portion of it with no better tool than a knife and hatchet made of stone, such as the Australian natives generally possess, would have been a work of very great labour. The head was two feet in length, and sixteen inches in breadth in the broadest part; the depth of the profile increased gradually from the edges where it was nothing, to the centre where it was an inch and a half; the ear was rather badly placed, but otherwise the whole of the work was good, and far superior to what a savage race could be supposed capable of executing. The only proof of antiquity that it bore about it was that all the edges of the cutting were rounded and perfectly smooth, much more so than they could have been from any other cause than long exposure to atmospheric influences.

One of the few people known to actually visit the area since Grey is Les Hiddins, the famous 'Bush Tucker Man'. He found the cave but was unable to find the carving until he used Google Earth, which revealed a passage Hiddins had missed on his previous visits. He intended to return in 2012 for another look but so far has not reported further.

Grey's outback adventure also turned up some other puzzling sights. He came across 'a native hut which differed from any before seen, in having a sloping roof'. Shortly after, on 7 April 1838, he found 'curious native mounds or tombs of stone'.

*T*his morning I started off before dawn and opened the most southern of the two mounds of stones which presented the following curious facts:

1. They were both placed due east and west and, as will be seen by the annexed plates, with great regularity.
2. They were both exactly of the same length but differed in breadth and height.
3. They were not formed altogether of small stones from the rock on which they stood, but many were portions of very distant rocks, which must have been brought by human labour, for their angles were as sharp as the day they were broken off; there were also the remains of many and different kinds of seashells in the heap we opened.

My own opinion concerning these heaps of stones had been that they were tombs; and this opinion remains unaltered, though we found no bones in the mound, only a great deal of fine mould having a damp dank smell. The antiquity of the central part of the one we opened appeared to be very great, I should say two or three hundred years; but the stones above were much more modern, the outer ones having been very recently placed; this was also the case with the other heap: can this be regarded by the natives as a holy spot?

We explored the heap by making an opening in the side, working on to the centre, and thence downwards to the middle, filling up the former opening as the men went on; yet five men provided with tools were occupied two hours in completing this opening and closing it again, for I left everything precisely as I had found it. The stones were of all sizes, from one as weighty as a strong man could lift, to the smallest pebble. The base of each heap was covered with a rank vegetation, but the top was clear, from the stones there having been recently deposited.

$\backsim$

Grey also reported other perplexing discoveries he referred to as 'an alien white race'. He found among the Aborigines he encountered 'the presence amongst them of a race, to appearance, totally different, and almost white, who seem to exercise no small influence over the rest'. Grey thought that these people were the main leaders of attacks on his party and speculated that they were of Malay descent.

At Roebuck Bay, an officer aboard the *Beagle*, the ship that carried Grey's expedition to Australia and picked them up at the end of the expedition, also described fair-skinned Aborigines in the area:

*A*t this time I had a good opportunity of examining them. They were about the middle age, about five feet six inches to five feet nine in height, broad shoulders, with large heads and overhanging brows; but it was not remarked that any of their teeth were wanting (as we afterwards observed in others); their legs were long and very slight, and their only covering a bit of grass suspended round the loins. There was an exception in the youngest, who appeared of an entirely different race: his skin was a copper colour, whilst the others were black; his head was not so large, and more rounded; the overhanging brow was lost; the shoulders more of a European turn, and the body and legs much better proportioned; in fact he might be considered a well-made man at our standard of figure. They were each armed with one, and some with two, spears, and pieces of stick about eight feet long and pointed at both ends. It was used after the manner of the Pacific Islanders, and the throwing-stick so much in use by the natives of the south did not appear known to them.

After talking loud, and using very extravagant gestures, without any of our party replying, the youngest threw a stone, which fell close to the boat.

These accounts have led many to since speculate about the origins of the hut, the carving, so unlike Aboriginal art and building, as well as the 'individuals of an alien white race'. An early suggestion was that these discoveries were linked to a mythical French sojourn in the unknown southland as early as 1503. Others have tried to link the finds with survivors of Dutch shipwrecks in the seventeenth and eighteenth centuries. But the carved head, the stone tombs, if that is what they were, and the fair-skinned Aborigines remain some of the many mysteries of Australia's past.

The marble man

In mid-1889 a curious object was discovered in a marble quarry near Orange.

It is the body of a man about 5ft. 10in. in height, well formed, and evidently from the shape of the head and the contour of the features a European. To geologists and scientific men generally, an examination of this strange discovery should prove interesting.

The marble in which the body was found is of various colours, but the body itself is petrified in white marble. With the exception of the arms, which are broken off at the shoulders, the limbs and features are intact, the left side of the body, however, being slightly flattened, due no doubt to the fact that it was found lying on this side.

The object was taken to Sydney where the discoverers placed it on display to the public. The body, if it was one, excited immense interest. Speculation ran wild. It was an Aboriginal. It was an escaped convict. It was a hoax. Doctors, geologists, government officials and just about everyone else examined it, to judge by the number of opinions and suggestions published in the press. Not all of these were very serious: one correspondent pointed out that the body took a size 12 hat.

Another correspondent claimed to have found a similar figure near Mt Gambier in 1854—'a petrified blackfellow had been found in a cave on Hungry M'Konnor's station at Mosquito Plains, between Jatteara and a place called Limestone, and now known as Penoli. The blackfellow was in a standing posture.' The governor was said to have visited the object, which was protected beneath an iron grating.

A Bathurst district local, probably tongue in cheek, claimed to know the true origins of the man:

deer mr. Headhitter—This here putrified man are a stature, mr. jones, the Bathurst stonemasing, sais he were sculpted at a old public at cowflat. the wurk tooke ten weaks, and arterwards the stature were berried in the ground, then dug up, and hexibetted as a putrified man.

The police were called and investigated the matter, their report being discussed in the Legislative Assembly. The mystery only deepened though. The police believed that the mummy had never been in the quarry but had been fabricated by a certain Mr Sala for nefarious commercial purposes.

Then the plot took another twist. Two, in fact. Sala claimed that he had found not only the marble man in the quarry, but also a marble woman and a marble child. People were now expressing their incredulity about 'the Sydney Fossil', as an Adelaide newspaper called the object, but despite this, the 'two shilling show' exhibition was a commercial success.

This did not stop a court case from which Sala emerged unsentenced and with costs awarded, the magistrates considering that the matter should never have been brought before them. Rumour, speculation and commerce careened on and the newspapers of the land milked the story for all it was worth, which seems to have been quite a lot. Officials partially dissected the body, claiming the results proved that it was once human. The geologists analysed some chippings with inconclusive results. The wags did not miss an opportunity:

'Don't you think,' said the lunatic, 'it'ud be a good idea to run that petrified man from N.S.W. for a seat in the Legislature of Queensland?'

'No,' said the practical one, 'I don't; there are too many darned old fossils there already.'

The marble man even appeared in a spoof advertisement for Milk Arrowroot biscuits—'Now with added bone ash!' He was featured on stage by the Watson's Bay Minstrels in 'a very laughable farce'.

By this time the story had rolled on for months, boosted by the marble man's travels as he was exhibited around the country. During that time, ownership of the marble man seems to have changed hands. Who actually owned the object and was therefore responsible for its debts became the subject of legal action, which, like everything else about the marble man, simply raised further questions without answers.

Then, in August 1889, Sala produced the marble woman he had earlier claimed to have found beside the man:

> The body is apparently that of a young woman of spare build, 5ft. high, with the facial features flattened. The body appears to be solid marble. The legs are raised at the knees; the arms, hands, nails, and fingers appear very natural. The head and an arm have been broken and re-joined roughly with plaster.

She was shipped straight off to Sydney for exhibition and caused a similar flurry of interest and disagreement. One newspaper wondered if further searching in the Orange area might reveal a whole family—'seven children, a cat, a dog, a frying-pan, and a broom handle—all petrified or all marble'. The article concluded with a reference to the great American showman and shyster, P.T. Barnum: '. . . as Barnum used to say, "the public like to be gulled".'

By the end of September, Sala was in the bankruptcy court where more accusations of fakery were levelled against him. Others felt it necessary to air their opinions in the press, and further farcical depictions appeared on stage. The same year, Harry Stockdale, one of the first marble man's early owners, published a book titled *The Legend of the Petrified or Marble Man*, adding further fuel to the furore and, of course, to the publicity blaze.

The following May, Sala's son was displaying yet another marble man in Orange, at a shilling a time. The reporter was so impressed he went out to the marble quarry and, under the supervision of Sala junior, managed to unearth a few items of his own, including a woman's skull, a hand and a breast. The place was also littered with fossil remains of fish, horses and other animals. By June a marble horse taken from the quarry was on show. The next October the marble man had graduated to the Great Hall at Sydney University and was said to be soon off to even greater things in Chicago.

From then the marble man, woman, child and horse seem to fade from the newspaper columns. Was the marble man really a petrified human being, of whatever kind? Or just a showground hoax? And what about the other fossils, allegedly human and otherwise, discovered in the area near the quarry? Opinions remained divided at the time and no one seems to have come up with any answers since.

Was Breaker Morant the Gatton murderer?

In 1898, Gatton was a small Queensland town with fewer than 500 souls, located on a busy route to and from Brisbane, and travellers passed through on a regular basis. The Murphy family were local farmers around 13 kilometres outside the town. On the evening of Boxing Day 1898, Michael Murphy, aged 29, with his sisters Ellen, eighteen, and Norah, 27, left home in a borrowed sulky bound for a local dance. When they arrived, the dance had been cancelled and they headed back sometime around 9 p.m. They did not return home and the following morning their mother asked her son-in-law, William M'Neill, to look for them.

M'Neill had loaned his sulky to the three and soon found its tracks. He followed them through scrub for over a kilometre from the main road, coming to a field where he found their bound and beaten bodies carefully laid out with their feet pointing westwards. Norah's body was lying on a rug; Michael and Ellen were found lying back to back, a few feet apart. The horse drawing the sulky had been shot dead. It was later established that Michael had been shot in the head as well as bludgeoned. His sisters had both had their skulls fractured. Norah was probably strangled with the harness strap found around her neck. Both women had been raped. The murders were thought to have taken place between 10 p.m. and 4 a.m. the following morning.

Investigation of the dreadful crime was botched from the very beginning, with crowds of gawkers destroying much forensic evidence at the scene. The police were slow to arrive and conducted their inquiries in an oddly slapdash way. The post-mortem was careless too, and resulted in the bodies having to be exhumed for further examination. The Royal Commission eventually held to examine the whole affair confirmed all this, but despite this level of official investigation and activity, the murders remained a mystery. Who had committed such a savage act? And why? The victims were three locals with no links to criminal activity, simply driving home from a dance that never happened.

Suspects included a newcomer to the area named Thomas Day, various itinerants and even family members. There were suggestions of a failed abortion attempt on Norah and also of incest. There was no sign of the victims having been forced into the paddock, strongly suggesting their acquiescence and the presence of someone they knew. None of these possibilities were ever substantiated and the Gatton murders remained unsolved, but ever since, there have been frequent revelations of the killer's identity, all impossible to prove.

One of the most intriguing, if apparently left-of-centre, possibilities is that the famed horseman, womaniser and poet Henry 'the Breaker' Morant was the murderer. This theory was put forward by the folklorist John Meredith, who conceived it while researching a book on the poet Will Ogilvie, a mate of the Breaker's. The theory depends on aspects of Morant's personality and personal history and on some suggestive chronology.

The man who was executed for murdering a prisoner of war during the Boer War was an enigmatic and sometimes disturbing character. The Breaker's early life is as clouded in myth as his later years, a situation made worse by his romancing of his past.

He was born Edwin Henry Murrant in Somerset, England, into very ordinary circumstances, though he often intimated that his ancestry was considerably more exalted. He arrived in Australia at age eighteen in 1883 like many other young Britishers of the time looking to make a fortune, a name or even just a living, under a false identity. Over the next fifteen or so years he made a rip-roaring reputation as a flamboyant bush character and outstanding horseman, earning his nickname 'the Breaker'. His feats of horsemanship, particularly riding a buckjumper few others could master, are still legend among horse fanciers. His amorous adventures included marriage to Daisy May O'Dwyer, later to become famous as anthropologist and journalist Daisy Bates. According to the story, Daisy gave the Breaker his marching orders when he—characteristically—refused to pay for the wedding. He took off on a stolen horse, also characteristically, and that was the end of the relationship (though not the marriage, as they never divorced). The Breaker continued his roistering lifestyle. He worked at whatever was available and developed a literary reputation as a bush poet, becoming friendly with other poets like 'Banjo' Paterson, Henry Lawson and Will Ogilvie.

The Meredith theory revolves around the Breaker's relationship with Ogilvie and correspondence between them, as well as with several other bush nomads of the period. Like Morant and many others, the Scots Ogilvie was drifting around the backblocks doing whatever work there was and writing verse and journalism whenever possible. They were all wild boys—womanisers, drinkers, gamblers and mostly exceptional horsemen. Some, especially the Breaker, were already bush legends. Meredith argues that despite his skills and image, Morant was effectively a kind of split personality. When sober he was charming, witty and even urbane. But after one too many he could turn into a very ugly and intimidating animal. Men who were not generally frightened by very much at all were known to fear and hate Morant.

The Breaker also lived a dissolute life, habitually out of funds, scrounging on his mates and not being too fussy where he obtained his mount. Despite all this, Ogilvie maintained contact with Morant until a few months before the Gatton murders. Morant simply disappeared and was not seen again by those who knew him until around February 1899, when he appeared at the Paringa Station on the South Australian section of the Murray.

Where had he been?

According to Meredith, the Thomas Day initially suspected at Gatton was Breaker Morant. Day turned up in Gatton at the same time Morant vanished from his mates further south. He took a job with a local butcher, an occupation in which he was skilled, and in just a few days developed a local reputation as a taciturn loner. He frightened his workmate so much that he asked their boss to get rid of Morant, and he was often seen loitering near the spot where the murders were committed.

The locals had Day—only in town ten days—pegged as the murderer, though the detectives from Brisbane concentrated their investigations on another suspect. Meanwhile, Day became increasingly abusive to his employer and family and he was paid off in lieu of notice. The police cleared Day to leave town, and he took the train to Toowomba, then travelled to Brisbane via Gatton a few days later. Then he disappeared.

According to Meredith, he joined the militia under another name but deserted a few weeks later and was never heard of again. This was around five or six weeks after the murders. About a month later Morant turned up at Paringa Station while a mob of cattle was being swum across the Murray. He did not stay for long. On the outbreak of the South African war he left to enlist, probably in hope of returning eventually to England.

While Breaker Morant's story had some years to run until his ignominious end, there is more to tell of Thomas Day. Before Day had arrived in Gatton, fifteen-year-old Alfred Hill and the pony he rode were lured into the bush and shot dead. The bullet was a .380 calibre. Police arrested and charged a man on suspicion but he was later released. No further action took place but in the course of the Royal Commission into the Gatton murders, it was established that the man charged with Hill's murder was Thomas Day. Morant was known to carry a pistol, and the bullet found in the brain of Michael Murphy was .380 calibre.

The evidence is circumstantial, but no more so than the many other theories put forward over the years. The Gatton tragedy remains one of Australia's most gruesome and enigmatic murders.

Vanishing vessels

Australia's history of maritime exploration and disaster has produced many legends of lost ships and vanishing wrecks. The well-known story of the Mahogany Ship, said to lie somewhere beneath the sands of Armstrong Bay near Warrnambool, goes back to at least the earliest newspaper account in 1847. However, the area was barely settled at that time, though it was visited by whalers and sealers. It also lay on an overland droving route, so Europeans were in at least some contact with the place. It has also been suggested that the story of the Mahogany Ship derived originally from earlier wrecks—probably of whalers or sealers—in the Hopkins River area.

In 1876, a local man, John Mason, wrote a letter to the Melbourne *Argus* detailing what he saw while riding along the beach from Port Fairy to Warrnambool during the summer of 1846:

*M*y attention was attracted to the hull of a vessel embedded high and dry in the Hummocks, far above the reach of any tide. It appeared to have been that of a vessel about 100 tons burden, and from its bleached and weather-beaten appearance, must have remained there many years. The spars and deck were gone, and the hull was full of drift sand. The timber of which she was built had the appearance of cedar or mahogany. The fact of the vessel being in that position was well known to the whalers in 1846, when the first whaling station was formed in that neighbourhood, and the oldest natives, when questioned, stated their knowledge of it extended from their earliest recollection. My attention was again directed to this wreck during a conversation with Mr M'Gowan, the superintendent of the Post-office, in 1869, who, on making inquiries as to the exact locality, informed me that it was supposed to be one of a fleet of Portuguese or Spanish discovery ships, one of them having parted from the others during a storm, and was never again heard of. He referred me to a notice of a wreck having appeared in the novel *Geoffrey Hamlyn*, written by Henry Kingsley, in which it is set down as a Dutch or Spanish vessel, and forms the subject of a remark from one of the characters, a doctor, who said that the English should never sneer at those two nations—they were before you everywhere. The wreck lies about midway between Belfast and Warrnambool, and is probably by this time entirely covered with drift sand, as during a search made for it within the last few months it was not to be seen.

⌐

Whatever the origins of the tale, it has attracted extensive investigation by historians, archaeologists, treasure hunters and history enthusiasts. One of the consistent, if controversial, themes in the story has it that the ship is a Portuguese—sometimes Spanish—caravelle wrecked in the area some considerable time before documented European occupation. It has also been claimed that the Mahogany Ship is of Chinese origin and that there is a local Aboriginal legend of 'yellow men' coming ashore. The few relatively reliable eyewitness accounts of the wreck before it disappeared beneath the shifting sand dunes suggest that the ship was of an unusual design. This could mean many things but has led to a suggestion that it might have been a roughly made craft from a documented Tasmanian convict escape attempt. Until the Mahogany Ship is rediscovered, or an authenticated document indicating contact found, speculation will continue.

A similar tradition exists on Queensland's Stradbroke Island, where the remains of a Spanish galleon are said to be disintegrating in coastal swamplands. The first documented sighting of the high-prowed timber ship dates from the 1860s. A local pilot and light keeper found the wreck at the southern end of the island and removed its anchor to use as an ornament in his home. His Aboriginal wife then told him of the local Indigenous knowledge of the wreck. There were further sightings in the 1880s, when the supposition that the mysterious vessel was of Spanish origin began to gain traction. This rapidly became a lost treasure tale and serious searches for the galleon began; one group in 1894 claimed to have found the wreck and removed a substantial load of copper fittings from it. When they tried to find the wreck again, the intriguing structure had disappeared.

Subsequent sightings have been either due to Aboriginal people taking settlers to the site, or after bushfires have revealed the smoking timbers through burnt-out vegetation. No sightings have been reported since the 1970s, though there are persistent suggestions that the locals hold secret knowledge of the galleon's treasure, fuelling continued searches for the site. A 2007 expedition unearthed a rusting coin that is said to date between the late 1590s and the 1690s.

Yet another intriguing mystery concerns the 'Deadwater Wreck'. In 1846, the surveyor and explorer Frank Gregory reported the 'remains of a vessel of considerable tonnage . . . in a shallow estuary near the Vasse Inlet . . . which, from its appearance I should judge to have been wrecked two hundred years ago . . .' The next recorded sighting of the wreck in the section of the

Wonnerup Inlet known as 'the Deadwater' was in 1856, though the account stated that it had been visible 'for years past'. There is a credible line of documentation back to the earliest years of European occupation in this area in the 1840s, and there is also the usual folklore surrounding this mystery. Unverified local tradition claims that early settlers massacred local Aboriginal people to obtain the gold ornaments that they possessed from some unknown source.

The decomposing ship was plundered in the 1860s, though almost certainly not by Aborigines, but there have been no credible sightings of it since. That has not quashed speculation and investigation about the ship's identity. Serious research and fieldwork into the wreck has been carried out, and based on estimates of the length of the Deadwater Wreck, it is suggested that the ship is a VOC *hoeker* named the *Zeelt*. This class of ship was around 30 metres in length and built in the high-stern style of many early East Indiamen, in accordance with some descriptions of the wreck before its disappearance beneath the sand and mud. The small 90-ton *Zeelt* went missing as early as 1672 on only her second voyage. This work may yet reveal the remains of the Deadwater Wreck, but there is also research suggesting *Zeelt* actually went down in southern Madagascar.

Yearning for yowies

What are we going to do about all these yowies? They're turning up everywhere around the nation in almost plague proportions. At least that is the impression given by the various websites dedicated to hunting the wild yowie.

Great Australian Stories included a solid section on yowies, as well as other mythical creatures of the bush, including the yarama, the bunyip and several other mysterious and usually unpleasant beings. Since then, the big, hairy creatures, reported from the time of the early colonial period, have been regularly sighted in the bush, and even in the suburbs: in 2010 a Canberra bloke met a hairy, apelike creature in his garage. Apparently, it wanted to communicate—but who knows what?

Canberra, Queanbeyan and surrounding areas have long been yowie hotspots. They became such a nuisance in the 1970s that a $200,000 reward was offered by the Queanbeyan Festival Board to anyone who could capture one of the elusive creatures. The money has never been claimed but that has had no effect on yowie sightings.

In 1903, Graham Webb of Uriarra recalled an encounter with 'some strange animal' that had taken place many years earlier:

We were out in Pearce's Creek (a small stream between the Tidbinbilla Mountains and the Cotter River) in search of cattle. In the early part of the day we came upon the remains of a cow of ours. We recognised this beast by the head, as the blacks would only take the tongues out. That the blacks had speared and roasted it was evidenced by their stone oven which was close by. We searched the creek during the day, and having seen no indications of cattle being there, we decided to return to where the cow had been killed, and camp there for the night, as it was a good place for the safe keeping of our horses. The weather was very hot and dry; it was in the month of March, there was no moon, none of us had a match. We had supper as usual, and lay down.

Some time during the night, I think it must have been late, I awoke (the others were asleep) and I heard a noise similar to what an entire horse makes. I heard it again and awoke the others. We heard it some four or five times, and the noise ceased, but we could hear it walking along on the opposite side of the range, and when in a line with our camp, we could hear it coming down in our direction. As it came along we could hear its heavy breathing. About this time the dogs became terrified and crouched against us for protection. On account of a fallen tree being on the side the thing was coming, it had to come on one side or the other to get to where we were. My brother Joseph was on the lower side of this tree, I was on the upper side and my brother William in the centre. Not many seconds passed before Joseph sang out, 'Here the thing is,' and fired a small pistol he carried at it. Neither William nor myself, coming to the scrub got a sight of it. Joe says it was like a blackfellow with a blanket on him.

We did not hear it going away. We then tried to set our dogs after it, thinking they might find out where the thing went, but we could not get them to move. Had this thing been a little later in coming we could have seen what it was, as the day began to dawn in less than a quarter of an hour after Joe fired at it.

Webb also mentioned another incident in which Aboriginal people had killed a creature like the one that had terrified him and his brothers:

*T*he locality where the blacks killed it was below the junction of the Yass River with the Murrumbidgee. The animal got into some cliffs of rocks, and the blacks got torches to find out where it was hidden and then killed it with their nullah nullahs. There was a great many blacks at the killing, and he saw two dragging it down the hill by its legs. It was like a black man, but covered with grey hair.

Many consider the yowie to be related to the yeti or 'abominable snowman' of the Himalayas. In 2013, an Oxford University geneticist claimed to have matched DNA from alleged yeti hair samples showing that they matched those of a polar bear. This claim raised enormous interest around the world, though it has been challenged on the basis that polar bears are not likely to have ever existed in Nepal. Probably not in Australia, either.

Other speculations about the yowie include the possibility that the creature is a remnant of an earlier species. Aboriginal legends are often put forward as evidence for this.

Meanwhile, the hunt for our very own long-armed and hairy monster goes on. Sightings are regularly reported, especially from hotspots in Queensland but also in many other places. In the Queensland farming town of Kilcoy, they are so enthusiastic about their venerable yowie legends that they have erected a yowie statue in the local park, now called Yowie Park. In another sighting hotspot, the town of Mulgowie, the locals speak enthusiastically of sightings and speculations on the nature of their mysterious monster, the poetic Mulgowie Yowie. They have yowies in Woodenbong, New South Wales; they're in the Blue Mountains, near Taree, throughout Queensland, as well as the ACT infestations. We love a good yowie yarn almost as much as newspapers, radio and television do, in which even the sniff of a yowie is elevated to a major event. It seems that we really don't want to let our yowies go. If only someone could actually produce one. Perhaps we could grasp it by the leg?

8

Romancing the swag

North, west, and south—south, west, and north—
They lead and follow Fate—
The stoutest hearts that venture forth—
The swagman and his mate.

Henry Lawson, 'The Swagman and his Mate'

THE SWAGMAN—ALSO KNOWN as a 'bagman'—is one of Australia's most colourful characters. We first hear the word around the mid-nineteenth century, but the itinerant way of life was established long before. The need to travel long distances between settlements and properties meant that the ability to live on the road was vital for many people, and as the frontier expanded it became even more important for those without horses to 'go on the wallaby'. The essential equipment included something to sleep on, a billy for cooking and whatever other personal items were needed to survive what were usually long, hot and dusty journeys, mostly in search of work but sometimes avoiding it.

As early as the 1860s, landowners were complaining about men 'on the tramp' and the

... reckless system of life assumed by the generality of the men who back [*sic*] their beds, and shift from one part of the colony to another, during the intervals between sheep shearing and harvest,

163

harvest and sheep shearing. Six months' work, six months' idleness—such is the year's programme of this gaberlunzie fraternity.

(A 'gaberlunzie' is an old Scots term for a beggar.) The writer went on to complain about the swaggies who 'knock down their entire earnings in the two great drinking bouts with which the two periods of industry are wound up.'

And there were plenty of others with the same view. Despite this, the nomadic labourer and bush worker was so necessary to the survival of the agricultural economy, especially the wool industry, that the swagman's way of life was followed by many.

Lore of the track

An extensive body of folklore grew up around the 'swaggie' who 'humped his drum' along the 'tucker track'. One of the many classic yarns highlights the legendary reluctance of swagmen to indulge in more conversation than was necessary.

A couple of swaggies are tramping along together in the usual silence. Around mid-afternoon they come across the bloated carcass of a large animal on the side of the road. That night as they settle down in their camp one says to the other, 'Did you notice that dead horse we saw this afternoon?'

It wasn't until lunchtime the following day that the other swaggie answered: 'It wasn't a horse, it was a bullock.' The next morning he woke up but his mate was nowhere to be seen. But he'd left a note. It read: 'I'm off, there's too much bloody argument for me.'

The swaggie's dry sense of humour features in more than a few yarns:

*O*ne day out on the track out the back of Bourke, a swaggie runs out of food. Somewhere along the Darling River he comes across a ramshackle selection. He knocks on the door of the tumbledown shack and asks the farmer's wife for some food for his dog, thinking perhaps that this would encourage her sympathy. But the wife refuses, saying she can't be handing out food to lazy tramps and flea-bitten mongrels.

'Alright then, Missus', say the swaggie, 'but can yer lend me a bucket?'

'What do you want that for?', she ask suspiciously.

'To cook me dog in.'

On another occasion, the same dry sense of humour was displayed by a one-time swaggie:

*B*illy Seymour was another well-known swagman of the 'Outback' tracks, but he has since turned cane-farmer, and the bush roads know him no more. Travelling somewhere over Muttaburra way one time Billy called at a roadside humpy, and appealed to the woman who presented herself at the door, to fill his ration bags. The woman was sympathetic but said that she had very little food in the house. Her husband had been away droving for three months, and she had received no money from him during his absence. If he didn't write soon she couldn't imagine what she was going to do.

Billy pulled his old battered tobacco-box from his pocket and opening it, drew from its interior a crinkled and worn one-pound note. 'Here, Missus' he said, 'take this; I was saving it until I got to town, but spare me days I reckon you need it more than I do.'

In this nugget from the 1930s, the swaggie is called a 'tramp' but his sense of humour and irreverence towards the archdeacon and his four white ponies is pure bush.

*A*rchdeacon Stretch, of Victoria, had been transferred to a big parish in New South Wales, where a kindly-disposed squatter, evidently somewhat partial to archdeacons, presented him with four handsome creamy ponies and a fine Abbott buggy. One day this Archdeacon was spinning along behind his creamies at a merry pace when he espied a tramp at the roadside whom he at once took aboard. Whether actuated by a purely generous impulse, or a wish to obtain the services of a gate-opener along the pastoral route, this article is little concerned. After a while, the tramp said: 'My word, that is a fine team of creamies, sir; when's the rest of the circus coming along?'

Sniffling Jimmy

Another colourful swagman ended up in the first AIF, where the skills of living off the land and often on one's wits stood them in good stead.

*N*omads of the long and dusty track!! Yes, I've met them and studied their habits and characteristics, and many of them have been strange folk indeed. Most of them belonged to the past generation of 'matilda-waltsers' [*sic*] who have since disappeared from the roads, and their place has been taken by others who will never possess the rare humor or suffer the hardships of the men I am now going to tell about. Throw a log on the fire, draw closer to the cheering blaze and listen:

Just before I left North Queensland in 1914 to enlist in the A.I.F. I met a well-known track character who was better known as 'Sniffling Jimmy'. He was a short nuggety-built fellow with a freckled face and a mop of fiery red hair that would have turned a Papuan green with envy. i.e., if the natives of our vast Northern island have a liking for red hair. He was about 35 years of age and said that in his time he had walked through nearly every city and township between Melbourne and Townsville. He rarely did any work, and with a merry twinkle in his eye he said that when a boy his mother was much concerned about his constitution, so he promised her that he would never do a day's work if he could help it.

Jimmy was one of the very few teetotal swagmen I have met, and when he refused my offer to come in and have 'one' he said that he never touched anything stronger than water in his life. However, his specialty was soliciting free rations at some wayside squatters' homestead or farmer's home. Rarely has a swagman ever uttered such a pathetic oration. If his appeal to have his bag filled met with an abrupt refusal he would rattle off something like the following: 'Oh, have a heart, lady. If it wasn't for me weak constitution I wouldn't be compelled to beg for food. You see, I was reared in poverty and besides me mother and an invalid father, there were 13 other children in our family. There wasn't enough money coming into the house to provide sufficient nourishment for all of us, and as a result I did not get much to eat.'

'But you appear healthy enough,' said a Proserpine woman one day.

'Ah yes, lady,' replied Jimmy, 'but you know that outside appearances are often deceptive; me constitution is injured in me interior.'

One day in 1915 I was carrying a bag of bombs from Monash Gully to Courtney's Post at Anzac, and about half way I came upon four men digging an eight-foot trench, through shaly ground, under snipers' fire. I instantly recognised one of the men as 'Sniffling Jimmy'.

'Hullo! You are working at last,' I said.

'Oh yes,' he replied, 'army rations agree with me constitution.'

Just then a sniper's bullet lifted the dirt a few inches away from where he was working and he began to dig the pick frantically into

the ground. I passed on and did not meet him again, but I hope he
returned to Australia without loss of health or limb.

The poetic swaggie

Others less literary and more unknown also caught the swaggie's
lifestyle and ethos from another angle:

> Kind friends, pray give attention
> To this, my little song.
> Some rum things I will mention,
> And I'll not detain you long.
> I'm a swagman on the wallaby,
> Oh! don't you pity me.
>
> At first I started shearing,
> And I bought a pair of shears.
> On my first sheep appearing,
> Why, I cut off both its ears.
> Then I nearly skinned the brute,
> As clean as clean could be.
> So I was kicked out of the shed,
> Oh! don't you pity me, &c.
>
> I started station loafing,
> Short stages and took my ease;
> So all day long till sundown
> I'd camp beneath the trees.
> Then I'd walk up to the station,
> The manager to see.
> 'Boss, I'm hard up and I want a job,
> Oh! don't you pity me,' &c.

Says the overseer: 'Go to the hut.
In the morning I'll tell you
If I've any work about
I can find for you to do.'
But at breakfast I cuts off enough
For dinner, don't you see.
And then my name is Walker.
Oh! don't you pity me, &c.

And now, my friends, I'll say good-bye,
For I must go and camp.
For if the Sergeant sees me
He may take me for a tramp;
But if there's any covey here
What's got a cheque, d'ye see,
I'll stop and help him smash it.
Oh! don't you pity me.
I'm a swagman on the wallaby,
Oh! don't you pity me.

Shopkeepers would often provide passing swaggies with the means to take them through to the next stage of their journey. Henry Lawson noted this during his trek to Hungerford in 1892:

We saw one of the storekeepers give a dead-beat swagman five shillings' worth of rations to take him on into Queensland. The storekeepers often do this, and put it down on the loss side of their books. I hope the recording angel listens, and puts it down on the right side of his book.

This was not because Hungerford was a prosperous place: 'Hungerford consists of two houses and a humpy in New South Wales, and five houses in Queensland. Characteristically enough, both the pubs are in Queensland.' It was one of the unspoken obligations of bush life in which it was customary to provide assistance to travellers down on their luck. One day you might be one too.

Swagmen were not necessarily poorly educated, and in some cases not even poor. There are many examples of swagmen who knew the classics, literature, art and philosophy, as well as some who were professors. Sometimes these were men who had fallen on hard times, frequently due to the grog, perhaps gambling or other problems. Some had the means to live a settled life but chose to carry their drums along the tracks of Australia. A well-known case is that of Joseph Jenkins (1818–98). After an early life as a successful farmer in Wales, Jenkins apparently suffered a breakdown of some sort aggravated by drinking and took passage to the colony of Victoria. Here he took to the road, taking whatever work he could get and writing award-winning poetry and campaigning in local newspapers to better the lot of bush workers. He kept a journal of his wanderings, later published as *Diary of a Welsh Swagman* (1975), in which he wrote about politics, social conditions and Aboriginal people, among many other topics.

Many men spent parts of their lives as swaggies, sometimes as a necessity, sometimes as a way of seeking their fortunes as in the classic fairy tales about ne'er-do-wells eventually doing well. Well-known examples include the bush entrepreneur R.M. Williams and the novelist Donald Stuart. Even aristocrats were known to shoulder their swags from time to time.

'There you have the Australian swag'

So, what was a swag? Obligingly, Henry Lawson has left us a detailed description of the typical swag of the late nineteenth century. He also gives an insight into the actual carrying of the swag.

*T*he swag is usually composed of a tent 'fly' or strip of calico (a cover for the swag and a shelter in bad weather—in New Zealand it is oilcloth or waterproof twill), a couple of blankets, blue by custom and preference, as that colour shows the dirt less than any other (hence the name 'bluey' for swag), and the core is composed of spare clothing and small personal effects.

To make or 'roll up' your swag: lay the fly or strip of calico on the ground, blueys on top of it; across one end, with eighteen inches or so to spare, lay your spare trousers and shirt, folded, light boots tied together by the laces toe to heel, books, bundle of old letters, portraits, or whatever little knick-knacks you have or care to carry, bag of needles, thread, pen and ink, spare patches for your pants, and bootlaces. Lay or arrange the pile so that it will roll evenly with the swag (some pack the lot in an old pillowslip or canvas bag), take a fold over of blanket and calico the whole length on each side, so as to reduce the width of the swag to, say, three feet, throw the spare end, with an inward fold, over the little pile of belongings, and then roll the whole to the other end, using your knees and judgment to make the swag tight, compact and artistic; when within eighteen inches of the loose end take an inward fold in that, and bring it up against the body of the swag.

There is a strong suggestion of a roley-poley in a rag about the business, only the ends of the swag are folded in, in rings, and not tied. Fasten the swag with three or four straps, according to judgment and the supply of straps. To the top strap, for the swag is carried (and eased down in shanty bars and against walls or veranda-posts when not on the track) in a more or less vertical position—to the top strap, and lowest, or lowest but one, fasten the ends of the shoulder strap (usually a towel is preferred as being softer to the shoulder), your coat being carried outside the swag at the back, under the straps. To the top strap fasten the string of the nose-bag, a calico bag about the size of a pillowslip, containing the tea, sugar and flour bags, bread, meat, baking-powder and salt, and brought, when the swag is carried from the left shoulder, over the right on to the chest, and so balancing the swag behind. But a swagman can throw a heavy swag in a nearly vertical position against his spine, slung from one shoulder only and without any balance, and carry it as easily as you might wear your overcoat.

Some bushmen arrange their belongings so neatly and conveniently, with swag straps in a sort of harness, that they can roll up the swag in about a minute, and unbuckle it and throw it out as easily as a roll of wall-paper, and there's the bed ready on the ground with the wardrobe for a pillow. The swag is always used for a seat on the track; it is a soft seat, so trousers last a long time. And, the dust being mostly soft and silky on the long tracks out back, boots last marvellously.

Fifteen miles a day is the average with the swag, but you must travel according to the water: if the next bore or tank is five miles on, and the next twenty beyond, you camp at the five-mile water to-night and do the twenty next day. But if it's thirty miles you have to do it. Travelling with the swag in Australia is variously and picturesquely described as 'humping bluey,' 'walking Matilda,' 'humping Matilda,' 'humping your drum,' 'being on the wallaby,' 'jabbing trotters,' and 'tea and sugar burglaring,' but most travelling shearers now call themselves trav'lers, and say simply 'on the track,' or 'carrying swag.'

Swags are still carried today, though they have been updated and redesigned for modern comfort and convenience. An exception is the swag of Cameron the Swaggie; Cameron lives the life of the traditional swagman, humping his blanket and billy from town to town and reciting bush poetry from his extensive repertoire to anyone who will listen. Billed by the occasional press article as 'the last swaggie', Cameron is but one of quite a few who still follow the Wallaby Track.

A swagman's death

One of the tensions between the swagman population and the people they worked for involved authority. The 'bloke' or 'cove' was the boss of the woolshed or station where those swaggies who were in work laboured for their wages. When times were good, which was often, relations were reasonably agreeable. But in hard times conflict was bound to arise. In the early 1890s much of the eastern Australian workforce was gripped by strikes and lockouts as depression strangled the economy. In the pastoral industries there was serious violence brought on by the graziers' refusal to pay the rate the shearers demanded due to the rapid fall in the market price of wool.

It was during this period that rural workers, most of whom were swagmen by necessity, established the labour movement in the form of organised trade unionism and the origins of the Australian Labor Party. Eventually, in early 1891, there was a serious possibility of insurrection as armed shearers gathered at Barcaldine and elsewhere in Queensland. There were riots, destruction of property including telegraph wires, and arson attacks. Armed troops were deployed and in May, thousands of striking shearers raised the Southern Cross flag and assembled beneath the famed ghost gum known as 'The Tree of Knowledge' at Barcaldine, giving birth to the Australian Labor Party. Significant as these events were, they are the subject of extensive romanticisation. The strike was called off in June in favour of direct political action through the ballot box, although fourteen shearers had been found guilty of conspiracy and imprisoned. The pastoralists had employed 'scab' labour from New South Wales but as tensions eased began to hire back the rebel shearers.

But all was not yet calm. In 1894, there were more strikes over an attempt to reduce wages. One of the most violent confrontations in this period had an influence on the creation of the best-known swaggie of all, the 'jolly swagman' of the famous song. On the night of 2 September 1894, a group of armed shearers attacked Dagworth Station, northwest of Winton on the Upper Diamantina River. The police magistrate at Winton wired the Colonial Secretary.

*D*agworth woolshed was burned down by sixteen armed men. The wire stated that at about half-past twelve on Sunday morning the constable and a station hand named Tomlin were on duty/guarding the shed. The first intimation they had of any attack was the firing of about a dozen shots through the shed. This woke the Messrs. Macpherson, and the others. The firing was continued, both sides engaging in it, for about twenty minutes. While this was going on, one of the unionists was seen to sneak up under cover of the fire of his comrades and set fire to the shed. The constables and the station hands kept firing at the party, and when this ceased it was not known whether anyone was wounded. About forty shots were exchanged. Three bullets were fired through the cottage where the Macphersons were sleeping. The unionists had taken up position in the bed of the creek, at the rear of the shed, where they were almost wholly protected from the fire of the defending party. Rain fell shortly after the men left. There is hardly any doubt but that this is the same gang that has been burning all the sheds.

A number of bullet-wounded unionists were later arrested in the shearers' strike camp and:

. . . a man named Haffmeister [*sic*], a prominent unionist, was found dead about two miles from Kynuna. The local impression is that he was one of the attacking mob at Dagworth, and was wounded there. There were seven unionists with Hoffmeister when he died, and these assert that he committed suicide. In consequence of the seriousness of this last event the Government are taking active steps to deal with persons who are found to be armed.

The story of swaggie 'Frenchy' Hoffmeister's death was the inspiration for Paterson to pen the verses that became 'Waltzing Matilda'. He was visiting the area the following year when the events were still on everyone's minds and tongues. Apparently hoping to impress Christina Macpherson, sister of the station manager, he wrote the poem for a tune she played on her autoharp. The rest is history, if of a kind complicated by folklore.

Where the angel tarboys fly

In 1908, a swaggie calling himself 'Vagrant' gave a blow-by-blow account of the great tallies of some legendary blade men. He managed to include a little verse, a yarn or two and a wonderful story made up of many stories about the competitive and boastful life of the shearer.

The shearing figures quoted in the 'Western Champion' of the 12th of September as to shearing tallies, are not quite correct. Andy Brown did not shear at Evesham in 1886. In 1887 Jimmy Fisher shore fifty lambs in one run before breakfast there. I do not know the time; but they used to ring the bell mighty early those days. I have seen spectral-like forms creeping across the silent space between the galley and the shed long before the kookaburra woke the bush with his laughing song, and he is a pretty early bird.

The same year Black Tom Johnson got bushed in the gloom of that space, and lost half a run before breakfast. Fisher shore 288 at Kynuna the following year: he was a wonderful man for his 8 stone of humanity. The same year Alf Bligh shore 254 at Isis Downs; he and Charlie Byers were the first two men to cut 200 sheep on the Barcoo. The same year Bill Hamilton, now M.L.A., shore 200 sheep at Manfred Downs, and to him belongs the credit of shearing the first 200 on the Flinders.

The next year Bill died at Cambridge Gulf; but as he is alive and all right now, the account was exaggerated. Bill says: 'That 200 at Manfred Downs was no "cake walk".' He used twelve gallons of water cooling down. Alick Miller shore 4163 sheep in three weeks and three days at Charlotte Plains, in 1885, and Sid ('Combo') Ross shore nine lambs in nine minutes at Belalie, on the Warrego, the year before.

In the early eighties there were a good number of 200 a-day men in New South Wales; but none of those celebrated personages ventured a pilgrimage northwards until 1887, when quite a number of fast men stormed the west, and their advent started a new era in the shearing world, improved tools and methods entirely superseding the old Ward and Payne, and Serby school, and the old rum drinking ringers of the roaring days were gradually relegated to the 'snagger brigade.' Paddy M'Can, Jack Bird, Tom Green ('the Burdekin ringer'), Ned Hyles, Jack Ellis (Bendigo), Mick Hoffman ('the Peak Downs ringer'), Billy Cardham, Jim Sloane, Jack Collins, and George Taylor ('the Native') had to give way to the younger brigade with improved Burgon and Ball tools, and new ideas, and, with the advent of Jack Howe, Christy Gratz, 'Chinee' Sullivan, Billy Mantim, George Butler, Jimmy Power, Alick Miller, Jack Reid, Allan M'Callum, and others, 180 and 200 were common enough.

Later, when machinery was introduced, tallies took a further jump. Jimmy Power shore 323 at Barenya in 1892 by machines. The same year Jack Howe shore 321 by hand at Alice Downs, his tallies for the week previous being 249, 257, 259, 263, 267, 144, a total of 1439 for the week. I doubt if this record has ever been beaten. I will say right here that Jack Howe was the best shearer I have ever seen at work. The only one approaching him was Lynch, of the Darling River, New South Wales.

No doubt figures get enlarged in circulation, and tall tallies in the bar-room mount up with the fumes of bottled beer—there is a lot of sheep shorn there. Shearers do not lie, as a rule: they boast and make mistakes casually. Jack Howe once told me the biggest mistake he ever made was in trying to shake hands with himself in a panel mirror in an hotel in Maoriland. He had just landed, and made for the first hotel. You see, he had grown a beard on the trip over, and looked like a chap he used to know on the Barcoo. The mistake was considerably intensified by the barmaid's smile, as she watched Jack's good-natured recognition of an old shearing mate from Queensland.

At Kensington Downs in 1885, a big Chinaman named Ah Fat rang the shed. He could shear all right, too. The men used to take day about to run him; but the Chow had too much pace. A shearer named George Mason made great preparations to 'wipe him out' one day, and, after nearly bursting himself up to dinner-time, discovered that Ah Fat was not on the board: he was doing a lounge in the hut that day. I think that Chinaman must have died; everyone loved him, and, like Moore's 'Young Gazelle,' with its gladsome eye, he was sure to go—

To that shed beyond the sky,
Where the angel tarboys fly,
And the 'cut' will last for ever, and
the sheep are always dry.

These records may be of interest to the survivors of the old school, and may, perhaps, stir up the dormant memories of the younger ones. They have been culled from past records, written on the backs of stolen telegram forms from almost every post office between Burketown and Barringun, and are given for what they merit.

Bowyang Bill and the cocky farmer

'Bowyang Bill' recalled an experience of his younger days, just around the turn of the twentieth century. If Bill is to be believed, on this occasion at least, he worked very hard for one of the notoriously tight-fisted and hard-handed cocky farmers. (A 'bowyang' was a length of string tied around trousers just below the knee to keep them up. They were commonly worn by working men in the nineteenth century and many illustrations of swaggies feature them.)

Bowyang Bill begins his story with a short verse that could be a memorial for the swaggies' way of life and death:

For they tramp and go as the world rolls back,
They drink and gamble, and die;
But their spirits shall live on the outback track.
As long as the years go by.

Remember those cockles who used to wake a fellow at 2 a.m. in the morning to start the day's work? They are not so plentiful as they were 30 odd years back, but there's still a few of them milking cows or growing spuds in this State.

All this takes me back to the time when I tied my first knot in the swag and started out along the dusty tracks to make my fortune. After many weeks I came to Dawson's place. He was a long, lean hungry sort of codger, and his bleary eyes sparkled when I agreed to work for five bob a week and tucker. I didn't know Dawson or I would have wasted no time in re-hoisting Matilda and proceeding on my way. I worked 16 hours a day on that place, and lived mostly on damper and flybog. I used to get up so early in the morning that I was ashamed to look at the sleeping fowls when I passed their camping place. I never saw those fowls moving about their yard. They were sleeping on their roosts when I went to work, and they were snoozing on the same roosts when I returned to the house at night.

Things went on like this until another young cove came along with a swag. It was also his first experience 'carrying the bundle,' and no doubt that was why he also agreed to work for Dawson. He said his name was Mullery. We had tea at 11 p.m. the day he arrived, and it was midnight when we turned into our bunks in the harness-room.

Before I went to sleep I told Mullery what sort of a place it was, but he said he would stick it—until he earned a few bob to carry him along the track. In the next breath he told me he was greatly interested in astronomy. I didn't know what that was until he explained he was interested in the stars. 'Well, by cripes,' I said, 'you'll get plenty of opportunities to examine them here.'

That cove was over the odds. I'm just dozing off when he leans over and says, 'Do you know how far it is from here to Mars?' Pulling the old potato bag wagga from my face I told him I hadn't the faintest idea, as I had never travelled along the road to the blanky place. He mentioned the millions of miles it was from here to there. 'Did you measure the distance with a foot-rule?' I asked as I again drew the wagga over my face.

When old Dawson pushed his head through the door at 2 a.m. I was awake but the new chap was dead to the world. Dawson went across and yanked the blanket off him. 'Here, hurry up,' he growled, 'and get those cows milked before they get sun-stroke.' 'What's going to give them sunstroke?' asked Muller, as innocent as you like. 'Why, the blanky sun, of course,' roared Dawson. The new chap made himself more comfortable in his bunk, then he drawled, 'There's no danger of that, sir, and allow me to inform you that at this time of the year the sun is 93 million miles from the earth.'

'You're a liar,' yelled Dawson, shaking the hurricane lamp in Mullery's face, 'and if you come outside I'll prove it to you. Why, the darned sun is just peeping over the tops of the gum trees half-a-mile from here, and by the time it's well above them you'll be on the track again. Yes, you're sacked, so get out of here quick and lively.'

The Mad Eight

So far into legend have the Mad Eight faded that no one can agree on the year of their amazing feat. Depending on the sources, it occurred in 1923, 1924 or 1925. Whichever of these dates is correct, the events took place in the Gascoyne region one shearing season. In those days shearers often formed 'teams', work groups who travelled together from station to station hiring out as a work unit.

In whichever year it was, the gun shearers Nugget Williams, Bob Sawallish, Vol Day, George Bence, Tiny Lehmann, Len Saltmarsh, Charlie Fleming and Hughie Munro got together and blazed their way across the country. In nine months they shore record-breaking tallies in eleven large sheds. But it was at Williambury Station where they propelled themselves into the colourful history of shearing; between them they shore nearly 18,000 sheep in two weeks—using hand shears. This was enough for the shearing team to enter shearing history. But when it was discovered that the average weight of a fleece that year was a solid 11 pounds, they moved from history into legend, where they remain firmly today.

In 1927, the fame of the Mad Eight even reached the federal Arbitration Court. During a hearing of a pastoral industry award claim, someone brought up the feat of the 'Mad Eight'. The Chief Judge, unaware of the intricacies of shearing culture, asked for an explanation and was told by the counsel representing the employers that 'the appellation was earned by the team because of the large number of sheep they shore in a day'. What the judge made of this was apparently not recorded.

The following year, the man who actually employed the Mad Eight published his account of the event and, incidentally, provides the most reliable date for their achievement. He began by pointing out that 1927 was not a good year for high tallies:

*T*herefore it is not likely that many teams this season will cut tallies such as were cut by the 'mad eight' which I had employed at Williambury in 1923. This was the team which came so much into prominence, and was commented on by advocates of the union.

They were known as the 'mad eight' on account of their pace, and the team consisted of A. Williams, R. Sawallish, Vol Day, F. Lehmann, L. Saltmarsh, George Bence, C. Fleming and H. Munro.

The tallies given for the Mad Eight were impressive by any measure and fully confirmed their claim to legendary status:

*T*he sheep shorn averaged 11 lb. wool, and therefore the following; figures showing the daily tallies of the eight shearers for two weeks are interesting. Commencing on September 3, the team shore 1509, 1708, 1577, 1748, 1698, 927 (Saturday, half day). Total for week, 9167.

Resuming on the second week the same team clipped 1189 on September 10, losing one hour through engine trouble, 1432, 1740, 2800, 1806, 803 (Saturday, half day). Total for week, 8770. The highest individual tally was 250, and two men obtained this figure. The shearers' highest daily averages were:- A. Williams, 213; R. Sawallish, 242; Vol Day, 242; F. Lehmann, 234; L. Saltmarsh, 216; George Bence, 222; C. Fleming, 226; and H. Munro, 205. Total, 1800, and average 225.

Eye-glazing though such statistics are for most city types today, they were lovingly collated and preserved by shearers and those in the wool industry back in the roaring days when the world was wide and the country rode on the sheep's back.

NED KELLY
(Sketched as he was Leaving Benalla).

9

After the Kellys

'I look upon him as invulnerable,
you can do nothing with him.'

Aaron Sherritt on Ned Kelly

THE NED KELLY story remains an important part of Australian history and folklore. Beginning as a fairly run-of-the-mill local conflict between free selectors, squatters and police, the murders at Stringybark Creek escalated the outbreak to the country's most serious episode of outlawry. The consequences of the Kelly saga continue to haunt us and the events, real and imagined, are continually recycled in books, films and the media. But there are many untold stories about what happened after the ironclad bushranger's execution. All have their origins in the events of 1878 to 1880.

The saga

Edward, the first-born son of Ellen and James ('Red') Kelly, grew up in the hothouse atmosphere of a combination of clan-like Irish-Australian families, the Kellys, Quinns and Lloyds. Each of these families had their own extensive histories of trouble with the Victorian and other police forces, surviving as they did by a combination of legal pastoral activities and stock stealing, or 'duffing'. The Kellys and their relations were by no means the only ones involved in this business. In fact, this was the normal means of existence for most free selectors at that time, the distinction between stock that had 'strayed' and that which had been stolen being a difficult one to make.

By 1871, at the age of sixteen, Ned Kelly already had numerous experiences with the law behind him, and had served one gaol sentence. In that year he was convicted of receiving a stolen horse and given three years in Melbourne's tough Pentridge gaol. He entered prison a high-spirited, 'flash' youth and came out a hard, bitter man in February 1874.

Ned went straight for a while, working as a timber-getter in the Wombat Ranges and keeping out of trouble—until September 1877. He was arrested for drunkenness and on the way to the courthouse attempted to escape. The ensuing brawl with four policemen and a local shoemaker is notable only for the fact that two of those policemen, constables Fitzpatrick and Lonigan, were to play small but significant roles in the coming Kelly drama.

Fitzpatrick was the first to make an entrance. Seven months after the fight with Ned, the constable, probably drunk, rode up to the Kelly homestead near Greta, alone and against orders, to arrest Ned's younger brother, Dan, on a charge of horse stealing. The truth of what occurred then will never be known, but Fitzpatrick later claimed to have been assaulted and shot by the Kellys, including Ned and Mrs Kelly. The family claimed that Fitzpatrick had tried to molest one of the daughters, probably Kate, and that their actions had been justified. Six months later, Judge Redmond Barry did not agree and sent Mrs Kelly to gaol for three years, saying that he would have given Ned and Dan fifteen years apiece, if they could have been found.

Of course, they could not be found; they were safely hidden in the rugged Wombat Ranges, accompanied by two other young friends, Joe Byrne and Steve Hart. In October 1878, a party of four policemen went into the ranges to hunt the Kellys down. In charge was Sergeant Kennedy, a good bushman and a crack shot. He was aided by constables Scanlon, McIntyre and Lonigan, the same Lonigan who had fought with Ned the year before. All these men had been hand-picked for their bush craft and general police aptitude, and they made it known that they intended to get the Kellys.

On the night of 25 October they camped along the edge of a creek known as Stringybark. The following evening the four-strong Kelly gang bailed up Lonigan and McIntyre, who were minding the camp while Kennedy and Scanlon patrolled the bush in search of the outlaws. McIntyre surrendered immediately, saving his life, but Lonigan was brave and foolish enough to clutch at his revolver. Ned Kelly shot him dead. On their return to the camp, Kennedy and Scanlon were called upon to surrender, but they resisted too, and Ned killed them both in the ensuing gunfight. During the fighting McIntyre managed to clamber onto a stray horse and ride for his life.

The Melbourne and provincial newspapers reacted to the shocking news, enabling the Victorian parliament to rush through an 'Outlawry Act' that rendered those persons pronounced outlaws totally outside the law. All rights and property were forfeit and the outlaw was liable to be killed on sight by any citizen. In addition, harbourers and sympathisers were liable to fifteen years' imprisonment with hard labour and the loss of all their goods.

Less than six weeks after Stringybark Creek, the Kellys struck again. This time they robbed the bank at Euroa, a busy town about 100 miles north of Melbourne, the state capital. The bushrangers escaped with around 2000 pounds in gold and cash. Ned also stole deeds and mortgages held in the bank safe, an action that endeared him to the struggling selectors of northeastern Victoria, most of whom saw the banks as 'poor mancrushers', as Ned himself was to describe them in his 'Jerilderie Letter'.

Acting on false information intentionally supplied by one of the Kellys''bush telegraphs', or informants, the police went looking for the gang across the border in New South Wales. Meanwhile, back in the 'Kelly country', the bushrangers divided up the Euroa loot between themselves, relatives and sympathisers. Over the next few months, many previously impoverished selectors managed to pay off their debts, usually with crisp, new banknotes.

Frustrated in their futile attempts to capture the outlaws, the police revenged themselves on the sympathisers. A score—including Isaiah 'Wild' Wright—were arrested and confined in Beechworth gaol for periods of up to three months without trial and without evidence against them. This misguided manoeuvre made the police even more unpopular in the district as many of the prisoners missed that year's harvest, causing severe hardship for their families.

The reward for the Kellys was increased from 2000 pounds to a total of 4000, a very large sum at that time. But this had no effect upon the loyalty of the sympathisers either. After the Kellys' next escapade the reward sum would be doubled again.

On 5 February 1879, the gang appeared at Jerilderie, 46 miles across the New South Wales border, where they locked the two astounded local policemen in their own cells. The Kellys spent that night and most of the next day in the town, masquerading as police officers in their stolen police uniforms. That afternoon they occupied the bar of the Royal Mail Hotel, handily adjacent to the bank, which they then robbed. Another 2000-pound haul was made and mortgages were burned to the accompaniment of cheers from the crowd held hostage in the hotel. Everyone was treated to drinks and a speech from Ned about the injustices he had suffered at the hands of the police, the government and the squatters. More importantly, he left with one of the bank tellers a 10,000-word statement that came to be known as 'the Jerilderie Letter'.

This fascinating document catalogues Ned Kelly's and his friends' complaints and grievances, and also gives an insight into the motives and attitudes behind their actions. Among other things, the letter complains of discrimination against free selectors and small farmers, like the Kellys, by the administration, which, it is claimed, was working hand in glove with the wealthy squatters against the poor. According to Ned, the police were:

> . . . a parcel of big ugly fat-necked wombat headed big bellied magpie legged narrow hipped splay footed sons of Irish Bailiffs or English landlords . . .

The letter ends with a stern warning for the rich to be generous to the poor and not to oppress them:

I give fair warning to all those who has reason to fear me to sell out and give £10 out of every hundred towards the widow and orphan fund and do not attempt to reside in Victoria but as short a time as possible after reading this notice, neglect this and abide by the consequences, which shall be worse than the rust in the wheat in Victoria or the druth of a dry season to the grasshoppers in New South Wales. I do not wish to give the order full force without giving timely warning, but I am a widows son outlawed and my orders must be obeyed.

In an earlier letter, written just before the raid on Euroa, Ned had cautioned his readers to 'remember your railroads'. The full implications of this mysterious warning became apparent on Sunday 27 June 1880. Glenrowan, a cluster of buildings and tents surrounding a railway station, fell to the bushrangers as easily as Euroa and Jerilderie. But this time they had not come to rob a bank; they had something more ambitious in mind.

The night before, Dan Kelly and Joe Byrne had 'executed' a

one-time companion named Aaron Sherritt. Sherritt had apparently been playing the dangerous role of double agent, playing the police off against the outlaws. But his murder also had another motive, to lure the bulk of the special district police force onto a train that would have to pass through Glenrowan on its way to the scene of the murder in the Kelly country. The bushrangers planned to wreck this train and pick off the survivors, particularly the Aboriginal blacktrackers who had several times brought the police a little too close to the Kellys for comfort. Exactly what the gang intended to do after this massacre remains controversial. It has been said that they merely aimed to rob as many unprotected banks as possible; others believe that their plans were far more enterprising, involving an insurrection to establish a 'Republic of North-eastern Victoria'. Whatever the bushrangers had in mind, they were well prepared for a hard fight.

During the months before the attack on Glenrowan, plough-shares and quantities of cast iron had been disappearing throughout the Kelly country. The reason for these unusual thefts became plain when the bushrangers herded most of Glenrowan's small population into Jones's Hotel that Sunday. In the back room were four rough suits of armour, consisting of back-plates and breastplates and an adjustable metal apron to protect the groin of the wearer. Each suit weighed about 80 pounds—almost 40 kilos—and there was one metal helmet, with eye slits and a visor, weighing about 16 pounds. Ned Kelly was the only member of the gang strong enough to wear both armour and helmet and still manage to handle a gun.

About ten o'clock that night, after a round of singing, dancing and drinking with the crowd in the hotel, Ned allowed a few prisoners to go home because the police train had not arrived as early as expected. This blunder ensured the failure of the bushrangers' plot. One of the freed prisoners, the Glenrowan schoolmaster Thomas Curnow, walked along the railway track and warned the police train just outside Glenrowan.

Hearing the train stop outside the town, the bushrangers realised what had happened, buckled on their armour and stood in front of the hotel to meet the police charge that very soon came. After a lengthy exchange of shots, Ned Kelly and Joe Byrne were wounded, and the clumsiness of their armour, together with the intensely painful bruises caused whenever a bullet smashed into the metal, had become apparent. Ned lumbered into the bush to reload his revolver and fainted from loss of blood. At about the same time, Joe Byrne was killed by a stray bullet that splintered through the wooden hotel wall.

The hotel was still full of prisoners, but the police raked the building with gunfire. A young boy and an old man were both wounded, and a woman with a baby in her arms and her family in tow was frustrated three times in her attempts to escape by the police's refusal to cease firing. She was finally helped to safety by the gallantry of a bystander who braved the gunfire to rescue her, though one of her children was wounded.

Shortly after this, Ned Kelly recovered consciousness and came crashing out of the bush, firing at the police from the safety of his armour. He was finally brought down by a shotgun blast to the upper legs fired by Sergeant Steele and taken into custody.

The police then sent to Melbourne for a field-gun to demolish the weatherboard hotel along with the two bushrangers left inside, Dan Kelly and Steve Hart. Long before the gun arrived, the prisoners were all released and the police set the hotel alight. A Catholic priest among the 500 sightseers who had gathered at the railway station rushed into the burning building. He found the bodies of Dan Kelly and Steve Hart, and rescued a badly wounded old man who had been forgotten by the prisoners in their rush to escape.

It was all over; the sightseers had nothing to do but wait for the blaze to subside and then hunt for souvenirs. The relatives of the dead bushrangers waited to claim the charred bodies for burial. Ned Kelly was taken to Melbourne, where he rapidly recovered from his 30 wounds and stood trial in front of the same judge who had sentenced his mother two years before.

Not surprisingly, the verdict was 'guilty' and Edward Kelly was sentenced to hang. Strong campaigning and a petition to have the sentence commuted were unsuccessful, and at ten o'clock on the morning of Thursday 11 November 1880, Ned Kelly dropped through the gallows' trapdoor and into legend. But that was not the end of it.

A Glenrowan letter

Young bank clerk Donald Sutherland wrote to his parents about what he saw in the immediate aftermath of the siege at Glenrowan.

My Dear Parents

I have your letter by the last mail all in good time. I am sorry to learn that Maggie Ben Hill had such a narrow shave in the neighbourhood of Spittal. By Jove she must have felt the cold pretty much I guess. The weather here just now is bitter cold. I was in Beechworth the other day and the snow was coming down in great flakes. Snow-balling being indulged in all the afternoon—the ground was literally covered. The mountains are all covered some time ago and the winter garments will continue being worn by them for about 6 months yet. We have hard frost every night and in the mornings the grass is quite brittle. The ice is not strong enough for skating though—in the shade in front of the Bank here and where the sun does not shine. We have frost all day—I sleep at night with three double blankets and a greatcoat and then feel the cold.

Fresh since I last wrote you we have had great doings here—the Kellys are annihilated. The gang is completely destroyed—you will see a long and full account of all that has been done in one of *The Australasians* which I send to you along with this letter. They had a long run but were captured at last. Glenrowan is only 8 miles from Oxley and 12 from Wangaratta being the next station on the line from the latter township to Melbourne. I always thought the Kellys were in the ranges about here although some people maintained that on account of their long silence they had got away from Australia altogether. On hearing of the affray, I at once proceeded to Glenrowan to have a look at the desperados who caused me so many dreams and sleepless nights. I saw the lot of them. Ned, the leader of the gang, being the only one taken alive. He was lying on a stretcher quite calm and collected notwithstanding the great pain he must have been suffering from his wounds. He was wounded in 5 or 6 places, only in the arms and legs—his body and head being encased in armour made from the moule boards of a lot of ploughs. Now the farmers about here have been getting their moule boards taken off their ploughs at night for a long time but who ever dreamed it was the Kellys and that they would be used for such a purpose. Ned's armour alone weighed 97 pounds. The police thought he was a fiend seeing their rifle bullets mere sliding off him like hail. They were firing into him at about 10 yards in the grim light of the morning without the slightest effect. The force of the rifle bullets made him stagger when hit but it was only when they got him in the legs and arms that he reluctantly fell exclaiming as he did so 'I am done I am done'. Steele was the man who dropped him and Kelly always boasted that he would burn Steele alive before he was captured. Steele is the sergeant in charge of the police at Wangaratta and a very nice fellow. The

Kellys this time had lifted the rails to upset the train and kill and shoot everyone on it. They were then going to make the engine driver run them down the line to Benalla where they would stick up all the banks, blow up the police barracks—in fact commit wholesale slaughter and then fly to their mountain fortresses.

Ned does not at all look like a murderer and bushranger—he is a very powerful man aged about 27, black hair and beard with a soft mild looking face and eyes—his mouth being the only wicked portion of the face. After his capture he became very tame and conversed freely with those who knew him. Not having the pleasure of his acquaintance I did not speak to him although I should have liked very much to ask why he never stuck up the Bank of Victoria at Oxley. Well he had it down on his programme at one time but a schoolmaster named Wallace and one who banks with us put him off it—at least Wallace got the news conveyed through Byrne, one of the gang that he had some deeds and papers here which he did not wish destroyed as it would ruin him. Ned had said I wont do it and he didn't do it and we were consequently saved from the presence of the gang. Poor Ned I was really sorry for him to see him lying pierced by bullets and still showing no signs of pain. His 3 sisters were there also, Mrs Skillion, Kate Kelly and a younger one. Kate was sitting at his head with her arms round his neck while the others were crying in a mournful strain at the state of one who, but the night before, was the terror of the whole Colony. The night that Byrne and Dan Kelly shot Sherritt at The Woolshed they rode through Oxley on their way to Glenrowan. Some of the people in the township heard the horses go by but I didn't being sound asleep. Byrne was shot in the groin early in the morning as he was drinking a glass of whisky at the bar. Then there remained only Dan Kelly and Steve Hart—whether they shot themselves or whether they were shot by the police will ever remain a mystery. At about 2pm a policeman named Johnstone whom I knew well at Murchison fired the house and it was only when no signs of life appeared that they rushed the place to find the charred remains of Dan and Steve Hart. They presented a horrible appearance being roasted to a skeleton, black and grim reminding me of old Knick himself.

Thousands of people thronged to Glenrowan on receipt of the news and not one of the crowd there had the courage to lift the white sheet off the charred remains until I came up and struck a match—it being dark—pulling down the sheet and exposed all that remained of the 2 daring murderous bushrangers. Dan and Steve are buried in the Greta Cemetery, Byrne is buried at Benalla and Ned is now in the hospital of the Melbourne gaol treated with every care until he is strong and well enough to be hanged. Such then is bushranging in Victoria so far. I may tell you however that it is not all over yet and my belief is that another gang will be out ere long to avenge the death of the present. I could tell you much more but time and space will not permit. You can read a full and correct account from *The Australasian*. I am quite well, hoping you are all ditto.

faithfully
D G Sutherland

PS The hair enclosed is from the tail of Ned Kelly the famous murderer and bushranger's mare. His favourite mare who followed him all round the trees during the firing. He said he wouldn't care for himself if he thought his mare safe.

'I thought it was a circus'

On Saturday 14 May 1881, less than a year after Dan's death and six months since Ned's hanging, the members of the Royal Commission investigating the causes of the Kelly outbreak rode up unannounced to the family home in Greta. They were met by Ned's mother, Ellen.

*H*er residence, a four-roomed slab hut, with a bark roof, stands in the middle of a paddock comprising about 10 acres. It is within a short distance from a mountain, called Quarry-hill, whence a good view of the surrounding country can be obtained. Within the paddock there were two or three horses and as many cows, and there were a few fowls and a tame kangaroo about the house. But the place presented a gloomy, desolate appearance. There was a very small kitchen garden, but there was no other land under cultivation. Some of the panes of glass in the windows were broken, and, excepting that some creepers had very recently been planted at the foot of the verandah posts, no attempt had been made to beautify the house, or make this home look homely.

When the commission pulled up on the road opposite the front-door that door was closed, there was no sign of any human being about. Presently, however, a child was observed peeping round the back of the house at the strangers. After a short consultation it was decided that it would be better for the commission, as they were near the house, to ask Mrs Kelly if she had any statement to make on the subjects that they have been appointed to inquire into. Accordingly, Messrs Graves and Anderson were told-off to go to the house and open up communication with Mrs Kelly. She came round from the back of the house to meet them, and intimated, when she was told of the object of the visit, that she had no objection to see the commission.

The remaining members were then called up, and introduced by Mr Graves to Mrs Kelly. She was dressed in black, and seemed to be between 40 and 45 years of age. In her younger days she was probably comely, and her hair is still abundant, and black as a raven's wing. Although looking careworn, she has evidently a large stock of vitality. Her eyes and mouth are the worst features in her face, the former having a restless and furtive, and the latter a rather cruel look. When Mr Graves introduced the other commissioners, Mrs Kelly said with a smile, 'I didn't know who you could all be; I thought it was a circus.'

. . . after a short and rather uncomfortable pause, Mr Longmore undeceived Mrs Kelly by informing her that they were the Police Commission and would be glad to listen to anything she had to say. She did not invite the commissioners into her house or open the front door, and two or three very young children—her offspring—could be seen inside the house, peering through a window. One of these children was a pretty little girl about four or five years old and her face reminded one very forcibly of Ned Kelly, whose hair and eyes were of a different colour from his mother's.

Ellen Kelly made the same charges she had made many times before and would make many times again:

The police have treated my children very badly. I have three very young ones, and had one only a fortnight old when I got into trouble [referring to her recent imprisonment in connexion with the assault on Constable Fitzpatrick at Greta]. That child I took to Melbourne with me, but I left Kate and Grace and the younger children behind. The police used to treat them very ill. They used to take them out of bed at night, and make them walk before them. The police made the children go first when examining a house, so as to prevent the out-laws if in the house, from suddenly shooting them.

Kate is now only about 16 years old, and is still a mere child. She is older than Grace. Mrs Skillian is married, and of course, knew more than the others, who are mere children. She is not in the house now. Mr Brook Smith was the worst behaved of the force, and had less sense than any of them. He used to throw things out of the house, and he came in once to the lock-up staggering drunk. I did not like his conduct. That was at Benalla. I wonder they allowed a man to behave as he did to an unfortunate woman. He wanted me to say things that were not true.

My holding comprises 88 acres, but it is not all fenced in. The Crown will not give me a title. If they did I could sell at once and leave this locality. I was entitled to a lease a long time ago, but they are keeping it back. Perhaps, if I had a lease, I might stay for a while, if they would let me alone. I want to live quietly. The police keep coming backwards and forwards, and saying there are 'reports, reports.' As to the papers, there was nothing but lies in them from the beginning. I would sooner be closer to a school, on account of my children. If I had anything forward I would soon go away from here.

Mrs Kelly was then asked if her children had any complaints:

Mrs. Kelly knocked at the front door, and called out to her daughter Grace to open it. Grace did so, and after much persuasion on the part of her mother, came to the open door, but speedily retreated behind it. She seems about 14 or 15 years old, and bears a much greater resemblance to her brother Ned than either Mrs. Skillian or Miss Kate Kelly do. Most of the party, seeing that the girl was bashful, withdrew from the house, and then Grace made a statement to Mr. Longmore and one or two others to the effect that one of her brother Ned's last requests was that his sisters should make full statements as to how the police had treated them.

She then continued as follows:—'On one occasion Detective Ward threatened to shoot me if I did not tell him where my brothers were, and he pulled out his revolver. The police used to come here and pull the things about. Mr. Brook Smith was one of them. He used to chuck our milk, flour, and honey, on the floor. Once they pulled us in our night clothes out of bed. Sergeant Steele was one of that party.'

Mrs. Kelly further stated that when she 'came out' her children's clothes were rotten, because of their having been thrown out of doors by the police. The police, also, had destroyed a clock and a lot of pictures, and threatened to pull down the house over their heads. She was understood to make a statement to the effect that the police had made improper overtures to some of her daughters, but she afterwards said that she had no such charge to make.

Mr. Longmore and one or two others went into the sitting room, which was very poorly furnished, and the ceiling of which was in a very dilapidated condition. All the inside doors leading into this room were shut, and it seemed tolerably certain that the commission did not see all who were in the house.

A death in Forbes

On 18 October 1898, the Forbes newspaper carried a report of an inquest held at the pub. A 36-year-old local woman known as Ada Foster was dead. A young police constable gave his evidence:

I received information that the deceased had left her infant, five weeks old, without any person to care for it. I made diligent search to try and ascertain her whereabouts, but failed to find any trace; the infant and other three small children were taken care of by a neighbour; I communicated with her husband, and saw him on Saturday evening; I continued making search to find her whereabouts till yesterday about 12.30 when I was informed that the body was floating in the lagoon; in company with Constable Kennedy I proceeded town [sic] the lagoon down the Condobolin road, and at the rear of Ah Toy's residence, I there saw the body floating face downwards, about ten feet from the bank against a log; the lower portion of the back was bare, the clothes having fallen over the head; we removed the body from the lagoon and conveyed it to the Carlton Hotel . . .

The medical officer deposed:

*Y*esterday afternoon I made an examination of the body of the deceased; owing to the advanced stage of decomposition it was impossible to form any definite opinion as to the cause of death, or to recognise the presence of marks of violence; if the body was in the water seven or eight days it would present the appearance it did; I should think the body by its appearance had been laying in the water from four to eight days.

A neighbour gave evidence that Mrs Foster was 'slightly under the influence of drink' and asked her to look after her five-week-old infant 'as she wanted to go away for a couple of days to get straight'.

William Henry Foster, estranged husband of the deceased, had been in the marital home the day before his wife's disappearance. She 'was under the influence of drink', he said. He had 'frequently heard my wife threaten to commit suicide when under the influence of drink, especially since her sister did so'.

The verdict surprised nobody: 'found drowned in the lagoon on the Condobolin Road, on the 14th instant, but there was no evidence to show how deceased got into the water'.

A week or so later, a stranger drove into town in a dray to collect the three Foster children. His name was Jim, surviving brother of Ned. The woman who had come to such a miserable end in the Forbes lagoon was the famous Kate Kelly.

Known to the magazines of the day as 'the girl who helped Ned Kelly', Kate had been one of Australia's first teen celebrities. The momentous events of 1878–80 had thrust her into the local, colonial and national limelight. The press and the police had her down as one of the gang's main accomplices, secretly taking them food, clothes and ammunition and eliding the traps on wild goose chases miles from where the Kellys were hiding. Most of it was fiction; elder sister Maggie had done most of the aiding and abetting. But Kate was young, good looking and, like

198

all the Kellys, feisty. They followed her movements, quoted her statements and made the ill-educated young girl a star.

Her notorious brother was hanged at 10 a.m. on 11 November 1880. That night, Kate and brother Jim, together with Ettie, Steve Hart's sister and reputed sweetheart of Ned, appeared on stage at the Apollo Theatre:

> A disgraceful scene took place last night at the Apollo hall, where Kate Kelly and her brother James Kelly were exhibited by some speculators. They occupied arm-chairs upon the stage, and conversed with those present. The charge for admission was one shilling and several hundreds of persons paid for admission.

The show was reported in Sydney a couple of weeks later. The police, worried about the impact on the local larrikins, closed it down. Subsequently, Kate was reportedly giving displays of her riding skills and working in an Adelaide hotel as a kind of celebrity barmaid. The press tracked Kate for a while but then she disappeared.

We now know that she went to live and work in the Forbes district. She married local man 'Brickie' Foster in 1888 and became Mrs Ada Foster to the world. She is buried in the Forbes cemetery under her married name, though 'nee Kelly' appears in brackets immediately below on her gravestone.

Living legends

One of the many Kelly legends had it that Dan Kelly and Steve Hart did not burn to cinders in the Glenrowan Hotel, but instead escaped to South Africa. In Pretoria, during the Boer War, the correspondent to the *London Daily Express* met them.

*O*ne night, when Pretorians, under martial law regulations, had long retired to rest, I was aroused by a knock at the door. On opening it my acquaintance, now nervous and excited, walked in. 'I have brought them,' he whispered mysteriously. 'What's that?' I asked. 'The boys.' 'What boys?' 'Dan and Steve.' 'Oh! you mean the Kellys? Show them in,' I said, flippantly.

He scowled reprovingly. He went out, and quickly returned with a deputation of two men of middle age, athletic, keen-eyed, sunburnt, firm-featured, typical Australian bushmen, who evidently knew what roughing it meant. There was no necessity for introductions. It was quite true I had met or nodded to them a score of times before that night. I did not know them, however, as 'Dan Kelly' and 'Steve Hart.' They sat down, and made themselves at home.

'Now, which is Dan Kelly?' I asked. 'Here,' said the darker-complexioned of the two, 'but you must not say that name again.' And don't say mine, either,' said Steve Hart. 'What! Are you afraid?' 'Well, we don't want it known,' said Kelly. Then he added earnestly, 'You promise never to mention this?' 'But why did you come to me?' 'Well, he,' pointing to the acquaintance, 'persuaded us. Now you promise that, or by—' His voice was husky, and I interrupted, 'You needn't fear, for, in the first place, I have only your word for it and, in the second place, I have no ambition to court the anger of the Kellys.' 'Well, that's all right.'

A bottle was opened, pipes were filled, and long after midnight Dan Kelly, who had listened enthusiastically to stories of Ben Hall, Frank Gardiner, Gilbert, Burke, Vane, O'Meally, and other earlier Australian bushrangers, combed his bushy hair with his fingers, and said:—'I don't mind you using this if it's worth while, but not before, say, three weeks, and we're safe away. Steve and me and Ned and Joe Byrne was in that hotel all right. Ned got away, and we wus to follow him; but Joe was drunk, and we couldn't pull him together.

'When we wusn't watching, Joe walked outside and wus shot. After that two drunken coves was shot dead through the window.

They wanted to have a go at the police, so we gave them rifles, revolvers, and powder and shot. The firing where they fell wus too hot for Steve and me to reach them, so our rifles and revolvers wus found by their remains. This wus why they thought we wus dead. I'm sorry these coves didn't take my tip, and go out with a flag, but they had the drink and the devil in them. I think Joe's recklessness maddened them.

'Well, me and Steve planned an escape. We wus in a trap and had to get out of it. We had with us, as we often had, traps' [police] uniforms and troopers' caps, and we put them on. We looked policemen in disguise all right, I tell you. The next question was how to leave the pub quietly. A few trees, bushes, and logs at the back decided us. We crawled a few yards and then blazed away at the shanty just like the traps. We retreated slow from tree to tree and bush to bush, pretending to take cover. Yes, cover from Steve and me!

'Soon we wus among the scattered traps, who, no doubt, reckoned we wus cowards. But we banged away at the blooming pub, more than any of them. The traps came from 100 miles around, and only some know'd each other. So how could they tell us from themselves? We worked back into the timber, and got away. Soon afterwards we saw the pub blazing. Then we thanked our stars we wus not burnt alive. Well, we got to a shepherd's hut, and we stayed there days.

'The shepherd brought us the Melbourne papers, with pages about our terrible end—burnt-up bodies and all that sort of stuff. We heard of Ned's capture, and we wus both for taking to the bush again; but the shepherd made us promise to leave Australia. He found us clothes and money. We got to Sydney and shipped to the Argentine. We've had a fairly good time since, and ain't been interfered with. We don't want to interfere with anybody either.

'A few days ago we crossed to South Africa. The war broke out, and, not having work, we went to the front. We had some narrer escapes, but nothing like the narrer escape from that pub. We're off in an hour or so, but we don't want the world to know where. You can say what I told you, but wait three weeks or a month. Now, listen! If you give Steve and me away, this little thing in the hands of a friend of mine will blow you out'—and he put the point of his revolver almost into my eye. I looked at him sharply, and the awful glare in his eyes convinced me he meant it.

Six weeks later I was surprised to encounter Dan Kelly and Steve Hart in Adderley-street, Cape Town. Dan Kelly said: 'Well, you kept y'r promise. We haven't heard nothing. You may write what you like after to-morrow.'

I did not inquire their destination, and they did not volunteer the information.

The stranger

Over six foot tall and weighing thirteen and a half stone, Isaiah 'Wild' Wright was one of the most colourful of the Kelly country's many brawlers. A relative of the Kellys by marriage, he had a fine eye for a horse and had done time for stealing some. He was a prominent sympathiser; after the shootings at Stringybark Creek, Wright and his brother were locked up for publicly goading the police.

On Monday, two friends of the Kellys came into the township from Benalla, viz, Isaiah (or Wild) Wright and his brother, a deaf and dumb man. Isaiah Wright underwent imprisonment about a year ago for horse-stealing. He stated in the hotel bars that he meant to go out and join Kelly, and somewhat in bravo style warned one or two persons to stay in the township to-day unless they wanted to get shot. He said he believed Kelly would torture Kennedy, and he was only sorry for Scanlan. Though a good many of Wright's remarks only amounted to his customary bluster, yet the police thought it prudent to lock both brothers up. They were about the streets when the party started, and had their horses ready, so it was not improbable that one of them meant to ride straight off with news to Kelly. The arrest of 'Wild' Wright was made so hurriedly that he had no time to resist.

Imprisonment had no effect on Wright. He continued to intimidate and insult the police at every opportunity:

*T*here was considerable excitement in Mansfield last night, just as the people were going to church, occasioned by the freaks and threats of Wild Wright, a relative of the Kellys. A body of police, numbering about 13, including a black tracker, had just arrived, and some of them were standing at the corner of the street. Wright called them dogs, curs, and many other opprobrious names. He told them to follow him, and he would lead them to the Kellys, as he was going to join the gang. He was mounted on a good horse, and just keeping a short distance between himself and the police, he then asked the police to come out in the bush with him a little way and he would pot them. Four of the police made towards Wright, but he rode away out of their reach, and still threatened them if they would come a little distance out of the town. He said, 'All the f***ing police in Mansfield can't take me.'

Sub-Inspector Pewtress then ordered two troopers to mount and arrest him. They pursued him for about two miles, but Wright was too well mounted, and gave the troopers the slip on the Benalla road. This morning Mr. Pewtress has sent a constable with a summons to Wright's house for him to appear for using threatening language. It is to be hoped he will not be let off as easy as he was last time.

Later the same month, Wright was again reported in the Mansfield pub:

*I*n the bar parlour of the principal hotel in Mansfield, this evening, Wild Wright said he had heard that Donnelly had turned policeman, and gone out with the traps after Kelly adding, if he had, he was a b***dy dog, and deserved shooting for so turning round; thus in the most open manner avowing his sympathy with the Kelly mob.

Wright was among the first fourteen sympathisers to be arrested in January 1879. Although there was no evidence to hold them, under the provisions of the *Felon's Apprehension Act*, they were continually remanded every seven days and would not be released for over three months. During the proceedings, Wild Wright addressed Superintendent Hare in court:

*N*o wonder you blush; you ought to be ashamed of your self'; and then turning to the Bench, 'Your Worship said you give me fair play, but you are not giving me fair play now. I don't know how some of these men stand it.'

Mr Wyatt said that he had been misunderstood and misrepresented on the previous Saturday. What he had meant was that he would give Wright fair play, and thought it best to be remanded.

Wright remained defiant, threatening the magistrate with violence when he was remanded yet again. He was not released until April, and was the last to be freed:

*W*hen the Kelly sympathisers were brought up yesterday, and Superintendent Furnell asked for a further remand, Mr Foster said it was his duty to act independently, and to do that which to his conscience seemed just and legal, and he did not feel justified in granting a further remand; he should there-fore discharge the accused. The whole of the men were then formally discharged. Isaiah Wright was brought up last, when Mr Foster said:— 'Isaiah Wright, your fellow prisoners have been discharged, and I propose to discharge you also. Several weeks since you, when in that dock, were foolish enough and cowardly enough to threaten me—foolish, because what you said could but prejudice your position; a coward, because you attempted to intimidate me when simply doing my duty, and that a very unpleasant one. My acts were official ones, and done in the interest of society, and it was a cowardly thing to make them the subject of personal enmity. It has been a subject of serious reflection with me whether I ought not to place you under substantial bonds to keep the peace, but this would probably cause your return to gaol, where you have so long been; and, trusting that the words were uttered in the heat of the moment, and that there is no ulterior intention of wrong, I discharge you.' Wright said 'Thank you,' and left the court.

Wild Wright missed no further opportunity to harass the police, even across the border into New South Wales after the Kellys robbed the Jerilderie bank.

*W*ild Wright has been in Jerilderie since Monday and is still here. He has been locked up and fined 5s [5 shillings] for being drunk and disorderly. To-day he was behaving in a most disgraceful manner, calling out in the street, when there was no police within hearing, 'Hurrah for the Kellys.' He is accompanied by another man.

⌐

Wright was one of the most important of Kelly's people, assisting with the preparations for Glenrowan and narrowly avoiding being arrested in the aftermath as he passed 'hot words' with the police taking the wounded Ned away. He tried to convince the police to give up the charred remains of Dan Kelly and Steve Hart and helped out at their funerals. After becoming involved with the petition to save Kelly from execution, he returned to his horse-stealing ways for a while, serving a seven-year sentence for one such crime.

He turned up again at Hartwood during the shearers' strikes of the early 1890s, where according to the memories of Hugh Eastman, Wright approached him for a job of shearing. Eastman asked the well-mounted bushman a few questions:

'Shearing anywhere this year?'

'Shure, I never shore a sheep last year.'

'Where were you shearing last year? You say you are a shearer.'

'Shure, I never shore a sheep last year.'

'What have you been doing in your spare time?'

'I've been doing a lot of jail, I'm just after doing seven years for stealing a horse along with Jim Kelly.'* (Wild now provided some helpful advice. 'If you are ever short of a horse, shake it on your own, don't go with another man or you are sure to be lagged.')

'What is your name anyhow?'

'You know my name right enough.'

'No, you are a stranger to me.'

'Well, I'm not woild at 'art, but they call me Woild Wright.'

'The devil you are. I wish I'd known that before giving you the pen.'

'Ah sure, you will not find me woild at arl.'

(* Not the brother of Ned, another Jim Kelly)

Wild Wright won the job and turned out to be 'one of the best blade men' Eastman had come across in a lifetime of sheep farming. He was still a prodigious drinker and still a show-off. Once while working for Eastman, Wright leapt onto the bare back of his horse, galloped straight at the shearer's dining area then vaulted over the animal's head to land on his feet inside. He sat down calmly to take his meal. Still 'flash'.

Wright then went to the Riverina, continuing his wild ways.

He turned up at the home of another old Kelly country mate, 'Bricky' Williamson, in Coolamon (New South Wales) around 1901, then disappeared. He died, probably in the Northern Territory in 1911. Or perhaps, as Eastman records:

*Y*ears afterwards, in the back country, a derelict, all broken up, was buried by the police on the roadside where he fell—the end of a queer misfit.

10

The child in the bush

Captain Cook
Broke his hook
Fishing for Australia,
Captain Cook wrote a book
All about Australia.

Colonial children's rhyme

THE LIVES OF colonial children were sometimes as hard as those of their parents. Often left to themselves, children developed their own ways to entertain themselves based on the venerable traditions of playing improvised games of chasing, hiding and running. Where there were any toys, they were few in number and so storytelling and, for younger children, nursery rhymes were important ways to learn and be entertained. Sadly, children were also vulnerable to the dangers of pioneering the bush.

The beanstalk in the bush

In the era before film, radio and television, people needed to entertain themselves. Much of this took place within the family and usually involved playing parlour games like charades, singing together and telling stories. So-called 'fairy tales' were popular, both with adults and children, to whom they were often told at bedtime. This very early version of the classic story about the naïve boy and his magic bean was told to a child in Sydney around 1860. Like many 'fairy' tales, there are no fairies in it.

*T*here was once upon a time a poor widow who had an only son named Jack, and a cow named Milky-white. And all they had to live on was the milk the cow gave every morning, which they carried to the market and sold. But one morning Milky-white gave no milk, and they didn't know what to do.

'What shall we do, what shall we do?' said the widow, wringing her hands.

'Cheer up, mother, I'll go and get work somewhere,' said Jack.

'We've tried that before, and nobody would take you,' said his mother; 'we must sell Milky-white and with the money start a shop, or something.'

'All right, mother,' says Jack; 'it's market-day today, and I'll soon sell Milky-white, and then we'll see what we can do.'

So he took the cow's halter in his hand, and off he started. He hadn't gone far when he met a funny-looking old man, who said to him: 'Good morning, Jack.'

'Good morning to you,' said Jack, and wondered how he knew his name.

'Well, Jack, and where are you off to?' said the man.

'I'm going to market to sell our cow here.'

'Oh, you look the proper sort of chap to sell cows,' said the man; 'I wonder if you know how many beans make five.'

'Two in each hand and one in your mouth,' says Jack, as sharp as a needle.

'Right you are,' says the man, 'and here they are, the very beans themselves,' he went on, pulling out of his pocket a number of strange-looking beans. 'As you are so sharp,' says he, 'I don't mind doing a swop with you—your cow for these beans.'

'Go along,' says Jack; 'wouldn't you like it?'

'Ah! you don't know what these beans are,' said the man; 'if you plant them overnight, by morning they grow right up to the sky.'

'Really?' said Jack; 'you don't say so.'

'Yes, that is so, and if it doesn't turn out to be true you can have your cow back.'

'Right,' says Jack, and hands him over Milky-white's halter and pockets the beans.

Back goes Jack home, and as he hadn't gone very far it wasn't dusk by the time he got to his door.

'Back already, Jack?' said his mother; 'I see you haven't got Milky-white, so you've sold her. How much did you get for her?'

'You'll never guess, mother,' says Jack.

'No, you don't say so. Good boy! Five pounds, ten, fifteen, no, it can't be twenty.'

'I told you you couldn't guess. What do you say to these beans; they're magical, plant them overnight and—'

'What!' says Jack's mother, 'have you been such a fool, such a dolt, such an idiot, as to give away my Milky-white, the best milker in the parish, and prime beef to boot, for a set of paltry beans? Take that! Take that! Take that! And as for your precious beans here they go out of the window. And now off with you to bed. Not a sup shall you drink, and not a bite shall you swallow this very night.'

So Jack went upstairs to his little room in the attic, and sad and sorry he was, to be sure, as much for his mother's sake, as for the loss of his supper. At last he dropped off to sleep.

When he woke up, the room looked so funny. The sun was shining into part of it, and yet all the rest was quite dark and shady. So Jack jumped up and dressed himself and went to the window. And what do you think he saw? Why, the beans his mother had thrown out of the window into the garden had sprung up into a big beanstalk which went up and up and up till it reached the sky. So the man spoke truth after all.

The beanstalk grew up quite close past Jack's window, so all he had to do was to open it and give a jump on to the beanstalk which ran up just like a big ladder. So Jack climbed, and he climbed and he climbed and he climbed and he climbed and he climbed and he climbed till at last he reached the sky. And when he got there he found a long broad road going as straight as a dart. So he walked along and he walked along and he walked along till he came to a great big tall house, and on the doorstep there was a great big tall woman.

'Good morning, mum,' says Jack, quite polite-like. 'Could you be so kind as to give me some breakfast?' For he hadn't had anything to eat, you know, the night before and was as hungry as a hunter.

'It's breakfast you want, is it?' says the great big tall woman, 'it's breakfast you'll be if you don't move off from here. My man is an ogre and there's nothing he likes better than boys broiled on toast. You'd better be moving on or he'll soon be coming.'

'Oh! please, mum, do give me something to eat, mum. I've had nothing to eat since yesterday morning, really and truly, mum,' says Jack. 'I may as well be broiled as die of hunger.'

Well, the ogre's wife was not half so bad after all. So she took Jack into the kitchen, and gave him a hunk of bread and cheese and a jug of milk. But Jack hadn't half finished these when thump! thump! thump! the whole house began to tremble with the noise of someone coming.

'Goodness gracious me! It's my old man,' said the ogre's wife, 'what on earth shall I do? Come along quick and jump in here.' And she bundled Jack into the oven just as the ogre came in.

He was a big one, to be sure. At his belt he had three calves strung up by the heels, and he unhooked them and threw them down on the table and said:

'Here, wife, broil me a couple of these for breakfast. Ah! What's this I smell?

Fee-fi-fo-fum,
I smell the blood of an Englishman.

Be he alive, or be he dead,
I'll have his bones to grind my bread.'

'Nonsense, dear,' said his wife, 'you're dreaming. Or perhaps you smell the scraps of that little boy you liked so much for yesterday's dinner. Here, you go and have a wash and tidy up, and by the time you come back your breakfast'll be ready for you.'

So off the ogre went, and Jack was just going to jump out of the oven and run away when the woman told him not. 'Wait till he's asleep,' says she; 'he always has a doze after breakfast.'

Well, the ogre had his breakfast, and after that he goes to a big chest and takes out of it a couple of bags of gold, and down he sits and counts till at last his head began to nod and he began to snore till the whole house shook again.

Then Jack crept out on tiptoe from his oven, and as he was passing the ogre he took one of the bags of gold under his arm, and off he pelters till he came to the beanstalk, and then he threw down the bag of gold, which of course fell into his mother's garden, and then he climbed down and climbed down till at last he got home and told his mother and showed her the gold and said: 'Well, mother, wasn't I right about the beans? They are really magical, you see.'

So they lived on the bag of gold for some time, but at last they came to the end of it, and Jack made up his mind to try his luck once more up at the top of the beanstalk. So one fine morning he rose up early, and got on to the beanstalk, and he climbed and he climbed and he climbed and he climbed and he climbed and he climbed and he climbed till at last he came out on to the road again and up to the great big tall house he had been to before.

There, sure enough, was the great big tall woman a-standing on the doorstep.

'Good morning, mum,' says Jack, as bold as brass, 'could you be so good as to give me something to eat?'

'Go away, my boy,' said the big tall woman, 'or else my man will eat you up for breakfast. But aren't you the youngster who came here once before? Do you know, that very day, my man missed one of his bags of gold.'

'That's strange, mum,' said Jack, 'I dare say I could tell you something about that, but I'm so hungry I can't speak till I've had something to eat.'

Well, the big tall woman was so curious that she took him in and gave him something to eat. But he had scarcely begun munching it as slowly as he could when thump! thump! thump! they heard the giant's footstep, and his wife hid Jack away in the oven.

All happened as it did before. In came the ogre as he did before, said: 'Fee-fi-fo-fum,' and had his breakfast of three broiled oxen. Then he said: 'Wife, bring me the hen that lays the golden eggs.' So she brought it, and the ogre said: 'Lay,' and it laid an egg all of gold. And then the ogre began to nod his head, and to snore till the house shook.

Then Jack crept out of the oven on tiptoe and caught hold of the golden hen, and was off before you could say 'Jack Robinson'. But this time the hen gave a cackle which woke the ogre, and just as Jack got out of the house he heard him calling:

'Wife, wife, what have you done with my golden hen?'

And the wife said: 'Why, my dear?'

But that was all Jack heard, for he rushed off to the beanstalk and climbed down like a house on fire. And when he got home he showed his mother the wonderful hen, and said 'Lay' to it; and it laid a golden egg every time he said 'Lay.'

Well, Jack was not content, and it wasn't very long before he determined to have another try at his luck up there at the top of the beanstalk. So one fine morning, he rose up early, and got on to the beanstalk, and he climbed and he climbed and he climbed and he climbed till he got to the top. But this time he knew better than to go straight to the ogre's house. And when he got near it, he waited behind a bush till he saw the ogre's wife come out with a pail to get some water, and then he crept into the house and got into the copper. He hadn't been there long when he heard thump! thump! thump! as before, and in come the ogre and his wife.

'Fee-fi-fo-fum, I smell the blood of an Englishman,' cried out the ogre. 'I smell him, wife; I smell him.'

'Do you, my dearie?' says the ogre's wife. 'Then, if it's that little rogue that stole your gold and the hen that laid the golden eggs he's sure to have got into the oven.' And they both rushed to the oven. But Jack wasn't there, luckily, and the ogre's wife said: 'There you are again with your fee-fi-fo-fum. Why of course it's the boy you caught last night that I've just broiled for your breakfast. How forgetful I am, and how careless you are not to know the difference between live and dead after all these years.'

So the ogre sat down to the breakfast and ate it, but every now and then he would mutter: 'Well, I could have sworn—' and he'd get up and search the larder and the cupboards and everything, only, luckily, he didn't think of the copper.

After breakfast was over, the ogre called out, 'Wife, wife, bring me my golden harp.' So she brought it and put it on the table before him. Then he said: 'Sing!' and the golden harp sang most beautifully. And it went on singing till the ogre fell asleep, and commenced to snore like thunder.

Then Jack lifted up the copper-lid very quietly and got down like a mouse and crept on hands and knees till he came to the table, when up he crawled, caught hold of the golden harp and dashed with it towards the door. But the harp called out quite loud: 'Master! Master!' and the ogre woke up just in time to see Jack running off with his harp.

Jack ran as fast as he could, and the ogre came rushing after, and would soon have caught him only Jack had a start and dodged him a bit and knew where he was going. When he got to the beanstalk the ogre was not more than twenty yards away when suddenly he saw Jack disappear like, and when he came to the end of the road he saw Jack underneath climbing down for dear life. Well, the ogre didn't like trusting himself to such a ladder, and he stood and waited, so Jack got another start.

But just then the harp cried out: 'Master! Master!' and the ogre swung himself down on to the beanstalk, which shook with his weight. Down climbs Jack, and after him climbed the ogre. By this time Jack had climbed down and climbed down and climbed down till he was very nearly home. So he called out: 'Mother! Mother! bring me an axe, bring me an axe.' And his mother came rushing out with the axe in her hand, but when she came to the beanstalk she stood stock still with fright for there she saw the ogre with his legs just through the clouds.

But Jack jumped down and got hold of the axe and gave a chop at the beanstalk which cut it half in two. The ogre felt the beanstalk shake and quiver so he stopped to see what was the matter. Then Jack gave another chop with the axe, and the beanstalk was cut in two and began to topple over. Then the ogre fell down and broke his crown, and the beanstalk came toppling after.

Then Jack showed his mother his golden harp, and what with showing that and selling the golden eggs, Jack and his mother became very rich, and he married a great princess; and they lived happy ever after.

Forgotten nursery rhymes

Most of us associate nursery rhymes with faraway times and other countries. But in the nineteenth century and well into the twentieth, they continued to be an important part of growing up in Australia. There was a surge of interest in creating distinctively Australian rhymes and many writers as well as interested amateurs contributed their efforts to magazines and newspapers. Ethel Turner, author of the famed *Seven Little Australians*, came up with a number, including this one:

Have you seen the cat of Dorothy Lee?
The one she calls her Catty-Puss?
If she's proud of her pet, then what should I be?
I've got a duck-billed Platypus.

Some were dreadful, but many provide an insight into the times in which they were written.

A couple of efforts relate to the gold rushes:

Little Brown Betty lived under a pan,
And brewed good ale for digger-men.
Digger-men came every day,
And little Brown Betty went hopping away.

And:

Little Tommy Drew
Went to Wallaroo
To search for a mine.
He walked by the road
And found a big load,
And said, 'What a rich man am I.'

Not surprisingly for a country that owed much of its wealth to wool, many nationalistic nursery rhymes involved sheep:

The man from Mungundi was counting sheep;
He counted so many he went to sleep.
He counted by threes and he counted by twos,
The rams and the lambs and the wethers and ewes;
He counted a thousand, a hundred and ten—
And when he woke up he'd to count them again.

These simple rhymes could even be made to serve a political purpose, as in the 'Nursery rhyme for young squatters':

Baa baa squatter's sheep
Where is all the wool?
Lost by the floods and drought,
Save three bags full.
One for the mortgagee
And one for debts to meet;
And one for the greedy boys
Who rule Macquarie Street.

Sydney also featured in one or two ditties:

Johnny and Jane and Jack and Lou;
Butler's Stairs through Woolloomooloo;
Woolloomooloo, and 'cross the Domain,
Round the Block, and home again!
Heigh, ho! Tipsy toe,
Give us a kiss and away we go.

A more ambitious treatment of children's rhymes came from William Anderson Cawthorne, who provided an Australianised version of the classic 'Who Killed Cock Robin?'

Who killed Cockatoo?
I, said the Mawpawk,
With my tomahawk:
I killed Cockatoo.

Who saw him die?
I, said the Opossum,

From the gum-blossom:
I saw him die.

Who caught his blood?
I, said the Lark,
With this piece of bark:
I caught his blood.

Who'll make his shroud?
I, said the Eagle,
With my thread and needle:
I'll make his shroud.

Who'll be chief mourner?
I, said the Plover,
For I was his lover:
I'll be chief mourner.

Who'll dig his grave?
I, said the Wombat,
My nails for my spade:
I'll dig his grave.

Who'll say a prayer?
I, said the Magpie,
My best I will try:
I'll say a prayer.

Who'll bear him to his tomb?
I, said the Platypus,
On my back, gently, thus:
I'll bear him to his tomb.

Who'll be the parson?
I, said the Crow,
Solemn and slow:
I'll be the parson.

Who'll carry the link?
I, said the Macaw,
With my little paw:
I'll carry the link.

Who'll chant a psalm?
I, said the Black Swan,
I'll sing his death song:
I'll chant a psalm.

Who'll watch in the night?
I, said the Wild Dog,
As he crept from a log:
I'll watch in the night.

Who'll toll the bell?
I, said the Pelican,
Again and again:
I'll toll the bell.

Then droop'd every head,
And ceas'd every song,
As onward they sped,
All mournful along.

All join in a ring,
With wing linking wing,
And trilling and twittering,

Around the grave sing:

Alas! Cockatoo,
How low cost thou lie;
A long, sad adieu!
A fond parting sigh!

Not satisfied with one attempt, Cawthorne went on to pen a second instalment to the story:

Then came the Wild Cat,
And the bushy-tail Rat,
With a squeak and a mew;
While, in a hop,
Up came, with a pop,
The big Kangaroo.

The Quail, and the Rail,
Were there without fail;
And the pretty Blue Wren,
With master Emu,
And screeching Curlew,
From a beautiful glen.

And the bird of the Mound,
In Murray-scrub found,
With its eggs in a row;
And the Parrot with crest,
In a green and blue vest,
As grand as a beau.

And the Lyre Bird, grand,
That ne'er still will stand,

Came in on tip-toe.
And straw-colored Ibis,
Once worshipped with Isis,
Was present also.

And the Bronze-winged Pigeon,
And the roly fat Widgeon,
From hill and from dell;
And he that doth build
A bower well filled
With spangle and shell.

Then flying very fast,
Came Laughing Jackass,
Hoo hoo hoo! ha ha ha!
While he gobbled a snail,
And wagged his big tail!
Hoo hoo boo! ha ha ha!

And the Snake, sneaking sly
With his sharp glittering eye,
As he searches and pries;
And the Lizard with frill,
Like a soldier at drill,
That fights till he dies.

And the saucy Tom Tit,
With his pretty 'twit twit,'
And his tail in the air;
And the wary quick Snipe,
With a bill like a pipe,
Hopping hither and there.

O wicked Mawpawk!
We'll have you caught,
For the deed you have done;
We'll slyly creep
When you're fast asleep,
And break your bones ev'ry one.

'Yes, Yes,' said the Hawk,
And the bird that can talk,
'We'll strike off his head.'
'Ah, Ah,' said the Owl,
'By fish, flesh and fowl,
'We'll bang! shoot him dead.'

So they all flew away,
And still fly to this day,
O'er hill and o'er plain;
But he dives in the rushes,
And hides under bushes,
And they search but in vain.

Written in 1870, Cawthorne's verses reflect the Victorian fascination with death, though it reads rather morbidly today. By contrast, most of the forgotten nursery rhymes of Australia were just for fun:

Billy had a gum-boil
Which made poor Billy grumboil.
The doctor said: 'That's some boil!
And does your tummy rumboil?
It seems to me abnormoil;
You'd better try some warm oil.'

So Billy got some hot oil,
And boiled it in a bottoil,
And on his gum did rub oil—
Which ended Billy's trouboil!

And, perhaps an authentic children's ditty:

Captain Cook
Broke his hook
Fishing for Australia,
Captain Cook wrote a book
All about Australia.

The lost boys of Daylesford

One of Frederick McCubbin's many admired paintings is simply titled 'Lost'. Completed in 1907, it shows a young boy crying and alone in the bush. Lost children were one of settlers' great fears, which were frequently realised as children wandered off into unknown and near-impenetrable terrain, especially in wooded country. A sombre gravestone in Daylesford cemetery commemorates the sad tale of William Graham, aged six, his brother Thomas, aged four, and their friend, five-year-old Alfred Burman.

The three were out looking for lost goats along the Wombat Creek on 30 June 1867. When they did not come home, a search was mounted but had to be abandoned at darkness. The worst frost of the year fell overnight. The search resumed the next morning, and over the next two days, more than 100 searchers found nothing but two small footprints. Word spread and soon there were more than 100 mounted searchers and over 500 on foot. Next day all shops were closed and a public meeting raised over 70 pounds for a reward. The police officer in charge was Inspector Smith.

. . . he had telegraphed to every place where there were black trackers to have them sent on; and Mr. Joseph Parker said that he, so soon as the meeting was over, would start for [home] and bring with him in the morning two young men who in following up a trail were equal to any black trackers. These statements were received with much applause, as was one made by Captain O'Connell, that the Volunteer Fire Brigade had, prior to the public meeting, resolved on turning out on the morrow to a man and making a search.

Mr. Inspector Smith suggested that all who intended to join in the search should meet at the Specimen Hill works, the manager of which had, in case anyone might lose his way, offered to keep the engine whistle, which could be heard two miles, continually sounding for their guidance after nightfall. He also impressed on every volunteer the necessity of taking a little bread and wine with him, in case of discovering the lost ones, and cautioned those who found them against bringing them too suddenly into a heated room, and gave instructions for their treatment.

By 4 July the numbers hunting for the children swelled further, including 200 dogs. But heavy winter rain set in and made it impossible to find any trace of the boys. The local paper published a letter of thanks to the local community from the fathers of the boys.

*n*ow that the public excitement has partially subsided with regard to the 'Three Lost Boys', we beg to return our sincere and heartfelt thanks to the inhabitants of Daylesford and surrounding districts, for the great and praiseworthy search they have made for the recovery of the children.

None have been more astonished than we have been at the mighty phalanx of human aid, aye, and brute aid too, that have been engaged in this search, and although all efforts have been unsuccessful, the public sympathy evinced has been a source of great consolation to ourselves and the distressed mothers.

When we have returned home night after night to tell the same sad tale of our want of success; when we have recounted to them the deeds of endurance and energy, and the great sacrifice of time and money, this community have suffered, their tears have been dried, and we have all been satisfied with the assurance that all that human aid can do, has been done on this occasion.

We still trust and hope that with Divine aid the bodies of the children may yet be found ere long, not forgetting 'There is a Divinity that shapes our ends, rough hew then how we will'.

In conclusion, we beg again to tender our heartfelt thanks to the public for the zeal and energy evinced to restore us our lost children. Our prayer is that, no parents will ever have to mourn for the loss and death of their children in the wild bush of Australia.

Later in the month an inquest was held, finding that the children probably died of exposure on the first night. Almost two months later a settler's dog came home carrying a child's boot still clinging to the remains of a foot. The dog later found a human skull. They found the bodies next day. The younger children were inside a tree cavity and the older boy nearby.

*T*he party named then formed themselves into a search party, going abreast at a certain distance from each other. Proceeding in this way for a short distance, David Bryan, in jumping a log forming part of a fence, discovered some bones and clothes lying about, and exclaimed, 'Here they are!' His brother Ninian was next to him, but on the opposite side of the log. Starting to join his brother, he went round a large tree standing and forming a corner to two fences. On rounding it he found it hollow, and a glance disclosed to him the bodies of two of the children. He started back, and said to his brother, 'Oh, Mike, here they are.' The others were speedily attracted to the spot, and watch kept over the remains till the police, who were sent for, arrived, and took them in charge. The remains too surely evidenced that they had been gnawed by dogs.

A witness favoured the local newspaper with a description of the scene with the kind of grisly details beloved of the era:

*T*he locality where the remains of the children who were lost from Table-hill on Sunday, the 30th June last, were found, in situate about a mile and a half from Wheeler's sawmills on the Musk Creek. The bodies of the two children which were found in the hollow tree were when discovered in a state of fair preservation, considering the length of time which had elapsed since they were lost; but the remains of the third consisted only of a few bones and the skull. The two bodies in the hollow tree when found were lying closely cuddled together, as if the children had by the warmth afforded by each other endeavoured to ward off the bitter wintry cold. The younger child had been placed inside, and the elder and stronger one had lain down beside him on the outer side. The backs of both were turned to the entrance of the cavity.

Here they must have lain and perished of cold and starvation. The elder boy had his legs completely under the body of the younger, and his cap lay on the floor of the cavity; the younger boy had his cap placed before his face. It is probable that the body of the third boy was also in the tree, but had been dragged thence by dogs. There are marks of hair outside on the roots of the tree. The elder boy had boots on, the younger had none, but a laceup boot broken at the heel was lying in the interstice of the tree just over his head. In the cavity were two sticks which they had evidently used in their wanderings. When the body of the elder boy was placed in the coffin, as the corpse sank into the narrow shell, his right arm was pushed forward, and his hand fell over upon his breast, and his face became uppermost. This hand was white, plump, and apparently undecomposed, but the whole of his features were gone, and nothing remained but a ghastly skeleton outline, with the lower jaw detached and fallen. The face of the younger child was, however, in a state of preservation, but perfectly black. The members of both bodies were much attenuated.

As so often happened in these cases, the lost children were within reach of help. But the density of the bush and difficulty of the terrain meant that even 200 yards was too far:

The position of the tree is at the corner of an old cultivation paddock in which potatoes are now planted. It is melancholy to reflect that these unfortunate children should have reached so near help and succour and failed to find it. Had they proceeded 200 yards farther up the fence, they would have come upon the hut of M'Kay. It would seem they had reached this place at night, and finding their passage impeded by the brush fence, turned into the hollow tree, not wishing to lose sight of it, thinking that the dawn of morning would set them right. Thus they must have lain down to sleep their last sleep.

Daylesford closed for the funeral. The streets were lined with mourners paying their last respects to the children and their families. Over 800 people attended the burial. The three boys were laid in their grave as they had been found, with the elder boy lying over the two younger ones in a forlorn attempt to keep them warm.

The town raised a fine monument above the graves of William and Thomas Graham and their friend Alfred Burman. The families founded a scholarship at the Daylesford Primary School as a mark of appreciation for the help they had received from the local people; known as the Graham Dux, it has been awarded every year since 1889. In 2013 the Daylesford and District Historical Society had the monument refurbished, including regilding the more than 400 characters that tell one of Australia's saddest lost child tragedies.

Fairies in the paddock

The flower fairy of European literary tradition is not a natural fit with the strongly realistic traditions of the Australian bush. Nevertheless, from around the middle of the nineteenth century writers began to adapt the fragile flower fairy to the local environment. Some also borrowed stories and ideas from Aboriginal tradition, a practice that eventually produced some of the darker elements of Australian children's stories in the form of the 'Banksia Men' in the *Snugglepot and Cuddlepie* stories by May Gibbs.

Most writers of local fairy tales were women, one of them just sixteen when she published her *Fairytales from the Land of Wattle* in 1904. Olga Ernst (Waller) presented 'What the Jackass Said' (i.e. the Kookaburra), 'The Opossum's Jealousy', 'The Bunyip and the Wizard' and 'The Origin of the Wattle' as tales told by herself as an older child to younger children.

> They are offered here as tales told by a child to younger children in the hope they will not only amuse the young, but will also win the approval of those to whom a loving study of tree and flower, bird and insect, and the association of familiar elements of old-world fairy love with Australian surroundings, commend themselves.

Olga Ernst provided a heady mix of European river sprites, goblins, little red elves, ugly gnomes and mermaids swimming near the mouth of the Yarra, together with bunyips and giants thundering across mountain ranges. There are magic runes, charms and magic elixirs aplenty, along with the 'Wizard of the Roper River' and the 'Mermaid of the Gulf of Carpentaria'. At the end of this story the mermaid is married to the Bunyip by a beautiful fairy and a witch turns the dust elves into the willy-willies or small dust storms.

In later life, Olga turned to writing mainly philosophical fantasy works and nursery rhymes. *Songs from the Dandenongs* was published in 1939 under her married name of Waller. It brought together Aboriginal names for natural features with the rhythms of British nursery rhymes, with music by Jean M. Fraser. The notes accompanying the verses included Olga's regret that many of the Aboriginal names had been lost or changed to banal English versions. In effect, this modest self-published collection was a pioneering attempt to familiarise children with Indigenous languages and appreciation of the landscape. 'A Mountain Jingle' began with the verse in the familiar rhythm of 'London Bridge is Falling Down':

We stand on top of Mt Dandenong,
Dandenong, Dandenong,
We stand on top of Mt Dandenong
And this is what we see:
Old Beenak has his cloud-cap on,
Cloud-cap on, cloud-cap on,
Old Beenak has his cloud-cap on
With a rainbow for a feather!

And so the book continued with information about local Aboriginal legends and practices, animals, birds, geology, weather and so on. Olga even had a rhyme for the recently completed dam, which she referred to as 'the Silvan Lake', 'only called a "dam" by the grossly unpoetic'.

It seems unlikely that many parents would have taken up any of the heartfelt recreations to sing to their children in those days. Olga died in 1972 and is remembered today only by her descendants and a few literary scholars.

Surviving Black Jack

In August 1835, two emaciated English youths staggered into the tiny settlement at King George Sound. They were little more than skeletons and had almost lost the power of speech. But they were alive. When their health began to return they told their strange tale of shipwreck, piracy and bare survival.

James Newell and James Manning sailed from Sydney aboard the schooner *Defiance* in August 1833. She was loaded with supplies destined to feed the ragtag bands of sealers, escaped convicts and deserters who haunted the islands around the southwest, near modern-day Albany. According to their own account they were cast away the next month when the *Defiance* was wrecked on Cape Howe Island. With the captain, another man and 'a native woman', they escaped aboard a whaleboat, eventually landing on Kangaroo Island. Here they built a house for the captain and his Aboriginal wife and planted a garden. The remainder of the schooner's crew, another six men, sailed for Sydney in another of the wrecked schooner's boats but were never heard of again.

In September, two black men arrived at the island, one of them a man named Anderson, a notorious local ruffian who would come to be known as the pirate 'Black Jack'. The young men took passage with Anderson to his stronghold on Long Island where they were compelled to work for their keep. A couple of months later, the captain of *Defiance* arrived and accused James Manning of stealing money from him. The captain, enthusiastically assisted by Anderson, took over 41 shillings from Manning at gunpoint.

While the two James were being held captive and robbed

on Long Island, another group of desperates resident on the island kidnapped five Aboriginal women, murdering two of their husbands in the process. Another Aboriginal man tried to swim to the island to rescue his wife but was drowned.

Not surprisingly, the two youths continually asked Anderson to put them ashore on the mainland, but he always refused. In January 1834 another small boat arrived under the command of a man named Evanson Janson. James Manning, apparently still with means, paid Janson for a passage on his boat to King George Sound. Instead, he was landed on Middle Island where Anderson again stole money from him, 50 shillings in English coins and Spanish dollars.

Eventually, in June, Manning and Newell convinced Anderson to land them. He did so but provided them with no gunpowder for hunting their food. They started walking, living on shellfish and grass roots. More than two months later they arrived at King George Sound, where they were cared for by local Aborigines of the White Cockatoo, Murray and Willmen groups who:

> . . . nursed, fed, and almost carried them at times, when, from weakness, they were sinking under their sufferings. This is a return which could scarcely have been expected from savages, who have no doubt been exposed to repeated atrocities, such as we have related in a previous narrative. Indeed, to the acts of these white barbarians, we may now trace the loss of some valuable lives among the Europeans, and more especially that of Captain Barker, which took place within a short distance of the scene of these atrocities.

The Aboriginal people were rewarded with gifts of rice and flour, and the sway of law and order in that wild part of the coast was lamented by the journalist who wrote up the story:

The habits of the men left on the islands to the southward, by whaling, or sealing vessels, have long borne the character given them by Manning and Newell; it appears, therefore, deserving of some consideration by what means their practices can be checked, as future settlers in the neighbourhood of Port Lincoln will be made to expiate the crimes and outrages of these lawless assassins.

It would be quite a few years before the law did rule the waves in this part of the country. But, as elsewhere, settlement eventually tamed the vast plains, mountain ranges and savage coasts.

11

Larger than life

They're a weird mob.
Nino Culotta (John O'Grady), 1957

FOR A COUNTRY that tends to pull down tall poppies, we seem to have an awful lot of them. The varied and often surprising stories of these lives are colourful cameos of the past. While some of the lives mentioned here have been mostly forgotten, in some cases the things they did have lived on in everyday Australian life.

The famous book *They're a Weird Mob*, later a film, picked up humorously on this aspect of the national character and is recognised as a classic. Tossed off, it is said, as the result of a ten-pound bet, John O'Grady was himself something of a character. He died in 1981, but his casual classic has become part of the national biographical tradition that includes all sorts and all comers.

The fate of Captain Cadell

Francis Cadell was one of those colourful, slightly larger-than-life characters who populate our colonial history and folklore. Along with such identities as the scoundrel 'Bully' Hayes (who also features in Cadell's life story), the fabulist Louis de Rougemont and the amazing Calvert, the sea- and river-going Captain Cadell made a lasting impact on many parts of the continent, including Western Australia.

Born in Scotland in 1822, Cadell went to sea on an East Indiaman at the age of fourteen. By the time he was seventeen he had taken part in the so-called Opium Wars between Britain and China. He followed this early adventuring with a swashbuckling life that took in piracy, ship design, commanding naval engagements during the Maori Wars, exploring what is now the Northern Territory, gun running, pearling and the trade in human flesh known as 'blackbirding'.

His main claim to fame, though, was his almost single-handed creation of the Murray River paddle-steamer trade from the early 1850s. As with many other periods in Cadell's fortunate life, this one left him with a number of high-level allies who supported him in some of his less glorious subsequent careers.

Largely forgotten to the history books, Cadell's adventures regularly filled the pages of the newspapers during his tumultuous life. He was one of those aspirational, adventuring types often encountered in the Australian colonies, described by his biographer as one of 'those over-achieving British Empire-builders who litter the Victorian world like soldier ants on a forest floor—so competent, so dependable, so energetic and yet so relaxed about it all. They never seemed to doubt what they were doing as they walked into other people's countries and—outnumbered thousands to one—imposed British law and order, built railways and ports, made fortunes and went to church on Sundays.'

While Cadell may have broken more laws than he imposed and rarely seems to have stepped inside a church, he was one of these driven pioneers, if a decidedly ambivalent one.

One of the many dubious periods of Cadell's life involved him in the early days of the Western Australian pearling trade. He was another of the variously optimistic, crazed or desperate band of entrepreneurs who created that industry and, it seems, contributed to its unhappy record of human misery. As well as apparently mistreating his indentured labourers, Cadell was rumoured to be running barracoons, or slave markets, on islands off the Western Australian coast.

Cadell had the knack of allying himself with unsavoury partners while managing to remain more or less respectable. Certainly the fame he earned from his pioneering of the Murray paddle-steam trade—which materially assisted the development of South Australia, Victoria and New South Wales—convinced many to give him the benefit of the doubt throughout his numerous escapades.

During his Western Australian troubles, Sir Dominic Daly, the ex-governor of South Australia, fortuitously turned up in Perth. His friendship with the mariner apparently provided sufficient establishment influence to defuse the very strong interest the authorities were showing in Cadell's pearling activities.

But despite his friends in high places, his lovable rogue personality and his acumen, Cadell met an untimely and mysterious fate in what are now Indonesian waters. Ever the entrepreneur, he was pursuing another of his business schemes and pushed his crew just a little too hard. The boat returned without its captain and Francis Cadell was never seen again.

The Fenian

On 10 January 1868, an Irish political prisoner and Fenian named John Boyle O'Reilly was marched into Fremantle Prison. O'Reilly had been guilty of little active subversion, though he had plotted much. Following a brief career as a journalist, in 1863 he enlisted as a trooper in the 10th Hussars, then headquartered in Dublin. He was recruited to the clandestine Irish Republican Brotherhood (IRB, also known as the Fenians), a forerunner of the modern Irish Republican Army (IRA), in 1865. Participating in the preparations for a planned rising that never took place, O'Reilly was arrested along with most of his co-conspirators in February 1866. After a trial he was sentenced to death by firing squad, but had this sentence commuted to twenty years' penal servitude. With 61 other Fenians, O'Reilly was transported to Western Australia aboard the *Hougoumont* in October 1867.

Sixteen of these men, plus O'Reilly himself, had been members of the British army and were segregated from the civilian Fenians and the common convicts. When advance news of this Irish 'weight of woe' reached the colony, segments of the Swan River community went into panic, fearing that the dreaded Irish, especially those with military training, would murder them in their beds. The fear was especially high in Fremantle, where the Fenians would be held. So great was the consternation, heightened by threats from some quarters to prevent the Fenians disembarking, that the disciplinarian Governor Hampton had his residence moved from distant Perth to Fremantle in an effort to calm the more excitable colonists.

When they did arrive, the entire complement of convicts and Fenians was disembarked at dawn, and marched in chains through Fremantle's forbidding limestone prison. They then underwent the same initiation into servitude as all other prison inmates: each was bathed, cropped, barbered and examined by a doctor, and their physical and personal details were recorded. They were then issued with the regulation summer clothing: cap, grey jacket, vest, two cotton shirts, one flannel shirt, two handkerchiefs, two pairs of trousers, two pairs of socks and a pair of boots.

O'Reilly and his companions were now 'probationary convicts'. If they behaved themselves for the remaining half of their sentence, they could be granted a ticket of leave, a dispensation allowing them to live and work much as any free colonist as long as they reported regularly to the magistrate.

Like most other transports, John Boyle O'Reilly the revolutionary was soon sent to work on the road-making around Bunbury from March 1868. There were over 3220 convicts in the colony at this time, though only a hundred or so on the road gangs in the Bunbury area. Later in his life O'Reilly would publish a classic novel, *Moondyne*, based on his experiences in this part of Western Australia. He dedicated this work to 'the interests of humanity, to the prisoner, whoever and wherever he may be'.

In the novel itself, O'Reilly provides some evocative details of the conditions. He begins by describing the bush and the work of the free sawyers:

During the midday heat not a bird stirred among the mahogany and gum trees. On the flat tops of the low banksia the round heads of the white cockatoos could be seen in thousands, motionless as the trees themselves. Not a parrot had the vim to scream. The chirping insects were silent. Not a snake had courage to rustle his hard skin against the hot and dead bush-grass. The bright-eyed iguanas were in their holes. The mahogany sawyers had left their logs and were sleeping in the cool sand of their pits. Even the travelling ants had halted on their wonderful roads, and sought the shade of a bramble.

He then goes on to contrast this with the lot of himself and the other convict toilers:

All free things were at rest; but the penetrating click of the axe, heard far through the bush, and now and again a harsh word of command, told that it was a land of bondmen.

From daylight to dark, through the hot noon as steadily as in the cool evening, the convicts were at work on the roads—the weary work that has no wages, no promotion, no incitement, no variation for good or bad, except stripes for the laggard.

Moondyne was written in the light of freedom, but it echoed some of the verse in which the unhappy O'Reilly cried out his fears and those of all transported to the Swan River colony:

Have I no future left me?
Is there no struggling ray
From the sun of my life outshining
Down on my darksome way?

Will there no gleam of sunshine
Cast o'er my path its light?
Will there no star of hope rise
Out of this gloom of night?

The light did shine for O'Reilly. The politics surrounding his fate and that of his rebellious companions was a cause célèbre of the time, resonating with the more romanticised aspects of the Irish struggle against English oppression. The correspondence files of the Colonial Office during this period are full of letters from respectable members of the British middle classes urging the release or pardoning of the Fenians, and there was also a considerable amount of correspondence relating particularly to O'Reilly's case. As well as these official representations, there were more clandestine plots in effect.

In early March 1869, the Fenian transportee was whisked away to freedom in the not-so-United States of America by a Yankee whaler. His rescue—an early example of globalisation—had been carefully plotted by the free Irish community in Western Australia, in league with elements of the Catholic Church, the American Irish community and its sympathisers. O'Reilly celebrated his 25th birthday in the middle of the Indian Ocean on his secret voyage back to England from where, under the noses of those authorities who badly wanted to capture him, he made his way to America, freedom and a promising future. In America he was influential in plans to free the Fenians remaining in Western Australia five years later. At Easter 1874, O'Reilly's six Fenian companions were rescued from bondage by an American whaler, the *Catalpa*, and taken to safety in the United States.

O'Reilly went on to a glittering journalistic and political career in America. He remained deeply involved in Irish patriotic activities and is remembered in that country, in Australia and in the country of his birth as an outstanding patriot.

The last bushranger

Jack Bradshaw, self-styled 'last of the bushrangers', was a spieler, or con man, who led a colourful life of crime, repentance and self-publicising that would not shame a modern marketing executive. He arrived in Australia from Ireland at the age of fourteen in 1860 and found work in the bush. He also worked as a petty trickster with a crook known as 'Professor Bruce', whose specialisation was reading people's heads and telling them amazing but true things about their character. This scam involved Jack arriving in town and finding out about the locals then slipping back to Bruce after a couple of days with the information. Bruce then entered the town in a flamboyant manner promising to reveal all—for a reasonable consideration.

Jack moved on to horse stealing with an accomplice endearingly named 'Lovely Riley'. But his real ambition was to rob a bank. He and Riley attacked the Coolah bank in 1876; they got the manager to open the safe but just as they began to rifle through its contents, the manager's pregnant wife came in. She gave the desperadoes a piece of her mind and they turned tail and fled, empty-handed.

Finally, at Quirindi in 1880, Jack realised his ambition and, once more in company with 'Lovely Riley', successfully robbed the bank of 2000 pounds. Escaping to New England, Riley's loose lips gave the game away and Jack decamped hurriedly to Armidale. Here, under a false name, he met, wooed and married the daughter of a wealthy squatter but was soon after unmasked and arrested. Fortunately, there was no bloodshed and he received a twelve-year sentence but was out again by 1888 and returned to his surprisingly amenable wife. Then, caught stealing mail, Jack went back to prison until 1901.

Inside, Jack saw the light and used the time to educate himself. When he got out he took up writing and lecturing about his highly glorified exploits. His first book, *Highway Robbery Under Arms*, told the story of the Quirindi robbery and was followed with several more, often overlapping titles that purported to tell the true stories of his relationships with many infamous bushrangers. Jack had made good use of his experience with Professor Bruce through all his years in prison, picking up inside knowledge of other criminals and their doings, real or not. He spun these into yarns that gave him a basic, if unreliable, living.

In 1928, the now ageing bushranger became a boarder in Phillipine Humphrey's grandmother's home. Phillipine recalled, 'He was the gentlest old man you could ever meet by then. He told lots of interesting stories and taught me many Irish songs.' Four years later, Jack moved to St Joseph's Little Sisters of the Poor Home in Randwick, New South Wales; Phillipine and her grandmother often visited Jack here, and he often said that the younger woman reminded him of his own daughter.

Jack died in 1937 at the age of 90 and was buried at Rookwood Cemetery in an unmarked grave, which has since been graced with a tombstone.

Lawson's people

People loved Henry Lawson not in spite of his failings and afflictions, but because of them. He was an extreme version of themselves, always struggling to make ends meet, battling the creature, looking for work, supporting—or not—a family. Forever striving and usually failing, just as they were, Henry Lawson's life was larger than their own but still essentially the same. His writing was infused with his life, and with theirs. 'My people', he called them.

The rugged contours of Henry Lawson's life began in 1867. Born to Peter and Louisa in Grenfell, New South Wales, he grew up in goldfields camps and bush huts, receiving an indifferent education, and from a young age was seen as an outsider. He did not mix well, was not good at physical activities, and was partly deaf. His schoolmates called him 'barmy Henry' and shunned him, as he ignored them in return.

Peter and Louisa's troubled marriage faded away in the late 1870s and Louisa moved to Sydney, where she eventually established a career as a writer and pioneer feminist. After working with his father on Blue Mountains building contracts, Henry joined his mother and siblings in 1883. He was apprenticed for some years as a coach painter. Aware of his educational failings, he studied at night school and twice attempted to matriculate, unsuccessfully, to Sydney University. Encouraged, if distantly, by his forbidding mother, Henry became interested in writing and slowly began to achieve some success. In 1887 he had his first piece, 'A Song of the Republic', accepted by the literary magazine *The Bulletin*. In the next few years some of his most popular verses appeared, including 'Faces in the Street' and 'Andy's Gone With Cattle'.

His fame grew and he published more and more verse, articles and later, short stories, the form in which he truly excelled. But his need to earn a living and to pay for his worsening addiction to alcohol meant that he needed to devote time and energy to finding work, time that took away from writing. In 1892, *The Bulletin* subsidised a trip to the drought-stricken regions of western New South Wales. He carried his swag for months, returning with the material that he would mine for the rest of his creative life. In the short term, the trip produced the classic stories 'The Bush Undertaker' and 'The Union Buries its Dead', among others. Four years later, his first important collection of stories, *While the Billy Boils*, was published, as was his verse collection, *In the Days When the World Was Wide*.

That same year he married Bertha Bredt. Family life began romantically, with a trip to Western Australia to dig for gold, but they only made it to Perth. Henry did some writing, house painting and other work but they were unable to make a go of it. Fed up with living in a tent, Bertha and Henry returned to Sydney where he soon took up again with his old mates and his old ways. Next year there was a futile trip to New Zealand where the family lived in deep isolation, teaching at a bush school. Once again, there was no alternative but to go home again. Through all this, Henry wrote, often drank and always struggled to make ends meet, particularly as children began being born. By 1898 his drinking had become so serious that he had to be institutionally 'dried out'. The treatment was successful and Henry remained sober for some years.

To say that Henry Lawson went to Britain would be inaccurate; he did take his family to London, but spent several years there without leaving the city. He succeeded in having a number of books published or re-published in Britain, but the event was a literary dead end. It also marked the effective end of his marriage. The return of his manic drinking, mood swings and frequent destitution were beyond even Bertha's toleration. She had her own serious mental problems requiring extended hospitalisation, and Henry's health also declined. In 1902, the family returned to Australia via Fremantle, where Bertha left Henry drinking and took the children home to Sydney. From that point Henry and his family were effectively estranged and he pursued his personal journey to hell, accompanied by the grog, madness, poverty, imprisonment and never-ending sponging off friends and colleagues.

With his marriage disintegrating, Henry tried to kill himself in December 1902. His drinking and inability to pay family support landed him in Darlinghurst Gaol on several occasions, accompanied by stints at the attached asylum, and there were a number of unsuccessful attempts to settle him in the country. Habitually drunk, impoverished and depressed, Lawson became a familiar pathetic figure on the streets of Sydney, cared for mainly by his long-suffering housekeeper Mrs Byers.

By 1916 Henry's loyal mates had become desperate and tried once again to save his life and the precious gift he had squandered so casually. A group of them gathered in the office of Labor Premier Holman. Led by F.J. Archibald, editor of *The Bulletin* and one of Henry's most loyal supporters and patrons, they discussed the need to save Lawson from himself, preferably by getting him away from the soaks of the city. There was the possibility of a pension, though this was difficult in an era before governments were expected to support the sick and elderly. Someone suggested that a better approach would be to give the writer a paid job of some kind. Why not post him to the recently initiated Murrumbidgee Irrigation Areas? He could have a regular wage and a cottage to live in, and in return would write verse and stories promoting the great experimental water dream. Best of all, the MIA was officially a 'dry' region in which alcohol was prohibited.

Henry Lawson's friends agreed and so the once passionate firebrand poet became a salaried bureaucrat of the New South Wales government service. Being Henry Lawson, though, it was not likely his career would proceed like that of any other public servant.

The Murrumbidgee Irrigation Areas scheme was the culmination of decades of water dreaming. As the early settlers and explorers confirmed the aridity of the vast continent they had colonised, the need for reliable water became a vital concern. In New South Wales, various ideas had been proposed and a Royal Commission recommended large-scale irrigation drawing on the Darling and Murrumbidgee rivers. It was the beginning of the troubles with the Murray-Darling basin waters that beset us still, but at the time it was a revolution given further urgency by the devastating 'Federation drought' from the mid-1890s. Construction of the Burrinjuck Dam began in 1906 and five years later the canals began to go in. The new towns of Leeton and Griffith were established and an official 'Turning on the Water' ceremony opened the scheme in 1912. The 'Area', as it was then known, was only a few years old when Henry's mates organised him into a cosy sinecure at Yanco, near Leeton.

Henry generally worked hard during his Leeton period. He and Mrs Byers shared a cottage provided by the Commission, probably the only dwelling he could even briefly call 'home' since childhood. He caught up with a few old mates from his swag days, all now settlers in the Area, and improved his health by working in the garden of his cottage. As well as his government post, he was receiving income from his other writing, from a successful stage adaptation of *In the Days When the World Was Wide*, and from several other occasional sources. But being Henry, he soon managed to establish a local supply of the supposedly unobtainable grog and returned to the bad old habits.

Between bouts of inebriation, depression and incapacity—together with many dashes by train back to Sydney for 'business'—Henry nevertheless managed to carry out a great deal of literary work, including rewriting and editing upcoming publications and composing new material. Some of this material was obedient to his brief of promoting the attractions of irrigation areas to sorely needed new settlers; some was of a more general nature or his response to the usually grim news of the war taking tens of thousands of Australian lives at the other end of the world. His plan was to first publish the poems and yarns in *The Bulletin* and anywhere else he could and then to write a great book, probably to be called *By the Banks of the Murrumbidgee*.

But life and the grog got in the way. Soon after his Yanco appointment came to an end his physical and mental condition began to deteriorate. He spent more time in asylums and hospitals and no more was heard of the Yanco book during these last grim years. His literary output drained away with his life force. He was hospitalised with a cerebral haemorrhage and although he recovered, it was to be only a few months before the inevitable.

On 4 September 1922, they sent Henry off in style with a state funeral, one of the largest in Sydney's history. The streets were so thronged with mourners that many of his old mates were unable to make it to the cemetery and were forced to stop at various pubs along the way to raise a glass or two to his memory. Henry would have been greatly amused by this and might even have spun it into a good yarn.

The Coo-ee Lady

One of the first words early settlers learned from Aboriginal people was 'cow-wee'. It was used in the Dharuk language around the Port Jackson area as a call to bring the community together. Later, other Aboriginal groups were heard using similar cries for the same purpose. Before very long, the drawn-out 'coo', followed by a high leap of the voice register to 'ee', rapidly became a widespread way to navigate the bush, find lost settlers and generally let anyone know you were around. By the 1840s it was said that visiting Australians would 'cooee' each other along the streets of London, hoping to find their way through the bustle and the fog, much to the bewilderment of the British.

So closely associated with Australia did the call become that it began to be used in popular literature. Even Arthur Conan Doyle had Sherlock Holmes solve a case through the great detective's knowledge of the call. In Australia, writers and poets featured 'cooee' and it became a popular subject for songs in the latter part of the nineteenth century. There was even a book titled *Coo-ee: Tales of Australian Life by Australian Ladies*. As national consciousness grew around the time of Federation, products of all kinds began to be branded with characteristically Australian names. It was possible to buy 'Coo-ee' wine, bacon and galvanised iron, among other items. Visiting or returning dignitaries such as Dame Nellie Melba were often greeted by cooeeing crowds. By the early twentieth century, the cooee was well established as a unique and characteristically Australian sound.

In 1907, an unhappy housewife in the dry dustiness of Kalgoorlie had a light-bulb moment. Maude Wordsworth James was in her early fifties when inspiration struck.

Most of Maude's childhood had been spent in Victoria with her English parents, Thomas and Alicia Crabbe. She married Charles James, a civil engineer, in 1875 and began a family. Charles took a job in Kalgoorlie in 1896 and the following year Maude and the children joined him but, used to the greener regions of Victoria, Maude was not happy in the west. She describes the country she experienced on her way to the golden city: 'After leaving Coolgardie, we continued on our journey over the same sort of country, through which we had come—only the farther we went, the redder the dust, and the drearier it all seemed.' She did come to appreciate the wildflowers and sunsets of the golden west but remained uneasy with her life in the dry and dusty land. Like most housewives of the time, though, she accepted her lot and busied herself with her home, garden and community life.

One night in 1907, her husband Charles, now the town surveyor, came home from work depressed about money. Maude lay awake wondering how she could make a lot of money very quickly. She wrote in her journal: 'Just as the dawn was breaking, an idea came to me that immediately arrested my attention.' Her idea—'entirely my own'—was that 'Australia has no Souvenir'. She was familiar with Tasmania's souvenir brooches in the form of gold maps of the state and the various other items produced by other states, all featuring native animals or plants. But Maude wanted a souvenir that would symbolise the whole country, and came up with the intention of 'making a fortune out of my favourite Australian word, "coo-ee"'.

From that day, Maude became the Coo-ee Lady, single-mindedly pursuing her idea of an all-Australian souvenir. She began designing, manufacturing and distributing a line of jewellery featuring distinctively Australian motifs, including the Aboriginal rainbow serpent, fashioned only from Australian gold, Kangaroo Island tourmaline, Broome pearls and Queensland opals. Her 'Coo-ee jewellery' began with brooches, cuff links, tie pins, bracelets and spoons, but Maude didn't stop there. She registered 'Coo-ee' as a trademark and patented her designs not only in Australia but also in New Zealand and in Britain. The *Australian Official Journal of Trade Marks* for 1907 shows there was little that Maude could not coo-ee-fy. It includes registrations for pendants, hat and scarf pins, earrings, photograph frames, hair combs, trinkets, pen handles, serviette rings, buttons, sleeve links, boxes, paper knives, scent bottles, blotters, bells, knockers, bangles, rings, parasol handles and even 'wishbones'. She began writing Coo-ee songs, ran Coo-ee competitions and expanded her wares to include chinaware and pottery. There was even a 'Coo-ee Calendar'.

Maude became completely obsessed with her empire and made a good deal of money, just as she had planned. Her most peculiar enterprise was the 'Coo-ee Corner'. Every Australian home would have one. It would be crammed with Maude's creations and would have a specially designed 'Coo-ee clock', an Australian version of the cuckoo clock. Every half-hour and hour the figure of an Aboriginal man waving a boomerang would pop out and call—you guessed it.

Maude came to think of the word as her private property. When a Heidelberg soldiers' welfare group made commemorative cooee medallions in 1916 she tried to claim royalties. But while it was possible to register designs using the word 'coo-ee', as Maude had astutely done, it was not legally possible to privately own the word itself because it was considered part of the national language: if you 'can't get/come within cooee' of something, then you're nowhere near or simply cannot hear it. They use the term in much the same way in New Zealand.

Maude left Kalgoorlie behind and moved to South Australia in 1908. During World War I she continued her 'Coo-ee' campaigns and even turned out a patriotic song on the theme. She lived in England for two years during the 1920s, then at Mosman in Sydney until 1931. That year she returned to South Australia and her son, Lieutenant Colonel Tristram James, came to live with her. Maude Wordsworth James died a widow at North Adelaide in 1936.

Australia's first Hollywood star

While most of us probably think of Errol Flynn as our first Hollywood export, he arrived there many years after a number of Australians who went to Hollywood in its very early years, including Louise Lovely (Louise Carbasse), Clyde Cook (The Kangaroo Boy) and the athletic stuntman Snowy Baker. American performers and crew also worked in Australia during the early years of our own industry.

But it was a South Australian railway worker's son who got there first. John Paterson McGowan (1880–1952) was Australia's first Hollywood star. In this country he is unknown rather than forgotten, but he is remembered in America as one of the pioneers of the movie industry.

Born in the South Australian railway town of Terowie in 1880, J.P. McGowan, or Jack as he liked to be known, had an average working-class childhood in Adelaide and Sydney. His father worked on the railways, a background that served McGowan so well that he became known in Hollywood as 'The Railroad Man'.

Before reaching the infant Hollywood of 1913, McGowan had many adventures that made him well suited for the various roles he would play in the cinema. He went to sea at seventeen and later worked as a stockman, becoming an expert horseman and sharpshooter. He won medals in the Boer War and then left Australia for the 1904 World's Fair in St Louis as part of a spectacular recreation of the South African conflict. For the next few years he acted in travelling theatrical troupes until employed by the Hollywood film studio Kalem Company, a buzzing whirl of enthusiastic amateurs keen to see what the developing technology of the silent screen could do. There was no union, no safety standards and no industry organisations; people just went there and made films.

McGowan was over six foot tall and strongly built, was handy with horses and guns, and could act at least as well as anyone else in those early years. His versatility as actor, director, writer, producer and occasional stunt man would result in over 600 productions in which he had one or several hands.

He began, as did just about everyone else in the business, with westerns. At that time the trend was for serials, which were churned out much like modern TV soaps. Some of McGowan's early titles were *The Railroad Raiders of '62*, *A Prisoner of Mexico* and *Captain Rivera's Reward*. As his career progressed he was involved in *The Bandit's Child*, *Whispering Smith* and *Medicine Bend*, among a slew of other stories about Ireland, ancient Egypt, pirates and espionage.

But it was in films about railroads, as the Americans call them, where he made his most celebrated contributions. He created many films on this theme, including *Fast Freight* and *The Express Car Mystery*. He also directed a 25-year-old John Wayne in *Hurricane Express*, an early role in which Wayne learned the skills that later propelled him to stardom.

Between 1914 and 1915 McGowan was strongly involved in many of the 119 episodes of *The Hazards of Helen* series, starring Helen Holmes, then McGowan's wife. Together they have a place in Hollywood history as the creators of the iconic scene in which the wicked villain ties the damsel to the train track; the episode was, of course, titled *The Death Train*.

The Australian continued his multi-skilled involvement in movie-making as actor, director, producer or writer—frequently more than one of these at a time. He also continued to be strong on westerns, with occasional productions of South Seas adventures, spy flicks and even a dog story. Later he developed a role in Hollywood industrial relations and eventually became Executive Secretary of the Hollywood Screen Directors Guild. The Guild recognised his service to the motion picture industry in 1950 with an Honorary Life Membership, together with such eminent Hollywood pioneers as D.W. Griffith, Walt Disney and Charlie Chaplin. No other Australian has attained this film industry acclaim.

A vision splendid

Kingsley Fairbridge was born in South Africa in 1885 and from the age of eleven was brought up in Rhodesia (now Zimbabwe). During a visit to England in 1903, he was deeply disturbed by the extent and depth of poverty in the industrial cities and especially horrified at the wasted human resources of children born into such poverty. He returned to Rhodesia a year later determined to do something to help these children, developing a vision that would initiate the Child Emigration Society, later the Fairbridge

Society, and lead to the establishment of settlements for orphaned and unwanted children in Rhodesia, New Zealand, Canada and Australia. The scheme that Fairbridge and his collaborators constructed was based on what he called his 'Vision Splendid':

> I saw great Colleges of Agriculture (not workhouses) springing up in every man-hungry corner of the Empire. I saw children shedding the bondage of bitter circumstances and stretching their legs and minds amid the thousand interests of the farm. I saw waste turned to providence, the waste of un-needed humanity converted to the husbandry of unpeopled acres.

To realise this vision, Fairbridge determined that he needed to become a Rhodes Scholar to provide himself with the education and contacts he correctly believed necessary to achieving his aims. After four attempts (his primary and secondary education had been sporadic) he became the first South African to be successful in winning this demanding scholarship and returned to England to study at Oxford University.

On 19 October 1909, Rhodes Scholar Kingsley Fairbridge addressed a meeting of 49 fellow undergraduates at the Colonial Club, Oxford, on the subject of child emigration. The government of Western Australia made an offer of land and in 1912 Kingsley and his wife established the first Farm School (now Fairbridge Village) at a site south of Pinjarra, receiving the first thirteen orphans from Britain in January 1913. In 1920, the school was relocated to its current site north of Pinjarra.

Although Kingsley Fairbridge died in 1924 at the age of 39, his 'Vision Splendid' lived on in England, Rhodesia, New Zealand, Canada, elsewhere in Australia and, most persistently, in Western Australia. In 1937, a farm school was founded at Molong, New South Wales, and another at Bacchus Marsh, Victoria. Two smaller schools were also established at Draper's Hall, Adelaide and Tresca,

Tasmania in the 1950s. Canadian schools were established in 1935 and 1938. Today Fairbridge Village in Pinjarra is the last surviving intact Fairbridge operation with an important historical role in regional, state, national and international affairs in relation to migration, welfare and community development.

The schools were generally modelled on similar lines, with a number of cottages or cabins grouped into small settlements within a working farm, catering for children between six and fifteen. Each dwelling had a 'cottage mother' and the boys were trained in agricultural work skills while the girls were trained in domestic skills, their labour also producing most of their food. Food, worship, education and health care were communally provided. The scheme also provided preschool care for those under six, who were looked after in England until old enough to emigrate. After children left the schools there was also an after-care operation catering for individuals up to the age of 21.

This arrangement lasted until after World War II when, in response to changing circumstances in the Dominions and in Britain, ongoing administrative and managerial changes were made. Throughout these changes, Fairbridge farm schools continued to send considerable numbers of boys and girls to their various operations. From the 1960s, changing attitudes to welfare and immigration, new arrangements for child welfare and a decreasing demand for agricultural skills increasingly rendered Kingsley Fairbridge's basic scheme unviable.

At this time the 'One-Parent' and 'Two-Parent' schemes were introduced to cater for the increasing numbers of children still in a parental relationship of some kind. These were effectively family reunion operations in which the Village would take the child or children into care and the single parent, in the case of the One-Parent scheme, would be found employment and accommodation in the same state. The Two-Parent version operated for families of five or more children where both parents were still in the family relationship. In this case the Village looked after the children but took no responsibility for finding employment and accommodation for the parents. The desired result of these arrangements was that families under threat of splitting could be assisted long enough for the parents to establish a home, at which time the child or children could be returned to them.

Despite these innovations, the era of child migration had long ended and the Fairbridge farm schools gradually closed down or were repurposed. In 1981, the last of the operations, Fairbridge Village at Pinjarra, ceased to operate as a farm school. In 1983, the current Fairbridge Western Australia Inc. was established, achieving charitable status in 1996. The Village is now a non-profit charitable youth organisation and location for the popular Fairbridge music festival, among other activities.

The extensive folklore of Fairbridge farm schools includes parodic ditties made up by the children who resided there over the years. To the tune of the hymn 'There is a Golden Land', they sang:

> There is a mouldy dump, down Fairbridge way.
> Where we get bread and jam, three times a day.
> Eggs and bacon we don't see, we get sawdust in our tea.
> That's why we're gradually fading away.
> Fade away, fade away. Fade away, fade away.
> That's why we're gradually fading away.

Whimsical ditties like this seem at odds with revelations of widespread abuse within the Fairbridge system and other institutions for lone children. But, like many oral traditions of the disempowered, they satirise poor conditions in such places and are a form of protest veiled in humour.

The illywacker

Australia once had an unenviable reputation in the world of crime as the home of numberless confidence tricksters. 'Illywackers', 'ripperty men' or 'spielers', among other names given by those who had been conned, were a real danger in the late nineteenth and early twentieth centuries. Journalist and author Ambrose Pratt was apparently well acquainted with some of these characters and wrote a lengthy exposé of their tricks for the English newspapers.

Pratt began by pointing out that the spieler was 'a swindler and a black-guard' who preyed on 'simple-minded country folk, unsuspicious foreign visitors, and fools at large', either with one or two accomplices or in a large gang. The police at that time reckoned there were at least 100 spielers in Sydney alone. In 1902, Pratt described the typical shyster:

*I*n person the spieler is a man of respectable appearance and affable demeanour. A skilful impersonator, his shape is protean; he is by turns a squatter, a lawyer, a millionaire, a lucky digger, a Supreme Court judge, a gentleman of private fortune, an English 'Johnnie,' fresh from 'Home'—sporting a lisp and the conventional 'Haw! Haw! Doncher know, deah boy!'—a parson, an eccentric retired merchant, a capitalist looking for investments for his money, or a bookmaker. He is always a man of gentlemanly presence, sometimes he is a gentleman by birth.

The spieler was always well dressed, adorned with plenty of jewellery.

*H*e puts up invariably at the best hotels, for at such places he meets the majority of his victims. He is a bird of passage, flitting quickly from State to State, and he never appears twice in the same character in the same town or at the same hotel. Finally, he is a man of brains, a keen student of human nature, and an exquisite comedian.

⌒

The article went on to describe some of the cons of the spieler and his many guises.

*H*is favorite character is that of the wealthy do-nothing, a blase man of the world. In this guise he attaches himself to young men whom he meets at his hotel, fast or giddy young men whose tastes incline to gambling. Singling out a particular victim, the wealthiest, or, at least, the most foolish, he feigns a fancy and flatters the pigeon to the top of his bent. When the time is ripe, he hires two rooms in the same office building in the city, which he furnishes lavishly on the time payment system. Choosing a particular evening, he has his luggage taken to the railway station (without his victim's knowledge), and then, after dinner, off-handedly invites his 'dear young friend' to stroll round with him to his club. The victim consents, and they repair to the aforesaid two rooms, the 'club' forsooth. A confederate, in livery, admits them. Other confederates are lounging in both rooms, who, however, affect to take no notice of the newcomers. The spieler calls for drinks. The victim unsuspiciously imbibes a drugged whisky and soda.

Presently the spieler introduces his protege to his confederates. A game of cards is suggested. The victim sleepily agrees. He plays and loses. When he has lost all his ready cash he signs blank cheques, which are presented to him for that purpose by the spieler. The spieler later on takes him back in a cab to the hotel, his 'dear young friend' apparently reeling drunk, and cashes his cheques over the bar, feeing the obliging barman liberally for the service. An hour later the spieler is comfortably seated in a railway carriage—on his way to another town—often hundreds of pounds richer for his trouble.

Then there was the parson collecting funds for the poor of his parish or feigning to lend money to a mug with a mortgaged property. Another was a special Australian favourite, selling shares in non-existent mines. In the 'lucky digger' con, the spieler:

. . . exhibits marvellous specimens of gold quartz from his 'mine!' He lavishes money about and shouts 'champagne' for anyone who will listen to his 'lucky digger' stories. One evening, when apparently 'half seas over', he offers in a well-stimulated burst of good nature, to give any of those present (he takes care to have a tipsy crowd about him) a half share in his mine for a mere song, say £250. Astounding as it may seem, his offer is invariably rushed, and some would-be rogue (for no honest man would traffic with a drunken man) presses the money into his hand, and induces him to sign a scribbled document.

I once saw two rascally young idiots fight in a crowded bar for the privilege of buying a half share in such an imaginary mine. They compromised by each handing the spieler £200, and agreeing between themselves to halve the share they had bought. Next morning, to their surprise, and, I confess, mine (for I thought the lucky digger genuine), the spieler had vanished, leaving no address.

The crook who pulled this one off turned out to be an especially notorious character who had carried out a number of 'long firm' frauds.

Pratt concluded with a warning:

His tricks are innumerable, the repertory of his characters unlimited. He is, indeed, an interesting and instructive body, but young Englishmen would do well to beware of them—those, I mean, who contemplate a visit to Australia, for their class furnishes him with an unceasing supply of victims, and from long experience he knows them well, their faults, their follies, and their frailties.

Although the term 'spieler' is no longer with us, the practice certainly persists and a mug is still born every minute, if not more frequently.

"For gorsake, stop laughing:
this is serious!"

12

Working for a laugh

We, the willing, led by the unknowing,
Are doing the impossible for the ungrateful.
We have done so much, for so long, with so little,
We are now qualified to do anything with nothing.

Anonymous

ONCE DESCRIBED AS 'the curse of the drinking class', work is
the lot of most people. To be endured, work needs to be laughed
at as well as laughed about. Australians have a fertile supply of
workplace humour, past and present. From outback yarns to
modern office jokes, from stump speeches to secret occupational
lingo, we have been working for a laugh since we began to work.

Droving in a bar

They were boasting in the bar about the biggest mob of cattle
they'd ever driven, here, there and every-bloody-where. One had
driven a mob of 6000 from Perth to Wave Hill. At least, he had
6000 when he started but when he finished over two years later,
he had 10,000. And so it went on.

An old bloke sat quietly in the corner, taking it all in. When
there was a cool moment in the hot air, he piped up. 'You blokes
talk about droving! Let me tell you about a real drive with a really

big mob. Me and a mate broke the Australian droving record. We picked up a big mob at Barkly. Took us two days to ride right round 'em, it was that big. Anyway, we started with this mob and drove them clear down to Hobart.'

The bar fell into a stunned silence before one of the young blokes piped up. 'Ow'd ya get 'em across the Bass Strait?' he asked sarcastically.

The old drover looked closely at him and said, 'Don't be stupid, son, we went the other way.'

A fine team of bullocks

They've been telling this yarn since Coopers Creek was first named, and probably long before. The story goes that a bullock driver had a crack team of beasts and on one particular trip was forced to get across a heavily flooded Coopers Creek. Usually this is an impossible task, but on this occasion the floodwaters didn't look too deep, so the bullock driver decided to give it a try.

He drew his team and wagon of wool up on the northern bank and spoke lovingly to them in the tender way that bullockies have, telling them that they now had a big challenge to get across the torrent. The bullocky then walked into the water and found that it was just up around his knees, showing his animals that it was not too dangerous.

He then went back and spoke lovingly to each and every one of the 22 beasts in the team. He told them what fine beasts they were and how he wanted them to pull together across the stream. Off they went, the lead bullock bravely forging ahead and the bullock shouting encouragement to the team.

After a titanic effort, the bullocks, the wool wagon and the bullock made it onto dry land at the other side. 'Whoa,' cried the bullocky, 'time for a rest.' As they settled down the bullocky looked back and saw with amazement that his champion team of bullocks had pulled the river 200 metres out of its course.

Without a word of a lie.

A stump speech

The 'stump speech' is a form of polished gibberish about nothing at all. Stump speeches featured in the United States during nineteenth-century political campaigns and were also used as entertainment and as forms of 'spruiking' a product, often of the snake-oil variety. Australia has a similar tradition of these absurd but entertaining rants. This one is thought to date from the early Federation period with its reference to George Reid, leader of the first Federal opposition, free trade advocate and eventually prime minister in 1904–05.

*L*adies and gentlemen—kindly turn your optics towards me for a few weeks and I will endeavour to enlighten you on the subject of duxology, theology, botanology, zoology or any other ology you like. I wish to make an apology, yes my sorefooted, black-eyed rascals, look here and answer me a question I am about to put to your notice. I want to be very lenient with you, but what shall it be, mark you, what shall the subject of my divorce (excuse me), discourse, this evening be? What shall I talk about? Shall it be about the earth, sun, sea, stars, moon, Camp Grove or jail? Now I wish to put before your notice the labour question. It is simply deloructious—isn't that alright? Yes, allow me to state the labour question is not what it should be.

Now look here, when I was quite a young man I worked very hard indeed, so hard, in fact, that I have seen the drops of perspiration dropping from my manly brow onto the pavement with a thud. Excuse me—yes, I say we shall not work at all! Then again, my wooden, brainless youths, answer me this: should men work between meals? No, no certainly not; it is boisterous!

Other questions I would put before your notice tonight are—why does Georgie Reid wear an eyeglass? Ha, ha my friends we don't know where we are; therefore where we are we do not know. Yes my noble-faced, flat-feeted, cockeyed, rank-headed asses, I will put before your notice other questions but no longer will I linger on these tantalising subjects. As time wags on and as I have to leave you; certainly I will not take you with me, therefore I leave you. Now the best of fools must part and as I see a policeman coming along I will go. Goodnight!

Working on the railway

The Australian railways have provided a living and even a way of life for very many people. Railway tradition is rich with poems, songs and yarns about the joys and irritations of keeping the trains running; old-time railmen will tell you about boiling the billy and frying eggs on their coal shovels as they stoked the boilers of steam trains. Or regale you with yarns about having to burn the sleepers lying beside the track when the coal ran out, just to keep the 'loco' going and get passengers to their destinations on time. Despite this level of commitment and effort, the slow train is a common feature of railway lore, with countless yarns on the same topic being lovingly retold across the decades and across the country.

On many rural and regional lines, trains were once so regularly and reliably late that passengers had long been resigned to very long waits. But one day on an isolated platform that shall remain nameless, the train arrived smack on time. A delighted and astounded passenger was so overcome by the experience that he ran up to the engine driver and thanked him profusely for arriving on time this once. The driver smiled faintly and replied, 'No chance, mate, this is yesterday's train.'

An anonymous poet expressed the desolate feeling of waiting for a train that may possibly never come:

All around the water tank
Waitin' for a train.
I'm a thousand miles away from home
Just a'standin' in the rain.
I'm sittin'
Drinkin'
Waitin'
Thinkin'
Hopin' for a train.

Service!

In this yarn, a passenger receives impeccable service.

a passenger boarded the train in Melbourne intending to get off at Albury. But when the conductor checked his ticket he had to tell him that the train didn't stop at Albury. The passenger went into a panic. 'I have to get off at Albury, it's a matter of life and death.' And pleaded with the conductor to stop the train for him.

The conductor said, 'Sorry, Sir, we can't stop the train at an unscheduled station but I do have a suggestion. I will ask the driver to slow down at Albury and I'll help you to alight from the train. It will be tricky and dangerous, but if I hold you outside the door by the collar and you start running we should be able to get you down without injury when your legs reach the right speed.'

The passenger was so desperate to get to Albury that he immediately agreed to this hazardous suggestion. 'Just one thing though,' said the conductor, 'after you're down be sure to stop running before you reach the end of the platform.' The plucky passenger nodded his agreement.

As the train approached Albury, the engine driver duly slowed down as much as he could. As soon as the platform came in sight, the conductor opened the door and held the passenger out over the platform. He began running in the air as he had ben instructed and the train was about halfway along the station before the conductor gently lowered him down. He hit the platform and staggered but managed to stay upright, losing momentum gradually as he slowed his running legs. He managed to come to a teetering stop just before the end of the platform. Just then the last car rolled past and he was suddenly grabbed again by the collar and hauled back onto the train. Shocked, he twisted around to see the guard smiling happily at him—'Expect you thought you'd missed your train, Sir!'

High-octane travel

This is an old railway yarn told in many places:

a couple of mechanics worked together in the railway sheds servicing diesel trains in Brisbane. One day there is a stop work meeting over some issue or other and the two find themselves sitting around with nothing to do. They'd like to go to the pub, of course, but they can't leave the workplace. Then one of them, let's call him Phil, has a bright idea. 'I've heard that you can get a really good kick from drinking diesel fuel. Want to give it a go?'

His mate, we'll call him Bruce, bored out of his mind, readily agrees. They pour a sizeable glass of diesel each and get stuck in. Sure enough, they have a great day.

Next morning Phil wakes up, gets out of bed and is pleasantly surprised to find that despite yesterday's diesel spree he feels pretty good. Shortly afterwards, his phone rings. It's Bruce. He asks Phil how he is feeling. 'Great mate, no hangover at all. What about you?'

'No,' agrees Bruce, 'all good.'

That's amazing,' replies Phil, 'we should get into that diesel more often.'

'Sure mate,' says Bruce, 'but have you farted yet?'

'What?' replies Phil, a bit taken aback. 'No, I haven't.'

'Well, make sure you don't 'cause I'm in Melbourne.'

Railway birds

This tongue-in-cheek description of various railway occupations in the form of a bird-spotting guide is at least as old as the 1930s, and probably earlier. No prizes for guessing which occupational group originated this item:

Engine Drivers—Rare birds, dusky plumage. Generally useful. No song; but for a consideration will jump points, signals etc. Have been known to drink freely near the haunts of man—especially at isolated stations. Occasionally intermarry with station-master's daughters (see Station Masters). Known colloquially by such names as 'Hell Fire Jack,' 'Mad Hector,' 'Speedy Steve,' 'Whaler,' 'Smokebox,' and 'Bashes.' Great sports, often carried from their engines suffering from shock—caused by wrong information.

Cleaners—Very little is known regarding the habits of these animals. How the name originated remains a mystery.

Guards—Fairly common. Red faces. Can go a long time without water. Easily recognisable by their habit of strutting up and down. Shrill whistle, but no sense of time. Sleep between stations, hence common cry of 'Up Guards, and at 'em.' Serve no generally useful purpose, but can be trained to move light perambulators, keep an eye on unescorted females, and wave small flags.

Porters—Habits strangely variable. Sometimes seen in great numbers: sometimes not at all. Much attracted by small bright objects. No song, but have been known to hum—between trains. Naturally indolent, but will carry heavy weights if treated rightly (i.e. sufficiently). Natural enemies of passengers (see passengers). Treated with contempt by station-masters.

Station Masters—Lordly, brilliant plumage. Rarely leave their nests. Ardent sitters. Most naturalists state these birds have no song, but Railway Commissioners dispute this. Have been known to eat porters (See Porters). Female offspring occasionally intermarry with very fast Engine Drivers.

Repair Gangs—Plumage nondescript. Migratory in habit. Nests are conspicuous and usually found in clusters near railway lines. No song but passengers assert their plaintive echoing cry of 'Pa-p-er' is unmistakable.

Passengers—Very common. Varied plumage. Will stand anything as a rule, but have been known to attack porters (see Porters). Often kept in captivity under deplorable conditions by ticket inspectors, guards etc. Will greedily and rapidly devour sandwiches and buns under certain (i.e. rotten) conditions. These birds are harmless when properly treated, and should be encouraged by all nature lovers.

Rechtub klat

Butchers in Australia developed a version of a secret trade jargon, or back slang, known as 'rechtub klat'—Butcher Talk, pronounced 'rech-tub kay-lat'. This descended from the similar back slang of migrating or transported butchers from London's markets, among whom back slanging was especially rife. In Australia there was little need for trade secrets to be protected but a secret language allowed butchers to converse while others were present, perhaps commenting on the price to be charged or admiring the physical qualities of a female customer. Another valued use of this lingo was to insult troublesome customers with impunity. Butchers in France traditionally uttered a similar convolution of language; it was known there as *loucherbem*, *boucher* being French for 'butcher'. Got that?

Although now spoken by very few, rechtub klat was once a relatively well-developed language. Today its vocabulary is fairly restricted to types of meat—*feeb* for beef, *bmal* for lamb and *gip* for pig—and crude but admiring comments such as *doog tsub* (good bust) and *doog esra* (good arse), among other such constructions crafted as required. A few other slabs of butcher talk are *kool*, *toh lrig* (look, hot girl), *gaf* (fag, as in cigarette) and *toor*, meaning root, as in the Australian vulgarism for sexual intercourse.

As well as commenting negatively on fussy customers and admiringly on young ladies, rechtub klat could be used to let the other butchers know that a particular cut had run out. So if there were 'on steltuc ni eht pohs' they should sell something different to any a customer who wanted 'steltuc'. It was not unknown for butchers to have complete clandestine conversations among themselves, as featured in the Australian movie *The Hard Word* (2002), when the language was used by the bank-robbing main characters to securely communicate their secrets to each other.

The garbos' Christmas

A characteristically Australian Christmas occupational tradition, now probably obsolete, involved the 'garbos'. For many decades the garbage men were in the habit of leaving a Christmas message, often in verse, for their clients. The message would generally wish the household well for the coming year and was also designed as a reminder of the traditional garbos' Christmas gift. This would be bottles or tins of beer left out along with the garbage bin on the last garbage day before the season began. Here are a couple of World War I examples of some Melbourne garbo greetings:

YOUR
SANITARY ATTENDANT
WISHES YOU
A Merry Christmas

Awake, awake, all freeborn sons,
Sound your voices loud and clear.
Wishing all a Merry Christmas
Likewise a glad New Year.

While referring to the Sewerage Scheme
As the greatest in the nation,
Until completed, I hope you'll give
Us some consideration.

The mission of our life just now,
Is to cleanse and purify.
We do our duty faithfully,
Be the weather wet or dry.

So while you're spending Xmas
In mirth and melody,
And friends to friends some present give,
Just spare a thought for me.

A MERRY CHRISTMAS

In recent years this custom seems to have dwindled, with only brief messages, if any, appearing. But even as late as 1983 it was possible to receive something like the following:

CHRISTMAS GREETINGS FROM
GARBO SQUAD
(Garbologists to you)

The year from us has gone,
Now it's time to think upon
Our blessings great and small:
May they continue for us all.

Your health, we hope, like ours is fine.
May 1984 be in similar line,
And in the New Year, we pray,
We'll serve you truly every day.

To you and yours joy we wish
That Christmas be a full dish
Of gladness, content and good health,
And the New Year bring you wealth.

Brian, Neville, Wayne

A Christmas message

Always a time for over-indulgence, Christmas at the OK Mine near Norseman, Western Australia, back in the roaring days was celebrated with enthusiasm, by some at least.

*I*t was Christmas Eve at O.K. in the days when the mine was in full swing and the local pub was the scene of a glorious general spree. In front of the building there lay many inches of thick red dust, also various stumps. On the following morning several booze-soaked individuals were slumbering in the layers of red powder after many hours of rolling and burrowing about. Waiting outside the pub for the breakfast bell to ring, the mine engineer was accosted by an aboriginal man named Jacky, who, after gazing thoughtfully for some time at the inebriated individuals sleeping in the dust, remarked, 'My word boss, white Australia all right today, eh?'

271

Total eclipse of communication

A favourite theme of workplace humour is communication—its failure, its absence or its distortion. One example is the shrinking memo, and the message it tried, at first, to convey. This item begins with a memo from the top levels of authority to the next level down, let's say from the managing director to the works director. The memo begins:

*M*emo: Managing Director to Works Director

Tomorrow morning there will be a total eclipse of the sun at 9 o'clock. This is something that we cannot see happen every day, so allow the workforce to line up outside in their best clothes to watch it. To mark the occasion of this rare occurrence I will personally explain it to them. If it is raining we shall not be able to see it very well and in that case the workforce should assemble in the canteen.

The next memo conveys this message down the line from the works director to the general works manager:

By order of the Managing Director there will be a total eclipse of the sun at 9 o'clock tomorrow morning.

If it is raining we shall not be able to see it very well on the site in our best clothes. In that case, the disappearance of the sun will be followed through in the canteen. This is something that we cannot see happen every day.

The general works manager then writes to the works manager an even briefer version of this rapidly disintegrating communication:

By order of the General Manager we shall follow through, in our best clothes, the disappearance of the sun in the canteen at 9 o'clock tomorrow morning.

The Managing Director will tell us whether it is going to rain. This is something which we cannot see every day.

In turn, the works manager passes this on to the foreman in another memo:

If it is raining in the canteen tomorrow morning, which is something we cannot see happening every day, our Managing Director in his best clothes, will disappear at 9 o'clock.

Finally, the foreman posts the message, or at least a ludicrous version of it, on the shop floor noticeboard. It reads:

Tomorrow morning at 9 o'clock our Managing Director will disappear. It is a pity that we cannot see this happen every day.

The laws of working life

Whatever can go wrong will go wrong. That's Murphy's Law. Even if you haven't heard of this universal truth, you'll be familiar with the general principle and the fact that whatever does go wrong at work will be at the worst possible time and in the worst possible way.

Things go wrong for us so often and with such devastating results that Murphy's Law alone cannot predict all the consequences of human error and disaster. There is a worryingly large number of similar laws, corollaries, axioms and the like, providing advice hard-won from bitter experience. You know the sort of thing. If you drop a slice of buttered bread it will unfailingly land butter-side down. And what about the curious fact that everything always seems to cost more than you happen to have in your pocket or bank account? Or, when you try to take out a loan you have to prove that you don't really need it? Here are some further helpful hints:

- The probability of a given event occurring is inversely proportional to its desirability.
- Left to themselves, things will always go from bad to worse.
- If it is possible that several things will go wrong, the one that does go wrong will do the most damage.
- Any error in any calculation will be in the area of most harm.
- A short cut is the longest distance between two points.
- Work expands to fill the time available.
- Mess expands to fill the space available.
- If you fool around with something long enough, it will eventually break.
- The most important points in any communication will be those first forgotten.
- Whatever you want to do, you have to do something else first.
- Nothing is as simple as it seems.
- Everything takes longer than expected.
- Nothing ever quite works out.
- It's easier to get into a thing than to get out of it.
- When all else fails, read the instructions.

Reading these little difficulties and dilemmas of work life suggests that none of us should bother getting out of bed in the morning. But of course, not everything in life goes wrong; sometimes you can have really great days when the sun shines, the birds sing and you feel on top of the world.

But next time you are having a day like this, just remind yourself of the last law of working life:

- If everything seems to be going well, you probably don't know what is going on.

Somebody else's job

Once upon a time there were four people, named Everybody, Somebody, Anybody and Nobody.

There was an important job to be done and Everybody was sure that Somebody would do it.

Anybody could have done it, but Nobody did it.

Somebody got angry about that because it was Everybody's job.

Everybody thought Anybody could do it, but Nobody realised that Everybody didn't do it.

It ended with Everybody blaming Somebody, when really, Nobody could accuse Anybody.

The basic work survival guide

This is an old favourite in Australian workplaces:

The opulence of the front office decor varies inversely with the fundamental solvency of the company.

No project ever gets built on schedule or within budget.

A meeting is an event at which minutes are kept and hours are lost.

The first myth of management is that it exists at all.

A failure will not appear until a new product has passed its final inspection.

New systems will generate new problems.

Nothing motivates a worker more than seeing the boss put in an honest day's work.

After all is said and done, a lot more is said than done.

The friendlier the client's secretary, the greater the chance that the competition has already secured the order.

Work expands to fill the time available.

In any organisation the degree of technical competence is inversely proportional to the level of management.

The grass is brown on both sides of the fence.

No matter what stage of completion the project reaches, the cost of the remainder of the project remains the same.

Most jobs are marginally better than daytime TV.

Twelve things you'll never hear an employee tell the boss

Wishful thinking is nothing new, as this list of helpful suggestions suggests:

1. Never give me work in the morning. Always wait until 5.00 and then bring it to me. The challenge of a deadline is always refreshing.
2. If it's really a 'rush job', run in and interrupt me every ten minutes to inquire how it's going. That greatly aids my efficiency.
3. Always leave without telling anyone where you're going. It gives me a chance to be creative when someone asks where you are.
4. If my arms are full of papers, boxes, books or supplies, don't open the door for me. I might need to learn how to function as a paraplegic in future and opening doors is good training.

5. If you give me more than one job to do, don't tell me which is the priority. Let me guess.

6. Do your best to keep me late. I like the office and really have nowhere to go or anything to do.

7. If a job I do pleases you, keep it a secret. Leaks like that could get me a promotion.

8. If you don't like my work, tell everyone. I like my name to be popular in conversations.

9. If you have special instructions for a job, don't write them down. If fact, save them until the job is almost done.

10. Never introduce me to the people you're with. When you refer to them later, my shrewd deductions will identify them.

11. Be nice to me only when the job I'm doing for you could really change your life.

12. Tell me all your little problems. No one else has any and it's nice to know someone is less fortunate.

Excessive absence

One of the great classics of workplace humour, this was old when it was kicking round the old Post Master General's department in the late 1960s. Versions can still be found on the internet.

*I*nternal Memo # 125
      RE: EXCESSIVE ABSENCE TO ALL PERSONNEL.

Due to the excessive number of absences during the past year it has become necessary to put the following new rules into operation immediately.

SICKNESS No excuse. The Management will no longer accept your Doctor's Certificate as proof. We believe that if you are able to go to your doctor you are able to attend work.

DEATH (YOUR OWN) This will be accepted as an excuse. We would like two weeks' notice, however, since we feel it is your duty to train someone else for your job.

DEATH (OTHER THAN YOUR OWN) This is no excuse. There is nothing you can do for them and henceforth no time will be allowed off for funerals. However, in case it should cause some hardship to some of our employees, please note that on your behalf the Management has a special scheme in conjunction with the local council for lunchtime burials, thus ensuring that no time is lost from work.

LEAVE OF ABSENCE FOR AN OPERATION We wish to discourage any thoughts you may have of needing an operation and henceforth no leave of absence will be granted for hospital visits. The Management believes that as long as you are an employee here you will need what you already have and should not consider having any of it removed. We engaged you for your particular job with all your parts and having anything removed would mean that we would be getting less of you than we bargained for.

VISITS TO THE TOILETS Far too much time is spent on the practice. In future the procedure will be that all personnel shall go in alphabetical order. For example: those with the surname being 'A' will go from 9.30 to 9.45; 'B' will go from 9.45 to 10.00. Those of you who are unable to attend at your appropriate time will have to wait until the next day when your turn comes up.

Have a nice day.

THE MANAGEMENT

Running naked with the bulls

Australians like to celebrate and enjoy themselves. No surprise there. But we seem to have a particular affinity for activities that are a bit off the wall and seem to take a perverse delight in parodying pretty well everything. The Darwin Beer Can Regatta is a light-hearted make-do event involving vessels made of empty beer cans. The Henley-on-Todd Regatta in Alice Springs features homemade craft racing along the dry bed of the Todd River. Cockroach Races were established as a regular event at Kangaroo Point, Brisbane on Australia Day 1982. In a similar spirit, they like to do things a little differently in Weipa.

Beginning in 1993 and intended to mark the first rain of the wet season, the locals invented a new tradition for themselves. They called it 'Running Naked with the Bulls'. Why? Because that's exactly what they did. The first event involved 150 local miners streaking nude along a two-kilometre course at 2 a.m. Other than their joggers, the miners carried only a plastic shopping bag for donations to the Royal Flying Doctor Service.

After that, things settled down, more or less, though the running has had what they call 'a chequered history'. The event rapidly established itself on the local calendar and became an international event as well. In 1998, it was believed to have set a record for the highest number of naked people ever to be interviewed; the ABC conducted the interviews from a telephone box along the course as the runners jogged past. Not wanting to appear sexist, the organisers also allowed women to run naked with the bulls in 1999.

Sadly, the event was closed down in 2001 due to complaints about indecency. There has been recent pressure to revive it, though, as Weipa is in need of the tourist income the event attracted. Local police are said to oppose its reintroduction. The future of the Running Naked with the Bulls remains uncertain at the time of writing.

But even when a local custom like this does spring up spontaneously, the commercial world is quick off the mark. A local resident and participant was heard on ABC Radio National back in November 1998, telling of the difficulties the event had encountered with sponsorship. It was not that the locals were against sponsorship for their start of the wet-season celebration; it was just that some sponsors were inappropriate. A large brothel chain wished to sponsor the event but the participants had to decline, not because there was a moral problem, but because the brothel wanted the runners to wear a T-shirt advertising their business. Reluctantly, the runners could not oblige.

Doing business

One of Australia's prominent businessmen was the founder of the airline he characteristically named after himself. Reg Ansett was very much the self-made man. Leaving school at fourteen, he worked as an axeman in the Northern Territory to earn enough to buy a Studebaker to start a road-transport company. This allowed him to buy a Gypsy Moth aeroplane and in 1938, aged just 28, he started Ansett Airways. He continued to display his legendary stubbornness and business acumen through the rest of his life, branching into car hire and other mostly successful businesses. He was a colourful character with a considerable public profile in his day, eventually being knighted for his achievements.

Reg Ansett entered Australian folklore in various ways, but particularly in a story often told about him by friend and foe alike. According to the yarn, a young man was keen to make a name for himself in business, just like the then ageing but incredibly eminent Reg Ansett. The young bloke couldn't believe his luck when he was in a restaurant for a meeting with an important client and he spotted Reg at a table full of other prominent business people, obviously settled in for a long session. Summoning up his courage, he approached the table and nervously addressed the great man, asking for a moment of his time and for a bit of a leg up the slippery ladder of business. Magnanimously, Reg condescended to help out and asked what he could do.

'Well, Mr Ansett,' said the young man, 'I have a very important client coming to lunch with me today. I need to impress this person with my business ideas and also with my contacts. Would you be kind enough to pretend that you know me?'

'Sure,' agreed Reg, mildly amused at the effrontery of the young man and probably reminded of his own early days.

'Thank you so much,' gushed the young man. 'When I leave the restaurant with my client I'll come past your table. Would you be good enough to stand up and greet me as if I were a valued business colleague?'

Reg was bit taken aback, but he was in a good mood over his latest business deal. 'Okay, young fella,' he replied condescendingly, always happy to give a newcomer a helping hand.

Reg went back to his celebrations and the young man returned to his table to meet his client. When the meal was over, Reg and his mates were still hard at it. The young man paid the bill and carefully manoeuvred himself and his client to pass right next to Reg's table. Reg couldn't miss them and remembered that he had agreed to take part in the harmless deception. He got to his feet and enthusiastically held out his hand to the young man, saying, 'Good to see you again, how's business?'

The young man stopped, looked coldly at the great man and said, 'Piss off, Reg, you can see I'm busy.'

The end of a perfect day

Pigs do not fly, of course, but in the world of work they can—and sometimes must—be made to do so:

Another day ends . . .

All targets met
All systems in working order
All customers satisfied
All staff eager and enthusiastic
All pigs fed and ready to fly

Sources

1. THE WIDE BROWN LAND

Eaglehawk and Crow: Thomas, 1923. William Jenkyn Thomas (1870–1959) was a Welsh school master who wrote *The Welsh Fairy Book* as well as some educational texts. Unfortunately, he gives no sources for the stories he includes in his book, which was intended for a general audience and probably, given his profession, as a teaching resource. See also Berndt & Berndt, 1989.

Great floods: Smith, 1930, pp. 151–68. This is Smith's edited version of a story collected and written down by Aboriginal writer, activist, inventor and man on the $50 note, David Unaipon. Unaipon gave his work to Smith, a noted anthropologist, and Smith published it under his own name without acknowledging Unaipon. Smith's version is much shorter than Unaipon's but preserves the essential details of the story. David Unaipon's original collection was finally published by Melbourne University Publishing in 2001, edited by Stephen Muecke and Adam Shoemaker, who were instrumental in uncovering the truth.

Firestick farming: Gammage, 2011.

'The landscape looked like a park': Bride, 1899.

Captain Cook's Law: K. Maddock, 'Myth, History and a Sense of Oneself' in Beckett, 1988, pp. 11–30; Redmond, 2008, pp. 255–70; D. Rose, 'The Saga of Captain Cook: Remembrance and morality', in Attwood & Magowan, 2001, pp. 61–79.

The corners: Queensland Heritage Register.

2. UPON THE FATAL SHORE

Leaden hearts: The National Museum of Australia has a large collection of convict tokens. The selected messages reproduced here have had spelling and layout regularised to some degree.

The Ring: Warung, 1891.

The melancholy death of Captain Logan: The ballad is usually credited to the convict Francis MacNamara, though research by Jeff Brownrigg (Brownrigg, 2003) suggests that MacNamara was not the author. See also Meredith & Whalan, 1979, pp. 31–8 and R. Reece, 'Frank the Poet' in Davy & Seal, 1993.

A Convict's Tour to Hell: The poem exists in various manuscript versions, probably composed c. 1839. See MacNamara, 1839.

'Make it hours instead of days': *Sydney Stock and Station Journal*, 1902, p. 3.

Captain of the push: Mitchell Library scrapbook of clippings, 1830; Lawson, 1900.

The Prince of Pickpockets: The Newgate Calendar; *Australian Dictionary of Biography*: Barrington, George (1755–1804), *Argus*, 1956.

3. PLAINS OF PROMISE

'I was not expected to survive': Moger, 1840; Sarah Brunskill quoted in Haines, 2003. Despite the popular depiction of the Australian emigrant ships as floating hells, government-chartered vessels (the main focus of Robin Haines' work) delivered more than 98 per cent of their charges to their new land in good health in the period covered by the book.

The town that drowned: *Australian Lutheran Almanac*, 1939; Flinders Ranges Research.

Wine and witches: There are various, sometimes contradictory versions of these events. See Ioannou, 1997, pp. 63ff and *Relative Thoughts*, 2009.

Phantoms of the landfall light: Cape Otway Lighthouse.

Tragedy on Lizard Island: Falkiner & Oldfield, 2000; *Australian Dictionary of Biography*: 'Watson, Mary Beatrice Phillips (1860–1881). When that site was reclaimed for Central Station in 1904, the remains were transferred to what is now Botany Bay Cemetery, where they still lie. See also McInnes, 1983; Wemyss, 1837; Lahn, 2013; Kennedy, 2011.

Who was Billy Barlow?: *Maitland Mercury and Hunter River General Advertiser*, 1843; Hildebrand, 2011 (also contains a large number of Billy Barlow ballads).

Chimney Sweeps' Day: Leech, 1989.

The dragon of Big Gold Mountain: *Bendigo Advertiser*, 1874, p. 2; *Argus*, p. 6.

4. A FAIR GO

Black Mary: Wells, 1818; Clarke, 1871.

The Tambaroora line: Beatty, 1960. It is unlikely that the song was Bill Maloney's, though; see *North Queensland Register*.

Mates: 'A Sketch of Mateship' was published in Lawson, 1907b.

A glorious spree: *South Bourke and Mornington Journal*, 1879.

The Greenhide Push waltzes Matilda: Magoffin, 1987, pp. 82ff.

The Bunuba resistance: Pederson & Woorunmurra, 1995, p. 49. See also *Aboriginal History*, 1985, p. 98, note 26; Western Australian Folklore Archive.

The bagman's gazette: *Northern Standard* (Darwin), 1931.

Homes of hope: Gibbons, 2012; *Australian Dictionary of Biography*: 'Hammond, Robert Brodribb (1870–1946)'.

5. HOW WE TRAVEL THE LAND

Rangers and rouseabouts: Fahey & Seal, 2005.

The swagman's union: *Burra Record*, 1931.

The oozlum bird: The first mention of Goodge's poem is in the *Sunday Times* (Sydney), 1898. It was published a couple of months later, so he had probably been writing it since 1897.

The Tea and Sugar train: J.D. in *Railroad*, 1928; Mail (Adelaide), 1925; *Barrier Miner* (Broken Hill), 1943.

The black stump: oral tradition

The rise and fall of Cobb & Co.: Everingham, 2007.

The Long Paddock: *Sydney Morning Herald*, 1942.

The real Red Dog: Duckett, 1993.

6. DOING IT TOUGH

Depending on the harvest: *Argus*, 1880.

'Women of the West': *Argus*, 1901

Cures!: *Argus*, 1918; Edwards, 1997; fieldwork of Rob Willis.

A seasonal guide to weather and wives: Traditional, also fieldwork of Rob and Olya Willis; *Pageant of Humour*, 1920, but said to be from 1842 source.

Backyard brainwaves: Australian War Memorial; Ingpen, 1982.

Sugar bag nation: *Hindsight*, 1999; Lowenstein, 1998; Seal, 1977;

Happy Valley: *Sydney Morning Herald*, 1933.

Sergeant Small: Graham Seal, 'From Texas to Tamworth via New Zealand: Tex Morton sings an Australian song', in Dalziell & Genoni, 2013.

The farmer's will: Author's collection.

7. HOME OF THE WEIRD

Curious discoveries: Grey, 1841.

The marble man: *Maitland Mercury & Hunter River General Advertiser* (NSW), 1889, p. 4. Most of the Australian newspapers, large and small, carried items on the marble man.

Was Breaker Morant the Gatton murderer?: Meredith, 1996.

Vanishing vessels: Jeffreys, 2007; Gregory, 1861, p. 482; WA Maritime Myths, referencing Busselton Historical Society; Gerritsen, 2010; Van Den Boogaerde, 2009, p. 75.

Yearning for yowies: *Queanbeyan Age*, 1903, p. 2.

8. ROMANCING THE SWAG

Introduction: *Sydney Morning Herald*, 1869, p. 4.

Lore of the track: Wannan, 1976, p. 196 (from Mr J. Robertson, North Geelong); *Townsville Daily Bulletin*, 1924, p. 9; *Nepean Times*, 1933, p. 6.

Sniffling Jimmy: *Townsville Daily Bulletin*, 1924, p. 9.

The poetic swaggie: Paterson, 1906; Henry Lawson, 'Hungerford' in *Bulletin*, 1893.

'There you have the Australian swag': Henry Lawson, 'The Romance of the Swag', in Ross, 2011.

A swagman's death: *Morning Bulletin*, 1894, p. 5.

Where the angel tarboys fly: *Capricornian*, 1908 p. 47.

Bowyang Bill and the cocky farmer: *Narromine News and Trangie Advocate*, 1934, p. 6. 'Bowyang Bill' was probably Alexander Vennard, who usually used the byline 'Bill Bowyang'.

The Mad Eight: *News* (Adelaide), 1927.

9. AFTER THE KELLYS

The saga: Seal, 2002.

A Glenrowan letter: Sutherland, 1880.

'I thought it was a circus': *Argus*, 1881.

A death in Forbes: *Illustrated Australian News*, 1880; *Forbes & Parkes Gazette*, 1898.

Living legends: *Argus*, 1902.

The stranger: *Argus*, 1878; *Ovens and Murray Advertiser*, 1979; Eastman, 1850–52.

10. THE CHILD IN THE BUSH

The beanstalk in the bush: Jacobs, 1890—'I tell this as it was told me in Australia, somewhere about the year 1860.'

Forgotten nursery rhymes: Nursery rhymes from various sources, including Howitt, 1898; *Bulletin*, 1898 & 1917.

The lost boys of Daylesford: *Daylesford Express*, 1867a, 1867b; *Sydney Morning Herald*, 1867.

Fairies in the paddock: Ernst, 1904. The *Snugglepot and Cuddlepie* gumnut baby stories were first published in 1918 and have been with us ever since.

Surviving Black Jack: *Perth Gazette and Western Australian Journal*, 1835, p. 575.

11. LARGER THAN LIFE

The fate of Captain Cadell: Nicholson, 2004.

The Fenian: Evans, 1997, p. 98. See also Sullivan, 2001; O'Reilly, 1879; Hasluck, 1959, p. 75.

The last bushranger: *Courier-Mail*, 1937, p. 13; *Keep in Touch*, 2012.

Lawson's people: Lawson & Brereton, 1931; Roderick, 1982.

The Coo-ee Lady: Richard White, 'Cooee', in White & Harper, 2010.

Australia's first Hollywood Star: McGowan, 2005.

A vision splendid: Murphy & Muller, 1998; author's collection.
The illywacker: *Clarence and Richmond Examiner*, 1902, p. 6.

12. WORKING FOR A LAUGH
Droving in a bar: Edwards, 1997, pp. 235–6.
A fine team of bullocks: Anon., author's collection.
A stump speech: *Imperial Songster*, 1907.
Working on the railway: *Railroad,* various editions.
Service!: author's collection.
High-octane travel: author's collection.
Rechtub klat: Maddox, 2002.
The garbos' Christmas: Lindesay, 1988; Scott, 1976.
A Christmas message: *Townsville Daily Bulletin*, 1924, p. 9.
Total eclipse of communication: author's collection.
The laws of working life: author's collection.
Somebody else's job: author's collection.
The basic work survival guide: author's collection.
Twelve things you'll never hear an employee tell the boss: author's collection.
Excessive absence: author's collection.
Running naked with the bulls: Australian Associated Press report, in *West Australian*, 2002, p. 55.
Doing business: Seal, 2001.
The end of a perfect day: author's collection.

Bibliography

BOOKS AND MANUSCRIPTS

Attwood, B. & Magowan, F. (eds), 2001, *Telling Stories: Indigenous history and memory in Australia and New Zealand*, Sydney: Allen & Unwin

Australian Dictionary of Biography, 1976, vol. 6, Melbourne: Melbourne University Press

Beatty, B., 1960, *Treasury of Australian Folk Tales and Traditions*, Sydney: Ure Smith

Beckett, J.R. (ed.), 1988, *Past and Present: The construction of Aboriginality*, Canberra: Aboriginal Studies Press

Berndt, R.M. & Berndt, C.H., 1989, *The Speaking Land*, Ringwood, Vic: Penguin

Bride, T.F. (ed.), 1899, *Letters from Victorian Pioneers: a series of papers on the early occupation of the colony, the Aborigines, etc.*, Melbourne: Brain

Brownrigg, J., 2003, *'From Bondage . . . Liberated': Frank the Poet's Dreams of Liberty*, paper given at ESCAPE (An international and interdisciplinary conference on escape and the convict experience), Strahan, Tasmania, 26–28 June

Clarke, M., 1871, *Old Tales of a Young Country*, Melbourne: Mason, Firth & M'Cutcheon

Davy, G. & Seal, G. (eds), 1993, *The Oxford Companion to Australian Folklore*, Melbourne: Oxford University Press

Dalziell, T. & Genoni, P. (eds), 2013, *Telling Stories: Australian life and literature, 1935–2012*, Clayton: Monash University Publishing

Duckett, B., 1993, *Red Dog: The Pilbara Wanderer*, Karratha: self-published

Eastman, H.M., c.1850–1852, memoirs (manuscript on microfilm), State Library of NSW, MLMSS 130, B1341

Edwards, R., 1997, *The Australian Yarn: The definitive collection*, St Lucia: University of Queensland Press

Ernst, O., 1904, *Fairytales from the Land of Wattle*, Melbourne: McCarron, Bird & Co.

Evans, A., 1997, *Fanatic Heart: A life of John Boyle O'Reilly 1844–1890*, Perth: University of Western Australia Press

Everingham, S., 2007, *Wild Ride: The rise and fall of Cobb & Co*, Sydney: Penguin Viking

Gerritsen, R., 2010, *Geomorphology and the Deadwater Wreck*, a modified form of a presentation given at the Eastern Australian Region of the Australasian Hydrographic Society Annual Symposium in Sydney on 13 September, at http://rupertgerritsen.tripod.com/pdf/unpublished/Geomorphology_and_the_Deadwater_Wreck.pdf, accessed 14 April 2014

Grey, G., 1841, *Journals of Two Expeditions of Discovery in North-West and Western Australia, During the Years 1837, 1838 and 1839*, London: T. & W. Boone

Fahey, W. & Seal, G. (eds), 2005, *Old Bush Songs: The centenary edition of Banjo Paterson's classic collection*, Sydney: ABC Books

Falkiner, S. & Oldfield, A., 2000, *Lizard Island: The story of Mary Watson*, Sydney: Allen & Unwin

Gammage, B., 2011, *The Biggest Estate on Earth*, Sydney: Allen & Unwin

Gibbons, M., 2012, *Hammondville: The first eighty years 1932–2012*, online at www.melaniegibbons.com.au/sites/default/files/content/MENAI%20HAMMONDVILLE%20BOOKLET%20NOVEMBER%202012.pdf, accessed 15 April 2014

Gregory, F.T., 1861, 'On the Geology of a Part of Western Australia', *Quarterly Journal of the Geological Society of London*, vol. 17, pp. 475–83

Haines, R. 2003, *Life and Death in the Age of Sail: The passage to Australia*, Sydney: University of New South Wales Press

Hasluck, A., 1959, *Unwilling Emigrants*, Melbourne: Oxford University Press

Hildebrand, J., 2011, *Hey Ho Raggedy-O: A Study of the Billy Barlow Phenomenon*, e-book online at http://warrenfahey.com/fc_barlow_book.html, accessed 15 April 2014

Howitt, W., 1898, 'A Boy's Adventure in the Wilds of Australia' (1854), *The Bulletin*, 12 March

Ingpen, R., 1982, *Australian Inventions and Innovations*, Adelaide: Rigby

Ioannou, N., 1997, *Barossa Journeys: Into a valley of tradition*, Kent Town: Paringa Press

Jacobs, J. (ed.), 1890, *English Fairy Tales*, London: David Nutt

Jenkins, J., 1975, *Diary of a Welsh Swagman*, Melbourne: Macmillan

Jeffreys, G., 2007, *The Stradbroke Island Galleon: The Mystery of the Ship in the Swamp*, North Stradbroke Island, QLD: Jan & Greg Publications

Kennedy, M., 2011, 'Natural History Museum returns bones of 138 Torres Strait Islanders', *The Guardian*, 10 March

Lahn, J., 2013, 'The 1836 Lewis Collection and the Torres Strait Turtle Mask of Kulka: From loss to reengagement', *The Journal of Pacific History*, vol. 48

Lawson, B.L. & Le Gay Brereton, J. (eds), 1931, *Henry Lawson by His Mates*, Sydney: Angus & Robertson

Lawson, H., 1900, *Verses Popular and Humorous*, Sydney: Angus & Robertson

——1907a, *The Romance of the Swag*, Sydney: Angus & Robertson

——1907b, *Send Round the Hat*, Sydney: Angus & Robertson

Leech, K., 1989, *Jack-in-the-Green in Tasmania 1844–73*, London: The Folklore Society

Lindesay, V., 1988, *Aussieossities*, Richmond, Victoria: Greenhouse

Lowenstein, W., 1998, *Weevils in the Flour: An oral record of the 1930s depression in Australia*, Melbourne: Scribe

MacNamara, F., 1839, 'A Convict's Tour to Hell', in Nicholas, J. (ed.)

Macquarie PEN Anthology of Australian Literature, Sydney: Allen & Unwin, p. 83

Maddox, G., 2002, 'Behind that tray of snags, there's a rechtub talking', *Sydney Morning Herald*, 27 May

Magoffin, R., 1987, *Waltzing Matilda: The story behind the legend*, Sydney: Australian Broadcasting Corporation

McGowan, J.J., 2005, *J.P. McGowan: Biography of a Hollywood pioneer*, Jefferson, North Carolina: McFarland

McInnes, A., 1983, 'The Wreck of the Charles Easton: Read to a Meeting of the Royal Historical Society of Queensland on 24 February 1983', http://espace.library.uq.edu.au/eserv/UQ:241150/s00855804_1983_11_4_21.pdf, accessed 15 April 2014

Meredith, J., 1996, *Breaker's Mate: Will Ogilvie in Australia*, Sydney: Kangaroo Press

Meredith, J. & Whalan, R., 1979, *Frank the Poet*, Ascot Vale: Red Rooster Press

Moger, E., 1840 (28 January–18 March), letter, National Library of Australia, manuscript reference no. NLA MS 5919

Murphy, S. & Muller, A., 1997, *Fairbridge Village Interpretation Plan*, Research Institute for Cultural Heritage, Curtin University, Perth

Nicholson, J., 2004, *The Incomparable Captain Cadell*, Sydney: Allen & Unwin

O'Reilly, J.B., 1879, *Moondyne*, Boston: Pilot Publishing

Pageant of Humour, c. 1920, Sydney: Gayle Publishing Company

Paterson, A.B. (Banjo) (ed.), 1906, *Old Bush Songs*, Sydney: Angus & Robertson

Pederson, H., & Woorunmurra, B., 1995, *Jandamarra and the Bunuba Resistance*, Broome: Magabala Books

Redmond, A.J., 2008, 'Captain Cook meets General Macarthur in the Northern Kimberley: Humour and ritual in an Indigenous Australian life-world', *Anthropological Forum*, Special issue: You've got to be joking! Anthropological perspectives on humour and laughter, vol. 3, no. 18

Roderick, C., 1982, *The Real Henry Lawson*, Adelaide: Rigby

Ross, J. (ed), *The Penguin Book of Australian Bush Writing*, Camberwell, Vic: Viking

Scott, B., 1976, *Complete Book of Australian Folklore*, Dee Why West, NSW: Summit Books

Seal, G., 1977, *On the Steps of the Dole-Office Door*, (recording) Sydney: Larrikin Records

——2001, *More Urban Myths*, Sydney: HarperCollins

——2002, *Tell 'em I Died Game: The legend of Ned Kelly*, Flemington: Hyland House

Smith, W.R., 1930, *Myths and Legends of the Australian Aborigines*, London: Harrup

Sullivan, C.W. III, 2001, *Fenian Diary: Denis B. Cashman aboard the Hougoumont, 1867–1868*, Dublin: Wolfhound Press

Sutherland, D., 1880 (8 July), letter, Australian Manuscripts Collection, State Library of Victoria, manuscript reference no. MS 13713

Thomas, W.J., 1923, *Some Myths and Legends of the Australian Aborigines*, London: Whitcombe & Tombs

Van Den Boogaerde, P., 2009, *Shipwrecks of Madagascar*, New York: Strategic Book Publishing

Wannan, B., 1976, *Come in Spinner*, Melbourne: John Curry, O'Neill

Warung, P., 1891, 'The Liberation of the First Three', *The Bulletin*, vol. 11, no. 594, pp. 21–2

Wells, T.E. & Howe, M., 1818, *The Last and Worst of the Bush-Rangers of Van Diemen's Land*, Hobart: Andrew Bent

Wemyss, T., 1837, *Narrative of the Melancholy Shipwreck of the Ship Charles Eaton*, Stockton: Robinson

White, R. & Harper, M. (eds), 2010, *Symbols of Australia*, Sydney: National Museum of Australia Press/UNSW Press

JOURNALS AND PERIODICALS

Aboriginal History, vol. 9, part 1, 1985

Argus, 30 October 1878

——19 April 1880

——16 May 1881

——20 April 1892

——7 September 1901

——15 October 1902

——23 July 1918
——8 December 1956
Australian Lutheran Almanac, 1939
Barrier Miner (Broken Hill), 24 February 1943
Bendigo Advertiser, 7 April 1874
Bulletin, Christmas 1893
——March 1898
——November 1917
Burra Record, 11 February 1931
Capricornian, 14 November 1908
Clarence and Richmond Examiner, 6 December 1902
Courier-Mail, 14 January 1937
Daylesford Express, 4 July 1867a
——16 July 1867b
Forbes & Parkes Gazette, 18 October 1898
Hindsight, ABC Radio National, 1999
Illustrated Australian News, no. 29, 1 July 1880
Imperial Songster, no. 97, 1907
Keep in Touch (published by The Sisters of Charity of Australia), vol.
    13, no. 4, December 2012
Mail (Adelaide), 19 December 1925
Maitland Mercury and Hunter River General Advertiser, 2 September
    1843
——1 June 1889
Morning Bulletin, 4 September 1894
Narromine News and Trangie Advocate, 16 February 1934
Nepean Times, 1 April 1933
News (Adelaide), 28 June 1927
North Queensland Register, 18 September 1976
Northern Standard (Darwin), 29 September 1931
Ovens and Murray Advertiser, 27 February 1979
Perth Gazette and Western Australian Journal, 3 October 1835
Queanbeyan Age, 7 August 1903
Railroad, October 1928 and various editions throughout 1930s
    and 1940s

Relative Thoughts, 2009, quarterly journal of the Fleurieu Peninsula
    Family History Group Inc., vol. 13, no. 1
South Bourke and Mornington Journal, 19 March 1879
Sunday Times (Sydney), 9 October 1898
Sydney Morning Herald, 23 September 1867
——4 August 1869
——29 December 1933
——27 June 1942
Sydney Stock and Station Journal, 27 May 1902
Townsville Daily Bulletin, 4 June 1924
West Australian, 14 December 1891

WEBSITES

Australian War Memorial
The Australian War Memorial combines a shrine, a world-class
museum, and an extensive archive.
http://www.awm.gov.au

Cape Otway Lighthouse
Cape Otway Lighthouse is the oldest surviving lighthouse in mainland
Australia. In operation since 1848, it is perched on towering sea cliffs
where Bass Strait and the Southern Ocean collide. For thousands of
immigrants, after many months at sea, Cape Otway was their first
sight of land after leaving Europe.
www.lightstation.com

Flinders Ranges Research
Flinders Ranges Research undertakes research, evaluates information, presents reports and writes material for publication of South
Australian history.
www.southaustralianhistory.com.au/hoffnungsthal.htm.

Frank the Poet—Francis MacNamara 1811–1861
A research project by Mark Gregory.
www.frankthepoet.blogspot.com.au/2011/01/articles.html

The Legend of the Stradbroke Island Galleon
A research project by Brad Horton, Greg Jefferys and Cliff Rosendahl.
See also Jefferys, 2007.
www.stradbrokeislandgalleon.com

The National Museum of Australia
The National Museum of Australia has 314 convict love tokens in
its collection. These tokens were made by convicts around the time
of their sentencing and were given to friends and loved ones as
mementos.
www.love-tokens.nma.gov.au.

The Newgate Calendar
A searchable series of stories about criminals from the 17th century
and earlier through to 1840, this is a wonderful resource for anyone
interested in the criminal underworld of 18th-century Britain.
http://www.pascalbonenfant.com/18c/newgatecalendar

Queensland Heritage Register
The Department of Environment and Heritage Protection,
Queensland Government, is responsible for managing the health of
the environment to protect Queensland's unique ecosystems, including
its landscapes and waterways, as well as its native plants and animals
and biodiversity.
https://heritage-register.ehp.qld.gov.au/placeDetail.html?siteId=33360

WA Maritime Myths
A blog dealing with Western Australian wreck sites and early Dutch
explorers.
http://wamaritimemyths.wordpress.com/2007/11/

Western Australian Folklore Archive
The Western Australian Folklore Archive, Curtin University of
Technology, Perth, records, preserves and gives the public access to the
rich folk traditions, past and present, of Western Australians.
http://john.curtin.edu.au/folklore

Picture credits

1: WIDE BROWN LAND

Relation ov iovrnal dv voyage de Bontekoe avx Indes Orientales
[Relationship or log of Bontekoe's trip to the East Indies]. Separately
paginated section of *Thévenot's Relations de divers voyages curieux* that
comprises the accounts of the voyages of Bontekoe and Pelsaert, the
latter containing the third state of the map of Australia with the line
of the Tropic of Capricorn added.
John Oxley Library, State Library of Queensland, Neg: 855351

2: UPON THE FATAL SHORE

Convict love token from James Branch (undated). The engraved side
features the text 'Love & Union/JAB/James Blanch/Ann Harley/
SACRED TO FRIENDSHIP' around a design of two hearts joined
by a ribbon. The reverse side is the obverse of a cartwheel penny
showing the bust, in profile, of a man.
National Museum of Australia

3: PLAINS OF PROMISE

Wood engraving, 1876. The Opposum-Hill rush, near Berlin, Victoria,
published in *The Australian Sketcher*, June 10 1876. The upper view
is of Main Street showing timber and bark buildings, the Shamrock
Hotel at the left and next to it J. McLeish's store. Further along is the
Bank of Victoria and another store with the sign 'Kirwan' and a Skittle
Saloon at the right hand side. A sign advertising 'Mrs Sibley tonight'
is on the front of the Shamrock Hotel.

State Library of Victoria

4: A FAIR GO
Show at Hammondville, 1937.
State Library of New South Wales

5: HOW WE TRAVEL THE LAND
Horse-drawn coach with passengers outside Cobb & Co. Ltd, Coach Proprietors, Booking Office. Place unknown, but probably the Eastern Goldfields.
State Library of Western Australia, 2946B/1

6: DOING IT TOUGH
Happy Valley unemployed camp, La Perouse c. 1932.
State Library of New South Wales

7: HOME OF THE WEIRD
Henry 'The Breaker' Morant (1865–1902). A drover and horseman who began contributing verse and ballads to Sydney *Bulletin* in September 1891, he becoming widely known by his pen name 'The Breaker'.
Blue Mountains City Library

8: ROMANCING THE SWAG
Studio portrait of a swagman, Melbourne, Victoria, c. 1887. (Lindt, J. W. (John William), 1845–1926, photographer).
National Library of Australia, vn4312961

9: AFTER THE KELLYS
Wood engraving, 1880. Ned Kelly (sketched as he was leaving Benalla), published in *The Illustrated Australian News*, July 3 1880.
State Library of Victoria

10: THE CHILD IN THE BUSH
Wood engraving, 1867. 'The Lost Children of Daylesford' (A. C. Cooke (Albert Charles), 1836–1902, artist; W. H. Harrison, engraver) published in *The Illustrated Australian News*, October 26 1867. Shows men finding remains of lost children in hollow of large tree.
State Library of Victoria

11: LARGER THAN LIFE

Lobby card, 1921. Playgoers Pictures, Inc. presents J.P. McGowan in *Discontented Wives*. The caption reads: 'We'll keep it a secret from Ruth until it's assayed.'
Western Silent Films Lobby Card Collection, Yale Collection of Western Americana, Beinecke Rare Book and Manuscript Library, New Haven, CT

12: WORKING FOR A LAUGH

Drawing, 1933. 'For gorsake, stop laughing: this is serious!' (Stan Cooke, artist), part of the Stan Cross Archive of cartoons and drawings, 1912–1974. Reproduced with permission of Mr Simon Cross. National Library of Australia, vn4306283